C000163275

BOOK ONE

SAMIR AND GEORGHE

One

'What the hell do you want?'

Thierry did a quick check. His eyes darted around the foyer and the dank stairwell leading up to the upper floors. Anticipating trouble. But there was only Karim. Sounding unhappy.

'Well?' Karim said.

'You know why I'm here.'

The boy shrugged. Not the brightest button in the box. Liked to dress sharp, though. Oversized grey hoodie, designer jeans and a pair of brand-new Nikes. Slouched, like he wouldn't know any other way to hold himself. Halfway through a joint at ten in the morning. He was pacing back and forth in the area outside the lifts, which right now seemed to be out of order. Some humorous individual had stuck a sheet of A4 paper across one of them, with the words Take the Stairs, Arsehole scrawled across it.

This fetid entrance with its peeling walls was where they cut their deals. Thierry knew he could come back in two, five, eight hours time, and one or several of them would be here, in this exact same spot; working the mobile phones, shooting the breeze. Some might call it a pointless existence; others might look at the money and think it wasn't such a bad way to earn a living. The last big shipment Thierry's team had intercepted, a single carload from Spain, had contained 200 kilograms of cannabis. And last he'd heard, ten grams could fetch fifty euros.

A woman came through the door, pulling a shopping bag on wheels. She walked past the row of letterboxes without checking her mail. She didn't make eye contact with either of them. They heard her go up the stairs, the wheels banging on each step.

'How long have the lifts not been working?'

Karim shrugged again. An eloquent sort of guy. Thierry knew him better than the boy's mother did. He was two months short of his sixteenth birthday and the fuzz on his cheeks didn't amount to much.

'Karim –'

'Don't fucking call me that. It's Kevin, asshole.'

'Kevin! Since when?' Thierry couldn't help himself. He laughed. 'Give me a break.'

Alone, the kid wasn't a threat, not really.

 'OK, Kevin, whatever –'

'Who the fuck said you could call me Karim?'

'It's the name your mother gave you, isn't it?' Thierry said, suddenly impatient.

'Don't talk about my mother.'

'Just shut up, will you? Listen.'

'What do you want from me? If they see me talking to you...' His face contorted with anger but it was fear Thierry saw.

'Well they won't. I'll be gone by then. Look, I just want to talk.'

'What about?' He was jittery and Thierry wondered now whether maybe he was on something more than weed. Or maybe he had a guilty conscience. It happened, once in a blue moon but still.

'Maybe you need to unburden yourself.'

'What, you're a priest now? Dear Father, forgive me please, for I have sinned,' Karim mocked.

'I need to find Samir,' Thierry said. He was tired of the banter and he wanted to be in his car, leaving the housing project and its stench of hopelessness behind.

'What's that got to do with me?'

4

'Relax, I'm not after you about anything, OK? I'm just looking for Samir. I know you two hang out.

'I don't hang out with that loser.'

It was such a lie there was no point disputing it.

'That's the best you can do, is it? For Samir?' Thierry said wearily. That seemed to strike a chord. The boy looked unhappy.

'All I know is he was down at the station,' Karim muttered.

'And then?'

'Don't come near me.'

'I'm –'

'Don't – come – near - me.'

Thierry stepped back, even though he hadn't gone anywhere near the boy to begin with. Karim's paranoia was palpable, like a slippery presence between them.

I'm a complete idiot, Thierry thought. If his colleagues could see him now, they'd question his sanity. None of them ever came onto the estate alone. Preferably, there'd be half a dozen of them. One in the car, waiting with the engine running. He knew how stupid this was, but thirty years of doing this job and going around in circles could make you feel like you had to do things differently. Which wasn't to say he felt good. He could feel his heart hammering against his ribcage so hard it hurt.

'OK, relax. Karim. Kevin, fuck, I mean Kevin, OK? Tell me. Right now. Where the hell is Samir?'

'Ask your friend down at the station, man.'

'What friend?'

'Your *friend*. He took him to the station and scared the shit out of him.'

'Are you sure you haven't seen him since?'

They heard it at the same time. Laughter. The sound of footsteps approaching. Coming down the stairs. It was time to go, his car was parked right outside. He looked at Karim one last time. He was surprised to see the boy laughing, silently. There was no warmth in it.

Karim straightened his shoulders. Jabbed a finger in Thierry's face.

'Just wait,' he said. 'When they see you here, they'll skin you alive.'

Two

He was being smothered, he couldn't breathe.

Morel woke fighting for air, his hands held up before him, as if to ward off an attacker. But when he opened his eyes there was no one there. Nothing, except a disquieting stillness. Something you had to wade through. He took deep breaths and waited for his dreams to dissipate.

His body was covered in sweat and he was shivering. He took the thermometer from his bedside table and slid it under his tongue. Kept it there, as he got up and peeped through the curtains. For a moment, he was blind. Gradually, familiar shapes emerged from the whiteness. The stark outline of trees. A pattern of prints on the ground. The tyres of his old, trusty Volvo. It was all that stood out.

Snow! More snow than he'd seen in years. When was the last time it had been like this in Paris? Morel couldn't remember. Briefly, through a feverish fog, he saw a boy, chasing his squealing sisters across a frozen landscape, hands burning from the snow packed tightly in each palm. Where? He couldn't remember. It could have been Brussels, where he'd lived as a child. Or Russia, with its majestic winters.

He took the thermometer out of his mouth and peered at the result. Could be worse. He was relieved to think he would be going to work. Lucid enough to realize he wanted to escape the situation at home – he wasn't proud of it. Far easier to be Commandant Serge Morel of the *brigade criminelle* than to put up with his father's forgetfulness, and worse, the old man's intermittent awareness that he was losing his memory.

He turned his mind to the days ahead. *In 48 hours, I'll be seeing Mathilde again*, he thought. He felt dizzy with anticipation, or maybe it was just the fever.

A flash of colour outside Morel's window startled him, followed by the sound of barking. And his father's voice, indignant.

'What are you doing here? Stay out! Go home!'

Reluctantly, Morel stood up, slipped on a dressing-gown and a thick pair of socks before opening the door that led from his flat directly into the main house. He found his father standing at the front door, shivering in a pair of blue pajamas, his bare feet as painfully white as the surrounding snow. Descartes, their Bernese mountain dog, stood in the middle of the courtyard, casting baleful looks in their direction. Eager to get back inside, but disconcerted by Morel senior's tone.

'Papa, it's OK. Leave the dog alone.'

'But what is he *doing* here?'

'He's your dog, remember? Adèle got him for you months ago. Descartes, inside. Now.'

The dog looked as confused as its owner. But it opted for comfort and trotted in.

Morel's head was pounding. He steered his father towards the stairs. 'Let's get you dressed,' he said. He could never get used to this, he reflected. Babying his father. Philippe Morel followed his son up the stairs, looking like he'd already forgotten what he'd come down for.

'That's better,' Morel said, once his father was dressed more warmly. He'd noticed some time back that the old, familiar shrewdness in his father's eyes was gone. But he seemed uneasy at times, as if a small part of him still sensed that things were not as

8

they should be. 'Now, come back down and I'll make us both some coffee.'

'Don't speak to me as though I were a child,' his father told him.

'Sorry.' Morel took a deep breath and allowed Philippe to walk down the stairs ahead of him. Hostility radiated from the old man's body. Morel's head was pounding. It would take more than coffee to get him through the day, he thought. He left his father briefly to look for Nurofen in the bathroom cabinet. When he looked up, his face in the mirror was flushed, his eyes too bright.

Outside, the snow fell in gentle flakes and settled into something hard and unyielding.

*

'The Whites hate the Arabs, the Arabs hate us Blacks. Meanwhile, we are just trying to get on with things. Minding our own business, know what I'm sayin'?'

'Yeah, right,' Lila replied vaguely. She took the plastic cup from Alphonse and handed him the money for it. MC Solaar was rapping furiously about something or other. She had once been impressed by his verbal dexterity, now he bored her. It was always the same thing. Social injustice, racism. Not that she didn't care, but you could get tired of the discourse.

Alphonse, on the other hand, never tired of it. Lila took a careful sip of her drink. Takeaway coffee. That was one American import she was grateful for. She looked at Alphonse. His face was stiff from the cold despite the beanie and scarf. He was serving a man in a tracksuit who looked like he'd been running. At least he had earned his coffee. I should have gone to the pool this morning, Lila thought. Maybe then I wouldn't feel so bloody awful.

She couldn't go on like this. Since Akil had moved out, this time for good, she'd turned into a slob. The most exercise she got was her ten-minute commute past Alphonse's hole-in-the-wall coffee shop to and from the Metro station. She watched too much television and ate rubbish. Clogging up her arteries. She looked into the future and saw herself sitting in her GP's room, listening to the woman tell her she had type 2 diabetes.

'Don't you think? Alphonse said, and Lila realized she had no idea what he'd been going on about.

'We've forgotten how to be civilized,' he said, shaking his head slowly.

'When were we ever civilized?'

'I don't know. It just seems like everyone's pissed off at someone else,' he said.

'Except you and your fellow Africans, who are just trying to get on with things,' she said, earning a laugh.

She found she wasn't in a huge rush to get to work. Three days earlier, the body of a 35- year old male had been fished out of the Seine. The family had been notified. It turned out the man was a professional tennis player and his wife one of those plastic models favoured, in Lila's view, by men with small brains and big incomes. The man, Grégory Simic, had been drinking. At first, it had looked like a straight accident; Simic had slipped and drowned. But in the meantime, the man's laptop, seized by Lila mainly to annoy the bimbo wife, had revealed him to be some kind of sex addict. Now the superintendent wanted her to make sure that tennis man hadn't got involved in anything too kinky that might have got him killed.

She tested the coffee; it was OK to drink. A car moved slowly down the lane, its window-wipers moving to clear the windscreen.

There was still a thick layer of snow on the ground. It looked like it wouldn't melt anytime soon. Lila shook her head.

'What's with all this snow, Alphonse?'

'Ever heard of climate change?' he said, turning the music up.

'Sure. But this doesn't look like global warming to me.'

'It's warming and cooling and everything upside down. Exponential chaos, that's what it is,' he said. 'Know what I'm sayin'?'

'You sure do talk a lot of rubbish,' Lila said, before heading off with a half-wave. Halfway down the street she could still hear him laughing.

*

Outside police headquarters, the snow had turned to sludge. Lila entered the building and climbed the stairs to the fourth floor. It was quieter than usual. Early January was always like this. Crime was slow. People were probably still recovering from the holiday festivities. Too hungover to get into trouble.

Well, at least Christmas was over and done with, she thought. They said it was a tough time for people who lived on their own, disconnected from their families. As far as Lila was concerned, they were the lucky ones. Three hours with her family on Christmas Day and she felt like she'd been flattened by a bulldozer.

It didn't help that Akil had decided to come along. Even though they were fighting all the time. She should never have agreed. Being with Akil at her parents' was like being in a fishbowl. Her parents kept staring at them and there was nowhere to hide. The conversation was a nightmare. It was as though a bunch of bad actors had decided to get together for a film shoot, and everyone had forgotten their lines. Her mother was the worst.

'So…Where are you from, Akil?' she'd said brightly.

'Same place as you. Born and raised right here. In Paris, France.'

There was probably no need for the *banlieusard* accent, which made him sound like he'd grown up on a housing estate in the northern suburbs on the other side of the *périph'*, rather than in a three-bedroom apartment in Montmartre.

'What your mother *means*,' he'd told Lila later, as they sat side by side on the bed, not touching, 'is what the fuck do you think you're doing sleeping with my daughter, you Arab scum?'

'No, I think you're wrong. It's more like, What the fuck do you think you're doing sleeping with my daughter, you Arab piece of shit?'

They'd had a good laugh over that, and moved closer together.

Lila entered the office she shared with Morel and her two other colleagues, and dropped her coat and scarf on her chair. Jean and Vincent were in. Only Morel was absent.

'Morning, all.'

'Good morning.'

'How was everyone's weekend?'

'Good,' Jean and Vincent said in unison without looking up from their screens.

Lila dropped her bag on her desk and sat down.

'Mine was crap, thanks for asking.'

'You mean like last weekend?' Jean asked, looking up.

'And the one before that,' Vincent said. The two men exchanged a meaningful look.

Lila glared at them. 'What are you trying to say?'

'Nothing,' they replied in unison.

Lila turned her computer on. It annoyed her that everyone in the team knew about her relationship with Akil. Every time they broke up, or got together again, they seemed to guess. At least there would be nothing left to gossip about now. Though she had something new to worry about.

While her computer booted up, an infuriatingly long process, she lifted a black banana from the papers strewn across the desk's surface.

'Any sign of Morel?'

'He's on his way,' Jean said.

'Good.' She threw the banana into the bin.

She glanced at the empty desk facing hers – Marco had sat there, before Morel had shifted him to a different unit. It had been tough on the detective, he'd wanted so badly to stay – but Lila knew Morel was right. Marco didn't have what it took.

She knew Morel had a replacement in mind. Knew who it was. But still she hoped she was wrong.

Three

Being seventeen was tough. For a girl, it was hell on earth.

Aisha knew she was smart. She was also a coward. She didn't speak up. She didn't fight back. Most of what she thought and felt never got said. 'You're a bit of a mystery,' Monsieur Clément liked to say. He made her sound a lot more interesting than she was. But he was right about one thing: there *was* a lot going in her head.

When the bell rang, she didn't leave school as she normally would, straight after class. If she was late, her mother worried. Maman often said Samir and Aisha were all she had to live for, which was why they had to make sure nothing happened to them. She said the *cité* wasn't safe, not even during the day. *That's what you get for raising us in a suburb that has the highest crime rates in the country*, Samir told her. Aisha said nothing. The council estate wasn't so bad, as long as you stayed out of trouble. Maman's reply was always the same. *I had no choice*. She was so passive, so accepting, and Aisha could see it made her brother even angrier; it was like she was saying Aisha and Samir couldn't choose either. Typically, her mother and Samir would carry on bickering in this familiar way and she'd be quiet but all the while she'd be thinking that, actually, it wasn't the dealers and the gangs she was worried about. It was the girls.

Generally, she started walking home the minute school was over. Even if she knew what was coming. But today she couldn't face it. When she saw Katarina and the others at the gate, waiting for her as they always did, she nearly screamed. It was strange because it was like every other day. Except the day before Samir had been there, and she'd been able to bear it, and today he wasn't, even though he'd said he'd wait for her. Maybe she'd just reached her limit.

Katarina was looking around the snow-covered yard, really eagerly, like she was waiting for a friend. Aisha hid behind a wall before the girls could see she was there, and waited. She waited two hours. It was freezing. She did not pray to Allah; that was the sort of thing her mother would do. She tried to keep her mind busy. She thought of home and her side of the room she shared with Maman, with the Stromae poster from the concert she'd been to a couple of years back, the best night of her life, and she thought of Samir's scowling face at the dinner table, and of Antoine who wasn't really their uncle but she and Samir were supposed to call him that because he was the closest thing they had to a relative here and Samir needed a man in his life, Maman said. Aisha figured her mother was lonely and Antoine wasn't good-looking or anything but he was a ready listener and Maman needed someone she could talk to. When she looked sad or worried Aisha urged her mother to confide in her, but Maman said it was parents who were supposed to look after their children, not the other way around. *Be a good girl, stay out of trouble, that's all I ask of you.*

The hyenas – it's how she'd come to think of those girls because they were just like a pack of dirty dogs, they always looked like they could do with a bath; and their high-pitched laughter was like the strange sounds hyenas made, on those nature shows on TV. Katarina was scarier than those hyenas. She was the worst of them all with her acned face and long, greasy hair. She was from one of those eastern countries that joined the European Union, and now everyone said they too were invading France and taking people's jobs away. Antoine who had a sociology degree liked to say it used to be the blacks and the Arabs who copped all the flack and now it was also the pasty-faced people from the east. Maybe that explained why

Katarina was so unforgiving. She didn't want anyone to think that the two of them might have something in common. She called Aisha *bougnoule* and Aisha didn't think she even knew what it meant except she knew it was bad. All the way home, Katarina and the others walked behind her and called her names. In their shoes, Aisha would be ashamed. The worst was when they took her schoolbag. When she got it back the next day it was usually full of rotting food and other really disgusting stuff. Once there was even a used tampon at the bottom of the bag.

What was the use of praying to Allah then? Even if she believed, what sort of conversation would that be? Maybe she could ask for advice. *Please God, what should I do?* She wanted to kill them. Didn't it say somewhere in the Koran that it was okay to strike at your enemy?

The day before, Samir had waited at the gate, the way he sometimes did. Looking bored, and restless, like he had somewhere else to be. She never asked why he agreed to do this, in case he decided to stop. It didn't matter why, or whether he resented being there. The important thing was that he showed up.

She was so relieved, so grateful then. They didn't hurt her if he was there. They were too busy trying to get him to notice them, which he did, of course, but not in the way they wanted him to. Yesterday he'd looked different, Aisha wasn't sure why. He was dressed the same as always, with the puffer jacket and scarf Antoine had given him for his last birthday. His bag was slung over his shoulder, as usual, and he was smoking. Maman hated it. He was also letting his hair grow. Aisha wished he would stop doing things just to upset their mother.

Samir was eighteen months younger than her, but most people wouldn't know it. He was a head taller. And handsome. He seriously looked like Tahar Rahim in *A Prophet*. He'd inherited the best from their parents. Aisha had her father's big nose – she'd seen the photos - and her mother's bad eyesight. When she took the glasses off, she was blind.

The hyenas, especially Katarina, became so excited when they saw Samir; She wanted to shout, wait a minute, you know he's a *bougnoule* too, right? But of course, she kept quiet.

'Where's your girlfriend, Samir?' Katarina said. 'Have you got a girlfriend? Why not? A guy like you could have anyone.'

'Don't even look at them,' Samir hissed, and Aisha glanced at him. His face was dark with anger, his jaw tightly clenched. He felt humiliated, she could tell. She knew he despised these girls. Katarina was right: Samir could have anyone he wanted. The funny thing was, he didn't seem interested. She'd never seen him with a girl. And she was pretty sure it wasn't because he was into boys or anything like that.

'Fuck off,' he said to Katarina. 'Crawl back into the hole you came from.' The way she reacted, you'd think he'd paid her a compliment. Howls of high-pitched laughter. Aisha knew better. She knew she would pay for this, next time.

After a while, the girls drifted off, one by one. You could tell they just wanted to get out of the cold. Then it was just Samir and her, the rest of the way home. They didn't talk, not until they reached the estate. He was angry with her and with her, she thought, for losing control.

'I don't know why you let them treat you like that,' he said in a low voice, once they were in the building. His voice was filled with disdain. He stopped to light another cigarette, and just stood there, drawing deeply from it.

'What am I supposed to do?'

He shrugged his shoulders and didn't answer. Aisha waited. When he was done, he stubbed out the cigarette with his shoe and headed for the stairs. The lifts weren't working. They hadn't been working for weeks.

'I won't always be there, you know,' he said, without turning around.

Now, while she waited for him and he didn't show up, she thought about that. *Yes*, she thought. *I am a coward. He has every right to despise me. I despise myself*.

*

From the living-room window in El Chino's apartment, Samir could see the other three tower blocks and down below the concrete skateboard rink where he and his friends rode their bikes. The rink was deserted now, and covered in snow. Two men stood close together, smoking, near the entrance to one of the towers. A woman in a *djellaba* passed them, pushing a pram. The light was beginning to fade.

The blocks were collectively known as the Cité des Fleurs. Samir had lived here since his third birthday. He couldn't remember anything before then. This was all he knew. The estate. The two-bedroom unit he shared with his mother and sister, on the eleventh floor. Same block as where he was now, only four floors up.

For a couple of years now there'd been talk that they would be pulling the buildings down and replacing them with new ones. Fifteen months ago, after the Senegalese kid in Block B had been killed by a stray bullet, Sarko himself had visited the towers and made a speech

all about how he intended to clean up the neighbourhood. Someone
– a cousin of the kid's dad - had called the French president names he
probably wasn't used to hearing up close and the police had dragged
him away.

Down below, Samir heard the sound of glass smashing, followed
by shouting.

The Cité des Fleurs. What a fucking joke.

'Samir?'

He turned to find El Chino staring at him. Was the old man going
to start asking questions?

'I'm going to the shops. You'll have something to eat?' he said
instead. His real name was Alberto, but in the *cité* he was known as El
Chino on account of his slanted eyes. The Chinaman. His slit-eyed
gaze was directed at Samir now. His hand was in his pocket, jingling
coins. As he spoke, he buttoned up his jacket.

'I've put the heater on.' He hesitated. 'And I've left some clothes
for you in the bathroom. Yours are wet, you should take them off. I
won't be long. You wait here. OK?' Fifty years in France and he still
rolled his R's. Samir nodded quickly, to show he understood. He was
still shaking and he couldn't trust himself to speak.

Once he was alone, Samir washed his hands in the kitchen sink.
Only then did he get undressed, dry himself off and take the old
man's clothes. He wandered through the flat, looking in cupboards
and drawers. He found a twenty Euro note in the bedside drawer and
pocketed it. A half-empty bottle of wine stood on the kitchen
counter. He drank straight from it, quick gulps that sent shivers
through his body. The drink steadied him.

It was warm in the flat. And spacious. More space than at home.
Aisha, his mother, Yasmina – they all knew how to make a mess. He

19

didn't mind Yasmina so much, but his mother and sister – that was a different story. Shit everywhere. Hairbrushes with long strands of hair sticking out of them. Crumpled tissues. Stockings and bras hanging to dry in the bathroom, where his mother washed them by hand. In the evenings he came home to find Aisha and his mother watching reality shows and TV dramas together, sticky sweet wrappers piling up between them. They'd be crying together over a kid with a terminal disease or a woman whose husband had left her for someone younger and better-looking.

'What's the matter with you?' Samir asked his sister. It was one thing for his Mum to fill up on sugar and watch rubbish on TV. He couldn't stand to see Aisha do it. To think that maybe thirty, forty years down the track this would be her.

'Maman likes it. It makes her happy when we do these things together. You should try it.'

'Try what?'

'To make someone other than yourself happy.'

Right now, Aisha would be doing her homework. Listening to Stromae on her headphones. Anyone would think the man was a god, the way Aisha carried on. Their mother would be cooking dinner. The TV would be on in the background because his mother couldn't cope with silence. They wouldn't be worried yet. They were used to Samir coming in late. Only Aisha might be angry with him for not walking her home.

Samir's head was spinning. It was like the first time he'd tried marijuana. He'd felt panicky. Sweaty palms, racing heart. It didn't help that the others were all having a good time with it. Laughing at him like he was a big kid riding a bike for the first time. He took several deep breaths now. He knew he was avoiding thinking about where he'd just been.

He looked at himself in the mirror. On any other day, he might have laughed at his reflection. He was wearing the Spaniard's baggy corduroys and ratty cardigan. He'd lent him socks too; Samir's were soaked through.

'Stay as long as you need,' El Chino said. His voice was gruff but that didn't mean he was angry.

He never asked why Samir came. Why he'd turned up now, wild-eyed and shivering. At the door, Samir had kept his hands in his pockets, where the old man couldn't see them.

'I'll get you a hot drink. Some clothes. Here, put these on.'

No questions asked.

He was starving. He found bread on the counter and cheese in the fridge. Ate his sandwich standing in the kitchen. The wine was making him sleepy. There was coffee left in the pot and he finished that too. It was lukewarm and bitter. He wished he had a cigarette, but the Spaniard didn't smoke. Maybe he should have asked him to buy a pack while he was at the shops.

He pulled a chair up to the kitchen table with his back to the window. He was very still. Trying to identify every sound in the building. When his mobile rang he checked to see who it was. Karim again. He ignored it.

He didn't need to turn around to know what was down there, on the streets and in the spaces between the concrete blocks. In the wasteland behind the towers. Nothing but people's rubbish and kids looking for privacy. He knew every square inch, every corner where you could hide. Nothing shocked him.

Until today.

He tried not to think about it but that made it worse. How could a person's body look like that, like it wasn't made of bone and muscle and ligaments? The angle was all wrong. The sounds in the building receded and now Samir heard, all over again, the slow, shuddering breaths coming from the fragile torso beneath the jumper. The ragged sound escaping from those lips, like the sound of wet paper ripping. Snowflakes softly falling. Blood dripping on the ground. Still alive, but not for long. Surely not for long.

Samir wrapped his arms around his body, pulling the cardigan close. The light was gone now. He wondered when someone would find him. The boy in the shopping trolley.

Four

Alberto Rosales woke up in a cold room and checked the time. It was just past 7 a.m. He crossed into the living-room to turn the central heating on. Samir was fast asleep, curled up under the blanket the old man had covered him with before going to bed.

Samir, Alberto said quietly. Then, a bit louder. *Samir.* He needed the lad to wake up and call his mother. She would be worried sick. He should have let her know last night. Only Samir had seemed so distressed, though he'd done his best to hide it. He just needs a bit of time to recover from whatever it is that's upset him, then he'll go home, Alberto had thought. Now he felt like he'd made a mistake.

When the boy didn't stir, Alberto left him. In the kitchen, he made coffee and poured milk and cereal into a bowl. The bench was littered with crumbs and he wiped it clean.

'Morning.' Samir appeared, rubbing his eyes. 'Thanks for letting me stay.'

Alberto stared at him, momentarily confused. He'd forgotten that he'd lent his clothes to the boy. He looked comical in them, like a child playing at being a grown-up.

'You need to call your mother. She will be wondering where you are. We should have called her yesterday.'

'It's OK. I'll head home in a minute.'

'You're welcome to stay longer if you need, I'm not saying you have to go… just that you should tell her where you are.'

'Like I said, I'll just go home once I've had my coffee.'

'How do you like it?'

'Black, two sugars. Thanks.'

The boy hovered and Alberto spooned sugar into his cup, wondering whether he should say anything about the night before.

How did you talk to a teenage boy? Alberto had no clue. He and Emilia had never had children. That was just the way things had turned out. And he didn't think his own childhood was anything to go by. He'd been the eldest of thirteen. His parents' helper.

'Are you OK?' he finally asked. The boy was holding the cup with both hands. His face was drawn and his eyes red, as though he'd been weeping.

'I'm fine. Just wanted space, you know? Sometimes you need to get away from things.'

'I know,' Alberto said, though he didn't really. Away from things was where he stood most of the time. But Samir had been visiting him for years now. Finding something here that he couldn't get elsewhere. Ever since that first time when Alberto had found him sitting on the stairs. Seven years ago now. He didn't give much away. But still. A good kid.

Alberto told Samir to help himself to bread or cereal, and went to his room to give him space. Out of habit, he made his bed. Folded his pajamas and slipped them under his pillow.

Five years on, it was still strange to sleep alone in this bed, he thought. He and Emilia had been together throughout their adult lives. The first time he'd seen her dancing the muñeira on the village square, during the traditional mid-August festivities, he'd known she was the one.

Back in Spain, he'd been Beto to his friends and family. Here too, for a while. But for years now he'd been El Chino. He didn't mind the name. What he minded was the way things had changed on the estate. When he and Emilia had come here, it had been mostly working-class people. Spaniards like him, sick of struggling and sick of Franco, in search of new beginnings. Italians and Portuguese too. Alberto had found a job at the Renault factory and joined the Communist Party. He and Emilia, their friends and colleagues: they'd *believed* in something. He hadn't had much, but he'd had a voice.

Not long after that, things had started to change. The Arab-Israeli War of 1973 had driven oil prices up and people started worrying about the economy and about jobs; and all of a sudden France didn't want migrants anymore. But they kept coming. Different people moved into the *cité*. Most of them North African. Alberto still had his party card but that was pretty much all that he'd held on to. Nothing much remained of the old 'Beto'. He hardly knew himself.

Down below Alberto heard the sound of sirens and he stopped, clutching a pillow in his hand. The sirens were getting louder. He moved to the window and saw the flashing lights turn into the space between the tower blocks. Two police cars and an ambulance. Men in uniform got out of their vehicles and disappeared behind the buildings. The police remained but the paramedics returned to the ambulance after a while, and drove away.

What *now*? Alberto thought. He didn't like the fact that the paramedics had left empty-handed. No one to administer first aid to, in the ambulance, or to take to hospital. That's what happened normally when someone was hurt. This, what was happening now below, could be worse.

He finished what he was doing and went to check on Samir. But when he returned to the living-room, the boy was gone.

*

It was all over the news. Morel and his team watched in silence.

'Here we go again. Villeneuve makes the news. Poor kid,' Jean said once Morel had turned the TV off.

The boy had been beaten and dumped in a shopping trolley, outside a housing estate in Villeneuve. He'd died out there on his own. The trolley had been left on waste ground behind the high-rise council buildings. Someone had alerted police early in the morning. An anonymous caller. The camera zoomed in on the area. The height of the tower blocks made it a shadowy place. The snow had melted, revealing dirt. The camera then showed where the boy had lived. A shantytown built from cardboard and corrugated iron, half a kilometre from the towers. A broken-down caravan, surrounded by litter. Blank faces behind the dirty panes.

'Gypsies,' Lila said.

'What about them?' Jean said.

'Nothing. Just that no one likes them.'

'Is that a fact?'

'Yes, it is. This isn't about what I think. Even the *Beurs* don't want them there.'

'Do you really –' Jean began, but Morel cut him off.

'Don't. Let's get back to work.'

Jean wasn't easily offended. He searched Morel's face.

'You look like you should be in bed.'

'I'm OK.'

'The Cité des Fleurs,' Lila mused. 'The prettier the name, the shittier the place is. Have you noticed that?'

No one bothered to answer.

Morel returned to his desk. He kept himself apart from his team thanks to a Song-era, Chinese screen he and his ex-wife Eva had received for their wedding. When they'd separated, he'd taken the gift. Luckily, she hadn't known its value.

He knew the heater was on but he was still cold. His headache had returned. He took a couple of Nurofens and flushed them down with a glass of water.

When he looked up, Lila stood before him. She looked like she was gearing herself for a fight.

'What is it?' He realized now he was too sick to be here. A confrontation with Lila was the last thing he needed.

'I need to talk to you.'

'What about? Any luck with our missing man?'

He knew it wasn't that. Inwardly, he was bracing himself for a storm.

'Nothing so far. That's not what I want to talk about. You're thinking of taking Akil on.'

'I am. He's a good detective.'

'You should know that he and I have split up.'

'I'm sorry to hear that. But it doesn't change the fact that he'd be a great addition to the team.'

'If he joins us, it will make things very difficult for me.'

He looked at her and saw the turmoil he'd caused. Instead of softening him, it had the opposite effect. 'When it comes to the job,' he said coldly, 'I expect you both to behave professionally. Regardless of what's been happening in your private lives. I don't want you bringing your personal issues in here, compromising the team.'

Lila looked at him with disbelief. 'I can't decide whether you really are so devoted to this job that you can't or won't see the human consequences of your actions, or whether you're just an insensitive, cold-hearted prick.'

27

'Be careful, Lila.'

'I'm going with the former,' she continued, 'but I still don't like what it says about you. Tell me, when was the last time you invested yourself in a relationship? My guess is you don't even know what I'm talking about.'

'Lila —'

'Maybe the latter is right,' she said. 'Maybe you are a prick.'

She turned and left before he had a chance to say anything.

*

By the end of the day, the death of the Rom boy was the number one news item. For a long time now, Villeneuve had boasted the highest crime rate in the country, but it didn't make the news any less shocking. Over and over again, the different news channels replayed scenes from the streets in the zone where he'd been found. People came down from the tower blocks to hear what was being said. Few were willing to talk, though one elderly woman had plenty to say.

'What do you expect?' she said loudly. 'Have you seen the state of this place? The squalor? If you let people live like animals, they'll behave like animals.'

Morel didn't leave the office till five. He drove carefully. It seemed to take forever to get home. He turned the heater up high but as usual the car wasn't having any of it. He listened to the radio to stay alert. Already the 'experts' were commenting on the event, what it meant, who was to blame. Politicians were vying for air-time, taking the opportunity to pontificate in abstract terms about justice, dignity, integration. Marine Le Pen, it had to be said, did not waste time on such philosophical abstractions, even if she too had a flair for sidestepping questions. *This is what happens when you avoid a real debate on the question of immigration, when you sweep the issue under the table.* People were invited to call in. The general public, regardless of their political affiliation, tended to agree on one thing: the government was responsible.

By the time Morel reached Neuilly, the affluent suburb where he lived with his father, shops were closing. Only the Monoprix was still busy. At the lights, Morel watched a mother and three young children come out, loaded with bags. All four were blonde, and tanned, despite the time of year. They must have gone skiing over Christmas, Morel thought.

He turned into his street and drove into the courtyard. His hands on the steering wheel were numb and he was shivering. Augustine was putting her coat on when he walked in.

'Bonsoir, Augustine. Where is my father?'

'Watching television. He's had his dinner. Yours just needs heating up.'

'Thank you.'

'My pleasure. You look like you should be in bed. See you in the morning.'

After she'd left, he warmed up his dinner – Augustine had made a *boeuf bourguignon* – and took his plate to the living-room. He picked at his food, thinking that he wasn't that hungry after all. Despite his exhaustion, he forced himself to speak.

'Did you have a good day, Papa?'

'It was alright,' the old man answered. His eyes were glued to the screen. This was a man who'd never watched anything but the evening news on television. He'd despised every other TV programme, as a matter of principle.

'What are you watching?' Morel asked.

'I'm not sure. Looks like rubbish,' his father said.

Morel looked at the screen. It was a reality show whose name he'd forgotten.

'I think you're right,' he said. 'It's complete rubbish.'

The old man didn't respond, but Morel thought he caught a hint of a smile.

Later, in bed, he thought about his conversation with Lila. It bothered him. She'd crossed a line, but it wasn't that. What bothered him was the way he'd spoken to her and also the way he'd felt. As if, during his exchange with Lila, he'd been an observer rather than a participant, watching the scene from a long distance away.

It came to him, all at once. *Just like my father.* Cold. Unfeeling. Was he really becoming like the old man?

But Lila had crossed a line.

It isn't just me. She doesn't make things easy either, he thought.

He slipped under the covers and looked for a comfortable position. His limbs ached and his head still throbbed. Morel looked at the origami snowflakes strung across the window. He'd amused himself by making each one different and unique, but it wasn't taxing work, more like the sort of challenge a clever and somewhat dexterous child might choose to meet. It was a long time since he'd made something that mattered.

Still, the flakes were pretty, strung across the window. He reached out and gave each a twirl, creating the illusion of falling snow. In his fuzzy state, the illusion seemed real. His fingers brushed against the pane. The glass was cold. He pulled the covers up to his chin and closed his eyes.

*

Aisha lay in bed trying to sleep. She could hear her mother in the next room. Watching TV. Waiting.

Where the hell was Samir? She was trying to hold on to her anger in order to avoid thinking the worst. *Please*, she said out loud. *Please come home. Or call. Or text. We're worried.*

Her mother had turned up at school. They'd walked back together. Aisha had felt ashamed, then guilty for feeling that way about her mother. But why did she insist on covering her head and wearing a *djellaba* outside the home, and when people came around? Why couldn't she see what it did to Aisha? There were women who dressed like that in their community, of course, but they were generally older. Maybe her mother wouldn't dress that way if she knew what it cost her daughter. Out of the corner of her eye, Aisha had spotted Katarina and her friends, sniggering and muttering things under their breath. Her mother hadn't noticed; she'd been too upset about Samir.

We need to go to the police, she'd said. They'd caught the bus to the Villeneuve police station and filed a report. 'How old is Samir?' the desk officer had asked. When Aisha said sixteen, he looked like he wasn't all that interested anymore.

'He's probably with his friends. Or girlfriend. Does he have a girlfriend?'

She'd wanted to explain about her brother – that he would never stay away overnight, because he would never put their mother through so much worry and suffering, even if he could be unfeeling sometimes. However trying he could be, he would never go that far. But there was no point. She could see this man didn't care about Samir.

31

'Where do you live?' the officer asked. When she gave the address, he livened up a bit.

'That's where the boy was found this morning,' he said. She didn't know what he was talking about. But she saw the way the policeman looked at her. Like he was noticing her for the first time.

Now she heard a beep and sat up in bed. She reached for her phone and looked at the screen.

Didn't get a chance to talk to you today. How are you?

She hesitated before typing.

Samir has disappeared.

What do you mean, disappeared?

He didn't come home last night.

She waited for a reply. Nothing came. She typed,

I'm scared.

The reply came immediately.

You know I'm here for you. AS A FRIEND.

She looked at the last three words. After a while, she deleted the whole exchange.

Five

The next morning, Morel was finishing his breakfast when the doorbell rang. He went to the entrance, his father following close behind.

'Quiet, Descartes,' Morel said. The dog ignored him and continued to bark joyfully.

Morel opened the door and stood back in surprise. He hadn't seen her in a decade or more, but he had no trouble recognizing her.

'Virginie! What are you doing here?'

'Good morning, Serge.' His sister Maly's old school friend stood at the door. 'You look terrible. Like you're coming down with something. Friendly dog?' she asked, pointing at Descartes who was trying to squeeze past Morel to get to her.

Morel nodded.

'Embarrassingly so.'

'He seems friendly. But with a dog that size it's best to ask, don't you think?' She reached over and stroked Descartes head, earning a big lick across her wrist. 'I know it's very early but I need to talk to you.' With characteristic straightforwardness, even after all these years, she stepped closer and placed her palm flat against his forehead.

'You're very warm.'

Before he could say anything, she looked past him and spotted his father.

'Good morning, Monsieur Morel. Now *you* look well. This snow is unbelievable, no?'

*

'I can't remember the last time it was like this. I could barely find my car this morning; then it took me half an hour to start it. Were you intending to drive to work? Because I don't think yours is going anywhere this morning.'

Still a chatterbox, Morel thought. And the same, bright red curls. Though she must be doing something to keep her hair that way nowadays. Morel's was not as black as it had once been – it seemed that, with each passing week, he was finding more white hairs - and Virginie was a couple of years older than him.

Things were coming back to him. Late nights at his sister Maly's house, sitting uncomfortably around the table having fiery exchanges about love and politics. Virginie was always there, along with Maly's other university friends. They all interrupted each other and smoked as though their lives depended on it. Listening to them, you'd think no one had come up with a single original idea before. Even as a student, he'd never belonged in that *milieu*.

Morel handed Virginie a cup of coffee. He'd quickly got showered and dressed, while Virginie kept his father company. It didn't take her long to figure it out. 'How long has he been unwell?' she asked him quietly when he returned.

'A while now.' They both looked at Philippe Morel, who was staring into his cup as if to make sure it didn't contain poison.

'I'm sorry.' Virginie propped herself up on a kitchen stool, opposite Morel and his father. 'You're wondering why I've turned up here all of a sudden. Let me explain. You won't know this, but I work as a school counselor. At a school in Villeneuve. It wasn't by choice, initially, but now – ' She didn't finish her sentence, and went on. 'There's a girl I've been working with. Aisha. She's seventeen, nearly eighteen. Extremely bright. I'm fond of her. She's preparing her *baccalauréat* this year. Wants to be a journalist, she says.' Virginie smiled. 'She writes poems too, and they're surprisingly good.'

'Why are you seeing her?'

Virginie hesitated. 'Since the beginning of this school year, Aisha's behaviour has been different. She's been withdrawn. At times, she's rude and aggressive, which isn't like her. And her results aren't as good as they have been in previous years. Some of the teachers are worried she might be depressed. I spoke with her maths teacher, who's been observing her for some time. She seems convinced Aisha will try to harm herself.'

'It's a tricky age, isn't it? I would have thought that for an adolescent to be rude and withdrawn isn't so unusual.'

'These things aren't always easy to measure,' Virginie admitted. 'And I have to say not everyone's worried about Aisha's state of mind. Her French and philosophy teacher Luc Clément says she's engaged, taking an interest in her work. I think I'd rather err on the side of caution, though, so when there are concerns I tend to take them seriously. Another girl in the class tried to kill herself, halfway through the year. She nearly succeeded. You've got to be watchful with kids that age.'

'So what do you think is wrong? Is she suicidal?' Morel asked. He wondered where Virginie was going with this. What did any of this have to do with him?

'Suicidal? No, I don't think so. But I think something must have happened for her to be acting so differently. It's out of character. She's usually attentive and engaged in all her classes, and well-mannered. So, I've been spending a bit of time with her. Trying to draw her out. She's a bright, sensitive girl. But given the circumstances.... you can imagine what a place like Villeneuve is like.

The local schools don't receive enough funding; they don't have the staff and experience to cope with the challenges they face. Local youth unemployment is somewhere around forty percent. It's a tough environment.'

Morel considered this. 'Has something happened to her? Is that why you're here?'

'No.' She shook her head. 'It's her brother. Samir. He left for school the day before yesterday and hasn't been home since. When his mother called the school, they told her he hadn't come in at all. The poor woman is frantic.'

'How old is Samir?' Morel asked, before she could continue.

'Sixteen. Going on twenty-five.' She said it with an uneasy laugh.

'Has his mother called the police?'

'Yes. They didn't seem to take it too seriously. They asked whether he might be staying with friends.'

'And you don't think he's playing up,' Morel said.

'Do you think I'd be here if I thought he was playing up?' She put her cup down. 'Serge, I know this boy. I'm not saying he's a saint or anything. His mother's had a tough time with him lately. The family lives in one of our most troubled *cités*. The boy, predictably, spends more time with his friends than he does at home. He might be hanging out with the wrong crowd. I don't know. But this – this disappearing act – now that's not the sort of thing he'd do. He isn't always easy on his mother but he wouldn't leave her to worry like this.'

'Where's the father?'

'He went missing in Algeria before the family moved here. A local journalist. Just vanished one day. The kids were young, they don't remember him. Loubna moved her children here shortly afterwards, with the help of an elder brother who was already living here. That brother passed away several years ago.'

Morel nodded.

'I don't know how I can help,' he said. 'This isn't my jurisdiction, for a start.'

'If you could just come with me, to see Samir's mother,' Virginie said. 'And Aisha. You'll see straight away that something's wrong.'

Go with Virginie to Villeneuve? The idea was absurd and he would tell her that. Morel looked past her at the snow outside his window. Lila and the others in his team were investigating a drowning. It was the sort of case that should have gone to the local police, in the 4th *arrondissement* where the victim had lived. But Superintendent Olivier Perrin, Morel's boss, had assigned the investigation to his team. This time of year, it happened that you got landed with cases like this because people were still away on holiday. Plus, the man was a well-known professional tennis player. The story was in the papers and Morel's team had spent the past days fielding phone calls from journalists desperate for a story.

No one, on the other hand, was going to lose any sleep over a missing kid from the projects. Except his mother and sister, of course. *But it's not my problem. Let the local police take care of it*. Morel rationalized it all in his head. He was annoyed with Virginie for putting him on the spot.

'I don't really have time for this, I'm sorry,' he said, and he stood up, hoping she would take the hint and leave. His father stood up too, but as he did so, he knocked his coffee cup off the table with his elbow, spilling its contents across the counter. Virginie immediately grabbed a cloth from the kitchen sink and used it to clean the spill.

'It's okay, it's nothing,' she said, touching the old man's shoulder. Morel saw confusion on his father's face, and something else. Distress. He watched Virginie lean towards Philippe and say a few words to reassure him that it was a tiny incident, anyone could have spilled the drink. His father's body went slack and he let Virginie lead him out of the kitchen and into the living-room. Morel could hear her talking as if she was chatting to an old friend. *What's wrong with me?* He thought. *I feel nothing.*

After a couple of minutes, Virginie returned. 'Poor man,' she said. 'It must be hard for him.'

She clutched her car keys, and buttoned her jacket. 'I'd better get going.'

He made his mind up quickly. 'Wait. I'll do it. I'll come with you and meet the family.'

'Really?' She seemed astonished. When he nodded, she came around the kitchen counter and gave him a quick, awkward hug.

'But I really can't stay long,' he added.

'Let's go in my car, yours might take a while to start,' she said 'It won't take long at all and I'll drop you off at work afterwards.'

Philippe Morel was back in the kitchen, gazing at Descartes lying on the floor. They all heard the key in the front door and moments later Augustine appeared. Philippe frowned at her. She gave the old man a wide grin.

'Bonjour, Monsieur Morel. You've had breakfast, then? How about getting dressed, and we'll go for a stroll once I'm done cleaning the dishes? You wouldn't believe the amount of snow out there.'

Morel's father ignored her. Instead, he turned to his son and pointed to Virginie.

'Who is this woman?' he asked. 'And why did you let her bring that dog inside?'

*

'I'll get it.' Aisha looked through the peephole to see who it was. She stepped back and took the safety latch off.

'Monsieur Rosales. How are you?'

'Very well, thank you. I'm sorry to disturb you. I was wondering if Samir was here?'

'Why do you ask?'

It wasn't the response he'd been expecting and he looked down at his feet.

'I simply wanted to make sure he was OK.'

Aisha glanced back towards the flat before stepping into the hallway.

'I don't know if he's OK. We haven't seen Samir since yesterday morning,' she said.

The news seemed to distress the old man considerably.

'What – what do you mean?'

'What's happened, Monsieur Rosales?' Aisha asked. She reminded herself not to cry. Her mother was inside, Aisha had to hold it together for her sake.

'It's just that he came to me the night before last.'

'To your place?'

'Yes. He was – upset, I guess. I let him stay the night. I should have told your mother, I know now that I should have. But I thought Samir needed space.'

Aisha digested his words. She couldn't believe what she was hearing. 'My mother's worried sick.'

'I'm sorry, I should have – anyway, yesterday morning he said he would go home and I needn't worry. I thought he would come straight here. Why wouldn't he? After all he *said* he would.'

'He didn't come home.' All that worry and suddenly she couldn't hold it in any longer. 'Maybe he would be home with us now if you had told us about his visit, if you had called straight away when he decided to stay so late at your place.'

There was nothing he could say to that. He was guilty. 'Where could he be?' he asked, a quaver in his voice. Such a dumb question, Aisha thought. She resisted the urge to slam the door in his face.

'Have you tried his friends?' Alberto asked.

'What do you think?'

'Is there anything at all I can do?' He looked pitiful. Just then her mother came to the door.

'What is it, Monsieur Rosales?'

'Samir spent the night at his place the night before last,' Aisha said coldly.

'I should have said...' his voice trailed off. Aisha's mother took a step forward.

'Will you please tell him to come home?' she said.

'He's not *there* anymore, *Maman*.' Aisha turned to Alberto.

'I –' he began.

'Leave us alone,' Aisha said.

Six

In the 1950s, with foreign workers streaming in to the country and Paris bursting at the seams, urban planners and architects looked to the regions beyond the *boulevards péripheriques* – the motorways that marked the symbolic divide between Paris and its suburbs – as a means of resolving the housing crisis. In no time at all, Villeneuve turned into a vast construction site. Everywhere you looked, tower blocks and large council estates were going up. In the news, the Cité des Fleurs, erected on the old beet fields, was held up as a success. Families, French and foreign, praised their new neighbourhood with its spacious apartments and green, open spaces. In private, officials and architects congratulated themselves for what they saw as a prime example of successful social engineering. The architects had designed open spaces where people could meet and where children could play. Neighbours left their doors unlocked and balconies were decked with flowers, making the *cité*'s name seem apt.

Within a few decades, the buildings, built on the cheap, had fallen into disrepair. Drugs, mostly hashish and marijuana, became rife, and unemployment soared. One by one, shop-owners shut down their businesses, sick of being robbed. People started locking their doors and few bothered to adorn their balconies. All that remained was a grim, uniform landscape.

*

Looking at it now, it was hard to believe the Cité des Fleurs had started out as an utopian vision, Morel reflected as he and Virginie got out of her car and headed towards one of the tower blocks; a vision based on the belief that, somehow, architecture could shape social outcomes.

'The lift stopped working months ago. It looks like they still haven't done anything about it,' Virginie said as they pushed the door open and entered a dank hallway. Cigarette butts everywhere. A greasy, scrunched up McDonald's bag. The air smelt of stale cigarette smoke and piss.

'What floor?' Morel asked.

'Eleventh. You don't exactly blend in here,' Virginie said. He was dressed in a dark grey Hugo Boss suit, a Cucinelli cashmere sweater and a Pucci tie with a pink and gray design.

'I have a meeting today,' he said. 'I wasn't expecting to be here this morning.'

'Quite frankly, you'd be less conspicuous if you were naked.'

They walked up the stairs in silence. Morel's head was spinning. He had to stop on the fourth floor, and again on the seventh floor landing to catch his breath.

The woman who opened the door wore a black kaftan and house slippers. She was in her thirties, Morel guessed. Her kohl-rimmed eyes were filled with worry as she stepped aside to usher them in. Behind her, a teenage girl appeared in the dark hallway. Aisha, no doubt. The short hair gave her a boyish look. She gave him a frank stare.

'So you're the hot shot detective?'

'I don't know about that,' Morel said. The girl's eyes behind her glasses were striking, like her mother's.

Virginie turned to the mother. 'Loubna, this is my friend Serge Morel. He is a senior police detective. I asked him to come here because I know how worried you are about Samir.'

'Very worried. I think something must have happened to my boy. Why else would he not be here with us?' She seemed unsteady on her legs, and Virginie stepped forward. 'Perhaps we should all sit down?' she said. She steered Loubna towards the living area, a dark, single room with a sofa, a TV and a formica dining table with four chairs.

'Have you called the police yet?' Morel asked. It was Aisha who replied.

'We didn't just call. We actually *went* to the police station yesterday to file a report. They won't do anything,' she said, disgusted. They were all standing, except for Loubna who sat at the table, very still, her worry like a swarm of bees beneath the stillness.

'When exactly did either of you last see Samir?' Morel asked.

'The day before yesterday, at breakfast,' Aisha said. 'I didn't notice him at school but then I don't always. And Monsieur Rosales on the seventh floor says Samir stayed with him the first night he didn't come home.'

'Hold on. I thought you said he'd been missing for two nights,' Morel said, turning to Virginie. 'He hasn't, really, not if you know where he spent the first night.'

'I didn't know this,' Virginie said apologetically. 'Who is this Monsieur Rosales, Aisha?'

'El Chino,' the girl said. 'That's what everyone calls him. Alberto Rosales is his real name. His wife died five years ago,' she added *à-propos* of nothing.

'What's the connection with Samir?' Morel asked tetchily. He was thinking that he'd wasted his time coming here.

'For years now, Samir has been visiting him.' Aisha shrugged. 'He likes going there. I don't know why.'

'Could you tell us where his flat is exactly?' Morel said. He would be thorough, at least.

'Sure.' Aisha gave him the unit number. 'Are you planning on speaking to him?'

'No. I'll leave it with the local police. But I'll talk to them personally and make sure they follow up.'

'Samir would never do this unless he was in some kind of trouble. Why won't any of you take this seriously?' Aisha said shrilly. At the sound of her daughter's voice, Loubna came alive.

'Aisha,' her mother scolded. 'Don't be rude.'

Virginie stood up and turned to the girl's mother. 'Shall we have some tea? I'll help you make it.'

'I'm sorry, my manners...'

'Not at all. You're worried about your son. The last thing you need to be thinking about is your manners,' Virginie said briskly. With a meaningful look at Morel, she steered Loubna towards the kitchen. He could hear the clatter of dishes, the woman's high-pitched, hurried chatter, full of worry, and Virginie's voice, measured and calm.

Morel took in his surroundings. There wasn't much to look at. The cheap furniture; a shabby, mustard-coloured rug. A dozen postcards, tacked to the wall.

He turned to Aisha, who was looking towards the hallway, clearly wondering how she could leave the room without seeming rude.

'You're not going to school today?' he asked.

'I don't think so. I went yesterday. I didn't want to but Maman insisted. A couple of times I almost fell asleep in class. Neither of us has been sleeping properly.'

'I remember. Dozing in class, I mean. That used to happen to me when I was your age,' he said. 'I used to find it hard to concentrate. Still do, sometimes.'

Her eyes found his. 'Mostly it happens to me in physics. I hate it. I don't *get* any of it.'

He nodded. 'Tell me about the last time you saw Samir.'

'We were getting ready for school. Samir always takes forever. I left before he did. Sometimes we walk together.'

'You go to the same school?'

'For now. Though Samir will probably end up doing a technical degree. You know, a BEP. His teachers think he should. Train to be a mechanic or something. Which means next year he won't be at school anymore.'

'And he was supposed to wait for you after school? The day before yesterday?'

'He told me before I left home that he'd be at the school gate in the afternoon.'

'What for? Is it because your mother prefers it if you walk with him?'

'It's just so we can walk home together.'

'And he didn't show up.'

Aisha didn't reply. Instead, she seemed to close up.

'Does he usually walk you home?' Morel asked. There was something there. Aisha wouldn't look at him.

'Not usually. Sometimes though.'

'And you prefer it when he does?' Morel wasn't sure why he was asking. But he'd struck a chord. When the girl looked up, her eyes were filled with tears.

Before he could speak again, Loubna and Virginie re-entered the room. Aisha quickly looked down and Morel turned to the two women, aware that the girl did not want them to notice she was upset.

45

'It would help if you could draw up a list of Samir's friends,' Morel said. 'Have you called around to make sure he isn't with one of them?'

'He has nice friends,' the mother said in a tremulous voice. 'They are good boys.'

'That's not what he's asking, Maman,' Aisha said, exasperated. She turned to Morel. 'We've called everyone we know.'

'Any after school activities?'

'No. Sometimes he and his friends play soccer near the school. But Samir always gets home by six. Otherwise Maman gets worried.'

Morel thought about what he'd heard. Wondered what else there was to say.

'Is there anything in particular you're worried about? Anything that could help the police find Samir?' He addressed the question to both Aisha and her mother.

'Have you noticed where we live?' Aisha said. 'There is plenty to worry about.'

The mother nodded.

'I would like my children to grow up somewhere better than this,' she said. 'But it's not possible.'

They heard the front door open and shut, and steps down the hallway. Moments later, a diminutive, bald man entered the room. He'd let himself in to the flat, Morel noted. He stopped when he saw the visitors, but Morel had the distinct impression that he'd known they would be there.

'Antoine,' the man said, stretching out his hand.

'Last name?' Morel said.

'Carrère.'

'You're a friend of the family?'

'Yes.' He turned to Loubna, who had risen to greet him. She seemed animated suddenly, out of embarrassment or relief it was hard to tell.

'Any news?'

'No.'

'Let me drive you to work,' Antoine told Loubna. He glanced at Morel. 'After the policeman is done.'

'I'm done,' Morel said. He stood up. 'I'll drop in on the Villeneuve police station before I head back to Paris and talk to my colleagues here. In the meantime, if you think of anything else they should know, do get in touch. I'll make sure it's passed on.'

He noticed that all three women were looking at him now, with beseeching eyes. 'Is there really nothing more *you* can do for us?' Aisha said.

'There is a process that needs to be followed. There are rules,' he said, aware of how ineffectual that sounded.

Seven

For the first time since he'd left home, Samir was feeling good. He lay on his back and watched as Yasmina stood up from the bed and started to get dressed.

'You can't stay,' she said.

'I know.' He acted as though he didn't mind but inside he felt a pang of anxiety. He'd ended up spending his second night away from home in the cellar, in one of the box-like, storage rooms beneath the tower block where he lived. Wrapped in a pile of dirty blankets someone had dumped there. Generally speaking, it was safe to assume that anyone who used these rooms was up to no good. It was cold and dark down there and he'd spent a nightmarish night worrying that whoever had left the blankets might suddenly turn up and stick a knife in him.

He'd knocked on Yasmina's door at 10 a.m., when he was certain her brother would be gone. Convinced her not to go to work. She seemed to take pity on him. Fed him breakfast and run him a bath. He'd slept like a baby for an hour. Then woken up to find her naked beside him.

Now he wished he could remain here a while longer.

'What time does your brother get back?' he asked.

'Not for a couple of hours. But I've got to pick Leila up.'

'She's with the old lady?'

Yasmina nodded. She was a pretty, Moroccan girl, with curly black hair and long lashes. At twenty-one, she lived with her brother and her two-year old daughter, a child she'd had with a man whose name no one knew: Yasmina had never told anyone. Three days a week, Yasmina's grandmother took care of the girl, while Yasmina worked.

She held a job at a discount supermarket, and each month handed her wages over to her brother.

'One day I'll stop doing it. It's my money,' she often said. But Samir knew these were empty words. She was still paying for the shame of getting pregnant.

'I must be crazy. Sleeping with a 16-year-old,' she said now, looking at Samir stretched out on her bed.

'There are worse things.'

'Like what?' she teased, but she saw he was serious.

'What's the matter?'

He turned away so she wouldn't see his face.

'Nothing.'

She finished getting dressed and leaned over to give him a kiss. 'Time to get up, pretty boy.' He gripped her hand tightly, but she pulled away from him, laughing.

*

Virginie took Morel to the police station, a five-minute drive from the Cité des Fleurs. The circular, two-storey building was at least forty years old, Morel guessed. An ugly relic from the 1970s.

'I'll wait in the car,' Virginie said.

Inside the building, there were boxes everywhere. 'You're moving?' Morel asked the desk officer. He nodded. 'It's about time. The building's infested with rats. The plumbing's faulty. The power keeps tripping. You name a maintenance issue, this building's got it.'

The detective who came out to meet Morel introduced himself as Romain Marchal. There was an edginess about him, something sharp and watchful that made Morel choose his words carefully. 'Commandant Serge Morel,' the man said, making a show of being impressed. 'All the way from the Quai des Orfèvres. It's not often we have such illustrious visitors. I'm sorry the place is such a mess. If you'd come just a week later, we'd be able to welcome you in the new building. It's bright and shiny, at least for now. Things tend not to stay that way for long around here.' His handshake was brisk. They were more or less the same age, Morel guessed. 'To what do we owe this pleasure, then, Commandant Morel?'

'This is about a missing boy,' Morel replied, hoping the other man would stop rolling out his name and title to make some sort of point. He hesitated. 'I know his family. I'm interested in his welfare.'

'Is this the same boy whose sister and mother came in yesterday to file a report?' the desk officer piped up.

'That's right.'

'We've got the details already. Boy's a teenager. The family's Moroccan or something, right?'

'They're originally from Algeria. Look, I'm worried he may be in some kind of trouble,' Morel insisted. He was tired and feverish and he should probably let it go. After all, the boy had been seen the previous morning. But he remembered what Aisha had said about her visit to the station. *They won't do anything.* 'Samir spent the night before last at a neighbour's flat. He didn't come home yesterday either and no one knows where he's been since the neighbour saw him yesterday morning. It's not the sort of thing he would do.'

'So, he's only been missing for 24 hours?' Marchal sighed. He said 'missing' as though he didn't really believe it. 'Look, we've got our hands full at the moment. No doubt you've heard about the Roma boy.'

'I saw. It's all over the news.'

'It's a major headache, that's what it is. As if there wasn't enough going on.' Marchal turned to the desk officer. 'Let's see the report about the missing kid.' The officer handed it over. Marchal skimmed it and frowned. 'The Cité des Fleurs. That's where we found the Roma boy yesterday morning. Behind the towers.'

'I know. I said the same thing to the girl when she came to file the report about her missing brother.' The young officer looked pleased with himself, until he saw how Marchal was looking at him.

'You did, did you? And you didn't think it worthwhile to let any of us know about it? Given we're investigating a murder. A murder which, coincidentally, happened in the same area as where this kid lives who's now missing.'

The officer looked abashed. 'You think there's a link?'

'What I *think* is that you should have passed it on.'

Morel stepped in. 'So, you'll follow up on this.' More a statement than a question.

Marchal looked like he couldn't decide whether to be annoyed or amused. 'We'll keep an eye on it. Maybe you can let me know if the kid – what's his name again?' His eyes skimmed over the paper in his hand. 'Ah yes. *Samir Kateb*. Let me know if he doesn't show up at home tonight.'

'I will.'

*

'Where to now?' Virginie asked. 'Home, or work?' She gave Morel a quick appraisal. 'Thank you for coming out today and meeting the family.' She looked apologetic. 'I feel a bit bad, given how sick you are.'

Morel was mulling over Marchal's words. Thinking about an adolescent who'd left home two days ago, something he never did –

and, aside from his family's concern, the general indifference towards his fate.

'I didn't do much for them,' he said.

'You listened to them. That means something.'

*

Aisha's mother had left for work, with Antoine. He would drop her off and continue on to Clichy, where he taught at a university. Aisha's mother didn't dare take time off, she told her daughter. As it was, she'd left work early the day before to pick Aisha up from school. She was afraid of her manager. Aisha was glad to be alone, in a way. It was hard, having to pretend to be OK for her mother's sake.

On her bed, she pulled her knees up to her chest and rested her forehead on the window. It had stopped snowing but the sun had decided not to show up this morning. There was nothing to look at except grey skies and grey concrete.

Nothing on the horizon. Aisha couldn't see her future. Just these tower blocks, this empty sky. Graffiti-sprayed walls. *Welcome to Baghdad. Kamikaze. Fuck Police.* Burnt-out cars. Everything broken. The swing in the tiny playground, five minutes away. Even as a child, she'd seldom used it. Only the gangs did; the younger kids who were recruited as lookouts hung out there during the day, and the older kids sometimes used it at night, though for anything secretive – whether the intention was to make out or get high - the wasteland was best. There were no eyes on the wasteland, whereas the playground was smack in the middle of the estate, visible to anyone who cared to poke their head out their window to see what was going on. Within the community, news travelled fast. At night, sometimes from the eleventh floor you could hear the older kids, making a point of riling the residents. Day or night, the little kids who

52

just wanted to play rarely found it a welcoming place. Some came anyway, because where else could they go from here? Mahmoud, a boy in her class, lived in the towers, and Aisha knew that his Dad had fixed the swing the first couple of times it broke. For some reason, the dad had got really worked up about the broken swing. Mahmoud had a little brother, who was three. By the fourth time, the Dad had given up. Aisha felt for him. Why bother fixing anything, if it only got vandalized again?

Aisha sighed. She felt a longing to be elsewhere, some place where the colours were bright, fluorescent even, and the streets teeming with well-dressed people. People with a clear sense of purpose, all going to work or maybe to nice cafés where waiters brought you drinks on trays and you could sit for as long as you liked, watching passers-by.

From the top of her building, where she sometimes went with Samir when he wanted to light up – their mother wouldn't let him smoke inside - you could see the Eiffel tower. A year ago now, she and Samir had taken the RER into Paris. Half an hour later and they were walking down the Champs-Elysées where the trees were strung with lights and sprayed with fake snow – it hadn't snowed at all, then, not like this year. Couples walked past them, holding hands. An old lady strolled along the footpath, leading a poodle. Samir had joked that the poodle had better gear than they did. They had walked until their feet hurt, too shy to enter a café and order drinks, though neither would admit it. Aisha smiled, remembering. It had been a nice trip: just the two of them, in Paris.

She stretched out on the bed and closed her eyes. *If I count slowly to thirty, without breathing, Samir will appear.* She did, but nothing happened. *If I count to sixty without breathing, slowly, without cheating, Samir will come. He'll turn up and roll his eyes at us when we tell him how worried we've been.*

By the fourth try, she felt sick. She breathed deeply a couple of times. Then she turned her CD player on. Stromae's voice filled the room. Singing about absent fathers.

*

Lila took a deep breath and gave the tennis player's widow a smile, even though what she really wanted to do was throttle her.

'Madame Simic. We really need to talk about what I found on your husband's laptop.'

Valérie Simic did a good impression of looking bewildered. 'Yes, you mentioned that when you got here, and then we got sidetracked, didn't we? But I really don't understand why you're so interested in his laptop.'

Sidetracked? Lila had been with Simic's wife for twenty minutes now, twenty long minutes during which the other woman had talked incessantly, manically about the couple's life (tennis tournaments, social functions, holidays, more tennis). At Lila's request, she'd made a list of their friends, and of Simic's tennis partners, some of whom he had disliked and who had disliked him. And all the while Lila felt she was being bombarded with information that didn't matter, that only served to distract Lila from what actually did.

Every extra minute she had to spend in the couple's meringue-coloured living-room was making her feel more aggrieved. Why couldn't Vincent, Akil or Jean have done the job? Or Morel, for that matter. Looking at the pretty blonde woman before her, she reflected that any of her male colleagues would have got more out of their time with Madame Simic. She decided to speed things up.

'*Valérie*. I'm going to be straight with you here. I feel you're being evasive, and that's a real problem for me. I don't like wasting my time. That's at a personal level. More generally, I should warn you that by being coy, by holding back on anything you know that might shed some light on how your husband died, you're actually creating difficulties for yourself. It's called obstructing the course of justice.'

'What on earth are you talking about? What could I possibly be hiding? He was drunk when he fell into the water. It was a horrible, stupid *accident*.'

'That's something we have yet to confirm. The autopsy will hopefully tell us more,' Lila said. She went on before the widow could say anything. 'We have your husband's laptop, as you know. Yesterday, I spent some time looking at his correspondence. His e-mails. I found them, shall we say, quite informative. There is, for example, a long and rather graphic exchange with someone who calls herself Bijou. Quite a bit of back and forth banter going on there with this woman, which I won't go into now. Does the name Bijou ring a bell?'

'I can't say that it does,' Valérie said. She patted her hair and played with the pearls around her neck where the skin had turned red all of a sudden, as if from an allergic reaction.

'I think you do,' Lila said quietly. For a moment she almost felt sorry for Madame Simic. Despite appearances, she didn't strike Lila as a fool. Whatever games she and her husband had indulged in by mutual consent- Lila hoped it had been that, at least - it was becoming clear Simic had played a few without his wife's knowledge.

'It would be good if we skipped the part where you claim to have no idea what your husband was up to. It would make things a lot easier for us.' *For me especially*, Lila added inwardly. 'Going by your husband's search history, and the e-mails he's been getting, I'm guessing you two are regular swingers. And possibly into some pretty serious sado-masochistic stuff. Am I right?'

The widow crossed her stockinged legs and sat up a little.

'What of it?'

'I'm no expert on this, but I wonder what sort of people you come across at these sorts of places. S&M sex clubs. Plenty of perfectly nice people I'm sure, but some unsavoury types too I would imagine.'

'I'm not sure I like your tone, detective.'

'We're investigating your husband's death, Valérie. 'I'm told your husband had high levels of alcohol in his blood. If someone pushed him in to the water, he might have drowned. Too much to drink, and it was very cold too. His reflexes would have been slow. On the other hand, it may have been an accident. He may have tripped.'

'Who would want to kill Grégory?' his wife asked. For the first time, Lila detected a foreign accent; it was in the way Valérie had pronounced her husband's name.

'I don't know. But if you could bring yourself to answer my questions truthfully, then maybe we can get to the bottom of this.'

*

Morel refused Virginie's offer of a lift and got her to drop him at an RER station. He took the train back to Paris and then changed to the Pont de Neuilly Métro line that would take him home. On the way there, he called his boss, Superintendent Olivier Perrin, and told him he would not be coming in. He also called Jean to let him know.

Both his father and Augustine were out when he got home. He left a note for her on the kitchen counter, asking not to be disturbed. In his flat, he stripped off his jacket, shoes and tie. He took another two

Nurofens with a glass of water and went to bed, where he fell asleep almost straight away.

When he woke up it was three in the afternoon. He had no memory of the time at which he'd arrived home. Only knew that he felt much better. He propped himself up in bed and called Virginie.

'Any news?'

'No. Nothing.'

He had a missed call from his older sister Maly. When he dialed her number, she answered straight away.

'Everything OK?' she asked, sounding anxious. Sometimes she seemed to have a sixth sense when it came to his wellbeing.

'I've been ill, but it's nothing. A temperature. I'm at home, taking it easy.'

'That's not like you,' she said. A pause. 'Virginie called me earlier. She says you two have been getting re-acquainted.'

'She wants my help with something.' He told her about Samir and Aisha, and about the visit to Villeneuve. Realized as he was telling her that it was preying on his mind. He'd been uneasy all the way home. He'd blamed it on his run-down state and on the sobering effect of his visit to the tower blocks. But it was more than that. He was worried about Samir.

'You sound tired,' Maly said. 'Why don't I come over this evening? I can pick a quiche up on the way there. I'll prepare a salad. We can have a family dinner, with Papa. We haven't sat together and talked for ages.'

Morel thought about the evening ahead. He and his father in front of the TV set, or eating in silence at the kitchen counter.

'That would be nice. What about Noémie?'

Maly laughed. 'Karl can look after his daughter for a while. It'll do him good. And besides, I really need a baby-free night.'

Augustine was in the kitchen and Philippe Morel upstairs, resting. Morel sent her home and suggested to his father that they watch an old Francois Truffaut film. Watching films together wasn't something they'd done before the illness. Mostly they'd kept out of each other's way. Morel turned the heater on high and wrapped himself in a blanket. His father had insisted on changing into pajamas and a dressing-gown though it was still early. 'Look at us,' Morel said, once they were seated comfortably and the film was about to start.

'What?'

'Never mind.' Halfway through the film, his father turned to him and stared, as if aware of him for the first time. 'What's the matter with you? Why aren't you at work?'

'I'm not well. I haven't felt this sick in years, come to think of it.'

'You work too hard,' was all his father said. Nothing after that. A shutter had been raised and shut just as swiftly.

Maly arrived at six, carrying a quiche from Lenôtre and a Leclerc bag with the ingredients she'd bought to make a salad. 'Early dinner,' she said. 'I'm already hungry. Ever since Noémie was born I've been permanently hungry.'

'You're looking good,' Morel said.

'Fat is what you mean.'

'Don't be silly.' He meant what he said. Marriage and motherhood seemed to agree with Maly. She'd always been curvaceous and her figure was more rounded now. But she looked healthy; voluptuous, not overweight. And content, he thought. The three of them ate in the kitchen. Philippe Morel seemed livelier in his daughter's presence. He said little but seemed to be paying attention to what she said.

'How are things with Papa?' she asked when their father was back in front of the TV. It was just the two of them in the kitchen, sharing a bottle of wine. 'And how is it with the dog?'

'It's OK,' Morel said. 'I don't really know what else to say, except thank God for Augustine. I'm worried it may soon prove to be too much for her. It will, you know. One day, he's going to need proper care.'

Neither of them spoke for a while.

'As for Descartes –' Morel continued, glancing at the dog sleeping at his feet – 'he's thriving I'd say. I try to walk him when I can. Augustine does most of it.'

'Poor Serge,' she said. There was tenderness in her voice.

'Well I'm certainly in no position to go anywhere, now, am I.'

'Do you? Want to move out?'

Morel turned to the living-room. The volume on the TV was on high. Morel senior was losing his hearing as well as his memory. 'I don't really know. But I don't like the feeling of being stuck.'

'Perhaps it isn't just about Papa. Or the dog.' She smiled, then grew serious again. 'You create your own circumstances, Serge.' She hesitated. 'Any news of Mathilde?'

'We're meeting for a coffee. We finally managed to settle on a date.' He didn't tell her that it had taken him months to get back to the woman who had been his first love, more than two decades ago now. Just as his obsession with her had started to lessen, she'd tried to get in touch with him. Nearly four months ago. He'd been in Cambodia at the time, working on a case. Now he was about to see her again he didn't know how he felt about it.

59

He saw that his sister was observing him closely. She looked like she might be about to say more, but he cut her short.

'Shall we go and sit with Papa for a while?'

*

Before Maly went home, Morel received a call from Virginie to say there was still no sign of Samir. She told him that Marchal had visited the family and taken statements. He'd also visited Alberto Rosales, the old Spaniard. It was now sixty-two hours since the boy had disappeared.

'The police seemed more interested in the Roma boy's death and whether Samir might be involved than anything else,' she said.

After Maly left and his father had gone to bed, Morel called his ex-lover Solange. She and her husband Henri were about to head off to Aix-en-Provence, where they owned a house. After he'd hung up, he lay on his back for a while, staring at the wall. A familiar, not-altogether uncomfortable feeling took hold of him. He recognized it for what it was. Loneliness. *You create your own circumstances*. Maly's words.

After his nap, Morel found it hard to get to sleep. It was midnight when he heard his father in the kitchen, and he wondered whether to get up and check on him. But his limbs were heavy and it seemed like too much of an effort to get out of bed.

Around one, the snow started to fall. Morel closed his eyes and drifted into oblivion.

It was just past four in the morning when the ringing woke him up. As he reached for the phone, he realized he was sweating again. He should check his temperature. He had no idea what time it was, or how long he'd been asleep. It took a while to figure out who was on the line.

It was Virginie, calling to say that Samir was dead.

Eight

'Where do you think you're going?' Karim's mother grabbed him by his shirt collar and he quickly reached out for the edge of the table to avoid losing his balance. He managed to free himself, and backed away, though there wasn't much space. 'Where else? School, of course. Where did you *think* I was going?' Trying to sound annoyed. He hoped it was convincing. He hadn't gone back to school for nearly a week now, not since the last time they'd called him in to the head teacher's office. Asking questions. First the school, then that crazy *keuf*. All because of Samir. If it wasn't for Samir, Karim thought, no one would be after him for answers. He wouldn't be feeling as panicky as he did now.

At the table, his sister Mouna was drawing. Focusing on her picture like she was some kind of genius artist waiting to be discovered. She was rubbish at it. She kept her head down, looking all saintly and acting as as though she wasn't listening, but Karim could tell she was enjoying this: her brother getting an earful. His mother pointed at him, then at the kitchen table. 'Come here. Clear up, and wash the dishes. Then you can walk your sister to school.'

Karim rolled his eyes. 'Why? Why me, today? And why can't she just get on the bus? You know I'll be late to class if I have to walk her.'

'You want to let your nine-year old sister travel alone on the bus? Are you that irresponsible?' She took a step towards him and he tried not to flinch. His mother was a big woman. Not big as in jolly; Karim's aunt, who lived six floors down with her husband and three kids, had said once the accumulated weight represented all the grief his Mum had had to put up with over the years. Every disappointment; every

62

obstacle. 'This wasn't what she had in mind when your Dad brought her over from Algeria,' his aunt often said, shaking her head woefully. What had his Mum expected, Karim wondered. Paradise on earth? Meanwhile, his Dad was becoming more invisible by the day, slipping out at every opportunity so he didn't have to hear his wife nag him about how useless he was. Unemployed, and with qualifications that were of no use to anyone now, not with the car factories all moving to China where people worked for peanuts. Karim would have felt sorry for his Dad if he wasn't such a coward. All he did was hide. Where was he this morning? Probably still asleep. He could feel his anger rise and didn't notice his mother till she was standing right behind him, a large, oppressive presence.

'Hurry. I want you out of the house in five minutes. Five. Not a minute more,' she said.

'What about the dishes?' he asked. 'Five minutes doesn't leave me much time.'

'Don't talk back. You're not so old I can't smack you.'

'OK, I get it.' He sighed. He waited till she'd left the room before checking his phone. Nothing. Where was that bastard Samir? There weren't too many dishes and he did them quickly, making as much noise as he could. Just in case the old man was still asleep. Recovering from his night with that skanky redhead. Karim had seen them together twice. The second time, his father had seen him and looked so ashamed it had made Karim want to kick his teeth out. Useless, and a cheat.

As he pulled the soapy dishes from the water, he thought about the detective's visit. That Thierry had balls, or else he was a nutcase, turning up alone like that in the *cité*. What Karim couldn't figure out was what the guy wanted. He wished he hadn't told the *keuf* about seeing Samir with the other police officers. What if this Thierry went and told his colleagues what Karim had said? The first thing they'd do is come back and find him, right? Why hadn't he kept his mouth shut?

It wasn't just the police he needed to worry about. The police weren't such a big concern. Not compared to what would happen if Ali and the others discovered he'd been talking to the police. Just thinking about the conversation he'd had with Thierry in the building made him feel sick. How would Karim explain himself if it came out that he'd been chatting to the detective, right under his friends' noses? He'd have a hard time convincing them that it wasn't planned. It was over, for now. But Karim knew Thierry would be back. Asking questions that he, Karim, wasn't in a position to answer.

He rinsed the last plate and quickly wiped his hands. He'd walk as far as the bus stop with Mouna, and meet the others afterwards. No sense going to school now. Too much going on, and besides, what difference did it make? In his mind's eye, he could see the maths teacher, a smug bastard that one, smiling as though he found Karim mildly amusing. One of these days, he'd knock that smile off his face. Who the hell did he think he was, talking to Karim like that? 'Please, don't strain yourself, Monsieur Bensoussan.' His friends found it hilarious, while he feigned indifference. He knew what everyone thought, that he was an idiot. No one had ever thought that about Samir. Someday, he'd prove them all wrong. He'd prove Samir's sister wrong too.

The thought of Aisha stirred something within him. 'Hurry up,' he told Mouna. She yawned and swung her legs under the kitchen table. She was making a point of taking her time, doing everything in slow motion. Their mother glared at her. One good thing: she wasn't charmed by Mouna's antics anymore than she was by his.

'Get going. *Now,* Mouna. Or I swear -'

Outside the building, he zipped up his jacket and pulled the hood over his head. Kids with backpacks were heading for the bus stop. It was still dark. A man in a grubby overcoat stopped to inspect a wine bottle left on a bench. Lifted it, to see whether it contained anything, then dropped it to the ground and kept walking. Karim peered down the road to see if the bus was coming. Maybe he could convince Mouna to ride it alone. His sister caught him looking and immediately guessed what he was thinking.

'If you leave me, I'll tell Maman.'

'What a baby you are.'

'And you're a retard.'

There was no sign of the bus. No surprise there. If it did show up sometime this week, it would be packed. Without a word, Karim started walking. All along the path, the snow was turning to sludge. Preoccupied with his own thoughts, he ignored his sister. He walked fast and she kept up with him, sensing that he wouldn't wait if she lagged behind. 'I'm tired,' she complained. By the time they reached the school, they were both puffed. The sweat running down his back made his skin itch. His sister threw him a reproachful look.

'See you later,' was all he said. He turned and walked away, hands buried deep in his pockets.

Nearing the estate, he slowed down, wanting to make sure his mother wouldn't see him. She'd be leaving for her morning shift. He stopped at the *superette* to buy cigarettes, with the cash he'd found in his Dad's trouser pocket the night before. Even if his father knew he'd taken it, he'd keep his mouth shut. Karim's hands were cold and he fumbled with the change while the cashier waited. She looked like she might be his age, with pale blue eyes, bleached hair and green-painted nails. He could feel her eyes on him but when he handed over the change, her gaze was elsewhere, disinterested.

Outside, he stopped to light up. From a distance, the four towers built side by side rose before him, stark and unwelcoming. Inside, it got worse. Rubbish in the stairwells, broken panes, slogans scrawled across the walls. 'And they call themselves graffiti *artists*,' Samir had said once, laughing. He only said that sort of thing when it was just the two of them.

Karim inhaled deeply and felt the tobacco tear at his lungs. He finished his cigarette and walked towards the towers. His was the one furthest from Samir's, but identical. As he drew nearer, something at the foot of Samir's building caught his eye. Before he could make out what it was, he saw Ali and Réza heading towards him. His immediate reflex was to run, or hide, just as long as he didn't have to engage with them, but luckily he held himself together. Ali was busy talking and hadn't noticed him yet. But Réza had clocked him, Karim could tell. The expression on his face was insincere; every gesture deliberate. He was leaning towards Ali, nodding and smiling as though the two of them couldn't be tighter. When they drew near, Réza made a show of noticing Karim for the first time and raised his hand, the ubiquitous greeting sliding from his mouth like butter.

'What's up, *cousin*? What are you doing here?'

'Nothing much.'

'Got a spare cigarette?' Without waiting for an answer, Ali took Karim's packet and helped himself. Réza did the same, except he took two. 'One for now, one for later.' Karim didn't say a word. He ignored

Réza and looked at Ali, who was lighting up, one meaty hand thoughtfully cupping the flame though there was no trace of wind.

Ali. No one called him that to his face. At six foot two, with bulging muscles, he was known on the estate as the Boxer. Karim thought the Hulk would have been more appropriate. Managing his temper was not his strongest suit. Everyone knew what he could be like on a bad day, how quickly his mood could change. And when he got into a fight, he tended to win, while the other guy generally remained out of action for days, sometimes weeks. Now The Boxer rolled his shoulders, his face screwed up like he was getting rid of an ache.

'Kevin,' he said. 'What's up?' Karim, a.k.a. Kevin, took the hand that Ali proffered and endured a painful squeeze.

'We were looking for you,' Réza said.

'Oh yeah? What for?' Karim asked, doing his utmost to sound relaxed. He hated Réza, and trusted him much the same way he'd trust a fox with rabies, but the last thing he wanted to do was antagonize him. Karim attempted a smile, pretending not to notice the way Réza was looking at his leather jacket and smirking.

'What for?' Karim asked again.

'You in a hurry or something?'

'I'll tell him,' Ali said. The Boxer lay a hand on his shoulder. It felt heavy as a boulder. Karim looked away from Réza and turned to Ali. His face was a blank page. There was never much expression there. No clues, to anticipate what he was about to say. At the same time, as he waited for Ali to speak again, Karim found himself looking again at the building where Samir lived. He saw now what it was. A police cordon at the foot of the tower block. He couldn't see any police. A handful of residents stood close to the area that was taped off, talking to each other. No doubt gossiping about what had happened.

Karim turned back to Ali, who was staring at him in silence, about to speak. Karim suddenly realized he didn't want to hear it. Ali was hesitating, and Karim had never known him to hold back. He tried to speak before Ali did, as if that might change anything, but Ali spoke first.

'They've gone and killed Samir,' he said, and he took a drag from his cigarette, looking at the ground and slowly shuffling from side to side as if he needed to warm up.

'Can you believe it,' Réza said, before spitting on the ground. Karim thought he had never hated the slimy bastard as much as he did then. Then Ali looked at him as if something had just occurred to him. 'You're not doing anything important this morning, right? It's just that it would be good, you know, to have a bit of a chat.'

'About what?' Karim asked. He didn't want to spend another minute with them. He needed to think about Samir.

'You busy all of a sudden?' Réza took a step forward, but Ali placed a hand on his arm, letting him know to back off. 'It's business, Kevin,' he explained. 'That's all. Now that Samir's gone, we need to work a few things out. There might be a few changes.'

'Business,' Réza echoed. 'But also, the guys who did this,' he added. 'They need to pay.'

'Sure,' Karim said. What choice did he have? He was also confused. Even as he took the words in, absorbed their bitter truth, Karim had time to puzzle over what Réza had said.

They?

*

Aisha opened the door and got in. Luc Clément started the car. Neither of them said a word until they were well away from the estate. She looked through the rear window at the receding tower blocks before turning to face the road ahead. The heater was on and the warm air blew on her legs and made her feet tingle. They drove past the Roma camp, looking dirty and neglected and cold with snow everywhere and the makeshift dwellings exposed to the elements. Each home had been built from scratch with whatever was available and there were gaps where the freezing air would enter. Outside, a woman was throwing rubbish into a metal drum to keep a fire going. A snotty-faced kid stood by her side, watching the flames. His arms in a faded yellow t-shirt were bare. Aisha wondered which of these homes the dead Roma boy had come from and whether he too had a sister who was missing him now.

She looked away and tried to think about something else. She had discovered, some time back, that if you told yourself that you were doing something for the last time, then that moment could take on a special quality. Say you told yourself you had a terminal disease. Here you were, living your last moments. Things looked better that way, when you didn't take them for granted. When she looked up, she saw that the sky was the colour of tarnished silver. A flock of white birds – the non-migrating kind, she supposed – flew over the power lines, forming a shimmery pattern in the sky. Beauty was unexpected. So was tragedy. Samir was dead. Had he had time to realize what was happening to him? He must have. Aisha watched the birds' fluid escape. Right now, her mother was tearing her hair out. Mad with grief. Surrounded by well-meaning people, except for her own daughter who'd gone and left her. Slipped out while no one was looking. *I must be a cold-hearted bitch*, Aisha thought.

How long had they been driving? She didn't want to ask her teacher. All she knew was that they weren't in Villeneuve anymore. Strange, that you could be in the *cité* one minute and the next you were in a suburb so tidy, even the trees looked like they had spent time getting ready in the morning. They were planted at exact distances from each other, just as if someone had measured the in-between spaces with a ruler. Somewhere, she imagined, some *fonctionnaire* had a cushy job just making sure the trees were properly lined up.

Monsieur Clément turned into a residential street and found a space to park. He pulled the handbrake and left the engine running. She stole a quick glance at him. He sat still and looked straight ahead, as if waiting for something to happen. Somewhere close by, a train rumbled past. A man in a brown coat that floated about his ankles hurried across the footpath, carrying a briefcase. A jogger overtook him, a pair of oversized headphones stuck over his ears.

'Aisha.' The concern in his voice made her turn to face him again. 'I'm so sorry.' She felt herself shrinking from the look in his eyes, from the tenderness with which he spoke. Instead, she made a show of examining her surroundings, looking carefully as if she were making a decision about whether or not to move into the neighbourhood. Definitely not, she decided. It wasn't that flash but you could tell people would be stuck up and even if they didn't know you, they wouldn't want you living right next door. They'd dislike you just for being different. A bit darker, louder, or poorer than they were. Maybe they'd even want to hurt you, or hope bad luck would come your way. Then again, there were plenty of people who would hurt you right where you lived, worked, or went to school, she reflected, thinking of Katarina. *When it comes down to it, people are the same everywhere*. Except for Samir. No one was like him. In her mind, at least. It occurred to her now that she had always, always needed to see him as something special, different from everyone else. He was her brother, and by extension his special-ness made her special too. On her own, she wasn't enough.

'I don't know what to do,' she managed to say. *This* was the only certainty, right now. This conviction that she could not cope, that what had happened was too big, too painful to carry. Monsieur Clément didn't speak. Even without looking at him, she could feel the intensity of her teacher's gaze. For a brief moment, she was angry with him. What was wrong with him? Did he not have any friends of his own age? What kind of adult wanted to hang around a teenage girl? What sort of idiot would compromise himself like this, with a pupil? The white teacher with his favourite *bougnoule* student, she thought angrily, picturing Katarina's ugly sneer. Could it get any worse? If anyone saw them, sitting in his car like this outside of school hours, he'd probably get the sack and she'd become a social pariah. Even more so than now.

She turned to him, ready to say something hurtful, and was shocked to find him in tears. He cried without making any noise, which seemed somehow worse. Quickly, he seemed to realize he was making her uncomfortable and he took a deep breath, wiping his face with one hand and lifting the other as it to say he was sorry.

'One step at a time,' he said, as if to himself. 'I know that sounds like useless advice, but really all you can do is take it slowly. Don't think you have to be *mature* or that you have to be in control. Don't be afraid to feel. I know how frightening, how painful this must be.'

She snorted, her anger flaring again. 'You should be a psychoanalyst, not a philosophy teacher,' she said, and immediately regretted being flippant. A minute ago, she had found him stupid for crying, yet now all she wanted was to cry, for them to cry together, and for him to hold her. Nothing funny, just a warm, reassuring embrace. But he made no move to touch her. 'I know what you're going through,' he said. 'I've been there.'

She looked at him. He was funny-looking, with his tiny blue eyes and pink complexion. A bit on the pudgy side. Yet to her, he was a large, solid presence, exuding warmth. Not that she'd ever tell anyone that. And the way he laughed sometimes, the way he got really emotional about things like songs and books was really embarrassing, but it made you smile even when there was nothing to smile about. He wasn't tough on the students but he managed somehow to hold their attention, which was an achievement given some of the hard cases she had in her year.

'I'm scared,' she said. And angry, she wanted to add. But she couldn't explain the anger, and it frightened her. It felt like something she needed to hold close, like a rabid dog on a leash.

'I'm here for you, Aisha,' he told her, just as he'd done before, and he made that same gesture of wiping his face. Now he just seemed really tired. She could see he really meant what he'd said, and for the first time she was grateful.

She started crying then, thinking about Samir. Not caring what Luc Clément thought. After a while, she realized he'd turned the radio on. Or no, it wasn't the radio, it was a CD they'd listened to together before, in his car. Leo Ferré, reciting Rimbaud's Drunken Boat. Her favourite poem. The one that had made her start to appreciate words and how powerful they could be. She wanted someday to be able to express herself like that, using her own words.

The first time she'd heard it, they'd been like this together. Sitting in his car, listening in silence. At first, she'd laughed because Ferré was so earnest, so dramatic. It had all seemed so old-fashioned and ridiculous, sitting there listening to an old man with untidy white hair recite poetry like it was something cool you could perform on stage. She'd never seen or heard that before. By the end, though, it had given her goose bumps. Now, it pissed her off that he should think this was appropriate, given what had happened. Samir was dead and Luc Clément wanted to listen to poetry? But she found herself listening all the same, leaning back and surrendering to it. Just like the first time, the poem calmed her down. It took her somewhere foreign, away from the world she knew, away from the nightmare that was Samir's death. She saw that Luc had his eyes closed. He seemed to have forgotten she was there. She closed hers too and turned her back to him, her legs curled up beneath her, and let the words wash over her like medicine.

Nine

Morel didn't go back to sleep after Virginie's call. Instead, he lay in bed for another hour with a splitting headache before getting up. His body seemed to resist, to want to be left alone. He felt like an old and very grumpy man. Not so different, then, from the one sleeping in the upstairs bedroom, he reflected. He let Descartes out into the courtyard and made coffee for himself and for his father, who wasn't up yet. In the bathroom, he rummaged around for more painkillers. He washed the two last Nurofens down with a glass of water, thinking he would need to get more during the day. There was no point checking his temperature. Whatever the thermometer told him, he would go to work.

'What do you think of all this snow, Descartes?' he asked. He stood on the doorstep and drank his coffee. The dog was standing in the middle of the courtyard, looking morose. At the sound of Morel's voice, he lifted his head. There was none of the ebullience he'd shown the previous day, as though he too had been affected by the tragic news. Two young boys, dead within 48 hours of each other, Morel reflected. Was there a link? It was hard to think of the two as unrelated. When he tried to picture what might happen next, he felt uneasy. Georghe's death was one thing, but Samir's murder would further provoke a community that already had its share of grievances, a generation of kids Samir's age who were already marginalised, no matter what people like Morel's father said. How many times had Morel seethed in silence when his father stated that it was *their* fault if things weren't looking 'that great' for them? *They don't want to assimilate. It's unfortunate, but there it is.* Phillipe

Morel's words, back in the days when his mind was still sharp, if deluded.

The divide between Paris and its *banlieue* was not just geographical, it was psychological too, Morel thought. If you were a North African migrant living in a dump like the Cité des Fleurs, chances were that Paris would seem as distant as Timbuktu. The alienation was real and complex, its sources multiple. Whatever the reasons, in places like Villeneuve, the rage and frustration were always there, latent. Something like the death of a young Algerian boy could be disastrous. The events of 2005 were still fresh in Morel's mind: the accidental death of two adolescents running from the police had sparked protests in a northern Parisian suburb not far from Villeneuve. Riots had followed, swiftly spreading across some of the country's most disaffected regions. Would the same thing happen again? He felt certain it would. Maybe he was being dramatic, but Morel had the distinct feeling that the events of these past days would summon an avalanche that no one was really prepared for.

Morel watched Descartes amble back in and sag into a discontented heap at his feet. He scratched the dog's head and was rewarded with a limp thump of its shaggy tail. He finished his coffee and placed the cup on the kitchen bench. The silence made him restless. Even his father's muddled presence would be preferable to this emptiness. He went back inside and turned the lights and the radio on. When the news came on at 5.30, Morel listened carefully. There was nothing new about Georghe, and nothing at all about Samir. But he expected it wouldn't take long.

At six, he decided he could no longer sit around waiting for Augustine to come and he sent her a text, asking if she would make an exception and arrive earlier today. He needed to get to work. Augustine replied straight away. *Absolutely, be right there.* She arrived twenty-five minutes later, looking flushed. The thought of her running over at such an early hour made him feel guilty but he was also relieved. She would sit with his father while he had his breakfast and later they would go for a stroll around the neighbourhood.

Maybe Maly was right, Morel thought as he walked through deserted streets towards the Pont de Neuilly Metro station. He would need to find another solution. He couldn't ask poor Augustine to be there at the crack of dawn every time he wanted an early start. But neither could he be his father's keeper and still continue to do his job properly.

He took the metro but by the time he got to Concorde, he found he needed to get off the train. The air was stale underground, and his headache showed no signs of diminishing. He walked through the Tuileries, past the large round basin and the green metal chairs that were always occupied in summer, with only the bare trees for company. It was too early for the Roma girls with their fake petition forms, who normally prowled the park for gullible tourists. When he reached the Pont des Arts, its sidings sagging under the weight of hundreds of love locks, he pulled his collar up. A cold wind blew across the river, stirring the dark waters. On the Quai des Orfèvres, Morel stepped past the snow-topped line of police vehicles parked outside his building. He was about to enter when he noticed a woman on the quay, across the road from him. She was gazing at the water, her face turned to the wind. There was something familiar about her and when she turned, he recognized Virginie. She looked subdued, quite different to the last time he'd seen her. Her cheek when he kissed it was cold, lifeless.

'I should have called,' she said dully.

'Not at all. But you're lucky I came in early,' he said, rubbing his hands together. 'It's freezing out here.' He recognized one of his colleagues, who was entering the building, and responded to the man's wave by raising his own hand. 'How long have you been waiting?' he asked Virginie.

She shrugged her shoulders. Her face was pale, drawn. 'Come upstairs,' Morel urged. 'I can offer you a coffee, as long as you don't expect it to taste good.' She didn't respond and instead went ahead of him across the road, and into the building. They took the stairs. When they reached the fourth floor, she asked for directions to the bathroom and he pointed her in the right direction.

In the office, there was only Lila. She was looking at something on her computer with headphones on and didn't notice Morel until he was standing by her side. He pointed at the screen, where a couple posed in their underwear, doing their best to look seductive. 'A bit early for this sort of thing, don't you think?'

'It's research,' she commented. 'Swingers' website.'

'Is there a soundtrack?' he said, trying to draw her out. She raised her eyebrows and he gestured towards the headphones. Lila held them away from her ears and Morel heard what sounded like the desperate squawks of a wounded seagull. Whatever she was listening to, it wasn't restful.

'I should come in early more often, for your witty comments,' Lila remarked after he repeated his question. 'The music is mine. The website is one of Grégory Simic's favourite. His and his lovely wife's. Turns out they met up on a regular basis with other couples. Through this site, but also at a couple of clubs in town.'

She pushed her chair from the desk and rubbed her eyes. Morel searched her face, looking for some indication of her mood. He wanted to ask how she was but then Virginie entered the room. Morel introduced the two women to each other.

'Take a seat,' he told Virginie. 'I'll be right back, with the coffee.' He gestured for Lila to follow him. 'It's not like you to be here so early,' he said as they headed down the empty hallway.

'I can be unpredictable like that.' She wouldn't look at him. They would have to talk again, about Akil, Morel told himself. A part of him felt annoyed. *I can be stubborn too*, he thought.

'What's your friend doing here?' she asked. Morel explained about Samir. 'Virginie will be able to tell us more.' There was coffee left in the pot from the day before and he poured it into three cups, then warmed them up individually in the microwave.

'Are we investigating the two Villeneuve deaths?' Lila asked, puzzled. She added sugar to her cup and stirred. Her nails, Morel saw, were bitten to the quick.

'No, we're not.'

'Okay,' Lila said, looking skeptical, and Morel could tell what she was thinking: if you're not involved, why is this woman here, first thing in the morning?

Virginie was sitting at Lila's desk and quickly stood up when they returned. Morel handed her a cup and drew another chair up. 'Take a seat. Tell us what happened last night. When and how did you find out about Samir?'

'One of the residents found him. Around three a.m. this morning. Someone who lives in the same building. He was out, walking his dog – '

'At three in the morning?' Lila interjected.

'He says he suffers from insomnia. He thought it might help to get some fresh air.'

Morel wondered what sort of person would wander out in the middle of a cold winter's night, in a place like the Cité des Fleurs, but didn't say anything.

'On his way back into the building he found Samir. It was lucky he saw him, in the dark...' her voice faltered and she looked at Morel with haunted eyes. 'He stopped to light a cigarette and that was when he realized there was a body... it would have been a shock.'

'He called the police?' Lila said.

Virginie nodded. 'Yes. They knocked on a few doors before they were able to identify him... Loubna, Samir's mother, called me. I went straight over there.'

Morel had more questions but he kept them to himself, saying simply, 'It must have been very difficult.' There was a long silence, then Lila spoke.

'No doubt it'll be in the news today. Especially after what happened to the Roma boy. Georghe. Do you think the two are related?'

'I'm sure our Villeneuve colleagues will be looking at that,' Morel said.

'I wish it were you, leading the investigation. I don't know how much faith I have in the Villeneuve police. They seemed indifferent to Samir's fate,' Virginie said.

'That was before he died. Now things are different.'

The words, unconvincing, hung in the air for a moment. Then Lila stood up. 'I'll make more coffee,' she said. While she was gone, Morel kept silent. He told himself there was nothing he could do. Virginie was silent too, as if she knew there was no point wasting her

79

breath. In any case, Morel thought, looking at her, that she had run out of energy. She looked like she was about to collapse.

*

Once he'd walked Virginie to the metro station, Morel turned to the Simic case. When Jean and Vincent arrived, Lila briefed the team on what she knew.

'So you think he was killed because he and his wife like to get their kit off in sex clubs?' Jean asked.

'And swap partners,' Vincent added. He shook his head. 'I'm trying to picture the sort of life those two had.'

'Not your idea of an ideal partnership then?' Lila asked. There was an awkward silence, while everyone remembered Vincent's wife who had died of cancer a couple of years earlier. As far as they knew, he wasn't seeing anyone else, too busy with work and raising his children single-handedly. But Vincent smiled and said, 'To each their own, I guess.'

Morel turned to Lila. 'What does Richard Martin say?' Martin was the pathologist they worked with most closely. Morel respected his skills, knowing he was better at his job than anyone else in Paris. But the man had his faults. He was better equipped to handle dead bodies than live ones. His male colleagues tended to find him arrogant and his female colleagues found him, at best, offensive. A couple of women had filed sexual harassment suits against him and lost.

'He called me last night,' said Lila, who 'd turned down her fair share of date requests from Martin. 'He said either Simic bounced off a few walls before he fell into the water or someone gave him a good beating, then threw him into the river. Given his alcohol levels, and the state of his injuries before he hit the water, Martin says Simic didn't have a hope in hell of saving himself.'

'So what's next?' Morel asked.

'I want to check out this club that Simic and his wife liked to visit often. They were there every week. The night Simic died, his wife claims she was at home in bed, with a migraine, and that he'd told her he was going for a walk.'

'Maybe he went for a walk and took a little detour,' Jean said.

'A big detour, going by the level of alcohol in his blood.' Lila crossed her arms. 'And the club is within walking distance from where Simic's body was found in the water. I know that where he fell in isn't where he ended up exactly, with the current being what it is – but still

Morel looked at Vincent. 'I'd like you to give Lila a hand with this. Find out if Simic was at any of the clubs he and his wife visited that night; starting with the one closest to where he was found. Location might not mean much, given he was fished out of the water. So let's check them all out. And get a list of regulars and also the names of everyone who was at these places on the night he was killed.'

'Sure.' Vincent was writing everything down.

'Lila? Anything else?' Morel said.

'Yes. There's someone I need to track down. A friend of Simic's. A nice young lady called Bijou.'

'Her name is *Bijou*?' Jean smiled. 'I like her already.'

*

The superintendent showed up after lunch, preceded by the distinctive smell of his aftershave, a headache-inducing blend of patchouli and cinnamon. As Perrin entered the room, the scent became overwhelming and Morel felt his eyes water.

'Christ, can you believe the shit that's happening over in Villeneuve?' the superintendent said, not bothering to greet anyone first. 'First the gipsy in the supermarket trolley. Then the Beur kid. Did you watch the one o'clock news? Poor kid was stabbed repeatedly and bled to death outside his home. There's a bit of a ruckus in the neighbourhood. This morning, one of our Villeneuve colleagues working at the crime scene got hit on the head with a bottle. Thrown from a balcony. They had to take him to hospital. Thirty stitches. Fucking animals. Makes me grateful I don't work anywhere near that shithole.' He placed his hands on his hips and looked around the room.

'What's going on here? You all look like you're still asleep. Any progress on Simic? Come on people, it's wake-up time.'

After he'd left, Lila turned to Morel.

'Is it true that he might be moving on? A promotion, or something?'

'I certainly hope so.'

At that, she smiled. Morel smiled back.

*

Akil came in midway through the afternoon. Lila was out, getting help from the technical team to examine the contents of the dead tennis player's laptop, make sure they didn't miss anything that could be relevant in what was now officially a murder investigation. The Moroccan-born detective walked through the door with an air of studied nonchalance that was probably for Lila's benefit. His attitude changed the minute he realized she wasn't there.

'Welcome,' Morel said. 'Make yourself at home.' He gestured towards Marco's old desk. 'That's yours now.' Akil looked at the empty desk and at the one across from it and gave a tense smile.

'What has she said about this?' he asked, gesturing towards Lila's desk.

'She's not very happy,' Morel replied, then added, 'I hope you two can behave professionally towards one another.'

Akil nodded, suddenly grave. 'I certainly intend to. Behave professionally, I mean. I have a lot of respect for her, the way she does her job...' he trailed off awkwardly. Morel added, emphatically, 'She's the best. I couldn't manage without her.'

They both had their backs to the door and didn't hear Lila enter the room. She stepped up to her desk and set Simic's laptop there, among the empty coffee cups, hair clips and discarded chewing gum wrappers. They both looked at her expectantly. 'So you're the new guy,' she said, looking at Akil. He looked confused, before realizing she was trying to be funny. 'That's me,' he responded with a grin. She didn't return his smile. 'Just so you know. No one touches my stuff. And I don't do idle chatter.'

'I kind of know that about you,'' Akil replied.

Jean and Vincent walked in together. They greeted Akil warmly.

'Drinks tonight, I think,' Jean declared, clapping a hand on the younger man's shoulder. Morel stole a glance at Lila. She kept her head down. She unwrapped a piece of gum and stuck it in her mouth, her jaw working furiously.

Ten

Man is a wolf to man. Luc Clément wrote the words on the blackboard and turned to his students, trying his best to look engaged even though he was desperate to get away. Only this class to go before he could get out of here. Normally, he managed to stay focused, and there were even days when he enjoyed his job. But today was different. He'd spent his lunch break looking at his phone, wondering whether Aisha was okay and whether he should call or text. Before driving to school he'd dropped her somewhere near the estate. She was needed at home, she said. He pictured her there, surrounded by grieving relatives and friends, trying to comfort her mother. But who was comforting her?

'Did anyone bother to read the Hobbes text I assigned last week?' he asked angrily. A few in the classroom seemed to sit up and pay a bit more attention then, unused to that tone from their soft-spoken, head-in-the-clouds philosophy teacher. Luc scanned the room. Most of his students were distracted. Fidgeting in their chairs, chatting, rummaging in their bags for food and I-pods and cigarettes. Already preparing for recess. A couple of the kids had headphones on and one was fast asleep. Kenan Tanzir, one of Luc's favourites, snorted loudly at something his neighbour was telling him. Luc sighed. He still had high hopes for Tanzir, an introverted kid whose writing was thoughtful, imaginative. But the odds were against the boy. He was easily swayed, and his friends were not of the same calibre.

'Hobbes, Monsieur?' This, from Félix Orlan, a 19-year-old deadweight who seemed in no hurry to get anywhere in life. Luc knew he wouldn't finish high school and probably wouldn't go to technical college either. God only knew what he'd do.

'Thomas Hobbes. English thinker. Ring a bell? I mentioned his name four days ago, when I handed out a text of his for you all to read and reflect upon at home. No?'

'Monsieur, why an English thinker? Why can't we have a French thinker?' Moussa Keita asked. Luc had met his parents several times at parent-teacher meeting. They were from Mali and didn't speak French. Moussa's older brother had stepped in as translator.

'I must admit I didn't see that question coming. Why does it matter?' Luc asked.

'Well, we *are* in France…'

'Since when do you care?' Félix interrupted. He was leaning so far back, his chair was dangerously close to tipping. Luc half hoped it would. He ignored Félix's comment and addressed Moussa. 'So are you saying we should only focus on French things? French history and geography, French authors, French language…'

Moussa rolled his eyes. 'That's not what I mean. But…' He shrugged his shoulders and sat back, slipping his hood over his head and crossing his arms. 'Hoods off in class,' Luc said, gesturing for the boy to pull it back. Moussa rolled his eyes again, but did as he was told.

'So,' Luc continued. '*Hobbes*. Man is a wolf to man. What that saying is intended to illustrate is the brutish, anarchic and violent nature of man in his primal state, before civilization kicks in. A notion that other thinkers have challenged, though we won't go there yet. No point unless you've read this text. I have to say I'm disappointed, guys. I would have thought this was something that would grab many of you. What is our primal nature? Is good innate? Or is there only mutual distrust, driven by an instinctive need for survival?'

'Mutual distrust, no doubt about it,' Félix offered, earning a few laughs. The rest of them were silent. Luc searched the faces before him for a flicker of interest. Normally, he could get the kids involved. But today all he saw was apathy. Perhaps they sensed that his heart wasn't in it. His eyes flittered across Aisha's empty desk. She would have read the text and had something to say about it.

'Monsieur? Are you still awake?' This from Moussa, followed by laughter, which suggested to Luc that he'd been day-dreaming. How long had he been standing there, gazing at the blackboard with a piece of chalk in his hand? He turned and faced the class. He could see that, today, he'd lost the battle. Thirty-two kids, most of them with the attention span of puppies. He always had to work hard to hold their attention. Today, he didn't have the energy.

'Mehdi?' he called, choosing a student at random. 'Did you read the text?' The boy looked at him blankly. Someone sniggered.

Luc shook his head and scanned the room. '*Anyone*?' Laetitia, the girl who sat beside Aisha, shook her head. 'There wasn't enough time,' she replied lamely. 'My Mum's sick. I have to take care of her.'

'Sick of you, for sure,' someone in the back row sniggered, and Laetitia turned to him sharply. 'Shut up, moron.'

'Enough.' Luc pointed at Kenan. 'Maybe you could read the text for us now. That way we can all hear it.' Kenan glanced at his neighbour before shaking his head.

'No thank you, Sir.'

'I wasn't asking, Kenan. Just read the text.' A couple of the girls giggled, including Marianne, a large, big-bosomed girl, attractive in a fleeting sort of way. Nothing like Aisha, he thought. In one corner,

Katarina and her little posse of followers were sniggering about something. He couldn't be bothered, right now, engaging with any of them. He didn't like Katarina, and took great pains not to show it.

Luc looked at Félix's sprawling figure behind the desk, at the blank faces before him, and sighed. 'Never mind, Kenan.' He picked one of the students in the front row, a big girl with braided hair and fiery red nails called Mélodie.

'Mélodie, would you read the text out loud?'

'What, all of it?'

'All of it. From the beginning, to the end. For those of us who haven't had a chance to read it … I want you all to pay close attention. Because afterwards, I'll be asking questions.'

Groans and laughter. A clamour of insults, most of them good-natured. Nothing he hadn't heard before. Chairs were scraped back. Luc raised his voice in order to be heard through the noise and agitation.

'Mélodie, would you begin, please?'

'Fine, whatever.' As she began to read, haltingly, he looked out the window, at the stark courtyard and the high walls that surrounded the school. Not so much to keep people out, he reflected, but to keep the students in. Not that it made any difference. If a kid didn't want to be at school, there was only so much you could do. Warnings and threats of expulsion might work with some, but not all. And what use was it talking to the parents when half the time their French was too limited to hold a proper conversation? Luc remembered a recent lunch break in the staff room. As was often the case when it came to discussing the students and the education system, there had been heated exchanges. Some said it was up to the school to improve communication with the students and with their families. Others thought responsibility lay mostly with the parents and older siblings. *It starts with language*, the chemistry teacher had said. A sallow-faced man with a short fuse. *They need to become fluent themselves, and help develop the younger children's fluency.* Someone, Luc couldn't remember who, had butted in. *And what about our own capacity for reaching out and embracing the diversity? Making sure kids are not alienated from their culture of origin? Bollocks to that*, Matthew had said. His response had caused such an uproar that Corinne Tellier, the head teacher, had come in, asking if they could keep their voices down. Privately, Luc tended to agree with the majority but he agreed with Matthew too. Many of these kids came from families whose sense of belonging began elsewhere, not here in this neglected Parisian suburb. It was important to acknowledge and cultivate this. At the same time, language mattered. Not just the language of their forefathers, and of their parents, many of whom didn't speak French fluently, but also the language of their country of adoption. Without it, they would remain on the margins of society. Language was power. It was no surprise, Luc reflected, that France had made French a cornerstone of their colonial expansion. Without language, how could you articulate your needs and desires? How could you earn respect? Be seen, and heard?

Luc glanced again at the empty desk. His mind was full of her. *Aisha*. Fretting, wanting to reach out to her and offer comfort, friendship. What would happen now? Samir's death had shaken him, no doubt about it. Even after six years of teaching at this *lycée*, he wasn't immune to the violence he encountered, the messy background many of these kids shared. Still, he refused to think of his students as victims of the system. How did that help them? And he certainly never saw Aisha as one. But it seemed horribly unfair, that this tragedy should touch her and not someone else. She was top of the class, and he expected her to do well at her baccalauréat, in the subjects he taught, French and philosophy. How would she be able to focus on her studies now?

Mélodie was still reading. Heads turned and Luc saw that the classroom door had opened and someone was poking their head in. It was Marie, from the school office. 'Monsieur Clément, could you come for a moment?'

'What - now?'

'If you would,' Marie replied. Luc stepped out of the class and closed the door, hearing the noise erupt as soon as he'd shut it. There would be mayhem, but he didn't care. What did the head teacher want him for? Of course, the school would know about Samir by now. Could it be that Corinne wanted to question him about Aisha's dead brother, that somehow they thought he might be able to contribute something meaningful? Had anyone seen him with Aisha earlier, in the car? They had been careful, but it wouldn't take much for someone to notice. One of the kids, or a teacher, on their way to school. For the first time, he felt uneasy.

When he reached the end of the hallway, he found Corinne waiting for him. She led him into her office, where a man was sitting in the visitor's chair. He stood up when they walked in, and held out his hand.

'Monsieur Clément? Romain Marchal. I'm a detective with the Villeneuve police.'

'Has something happened?' Luc said. Marchal was short, no more than 1m65, Luc guessed. But there was something vaguely intimidating about the way he assessed Luc, coolly and in silence.

'Take a seat, please,' Corinne said. Luc did as he was told, aware that the policeman was looking at him still. The last time Luc had been in Corinne's office, just a few days before, had been with one of his students, who'd addressed him as 'tu' rather than 'vous' before going on a rant about the uselessness of getting an education in a dump like Villeneuve. A familiar refrain. Luc had brought him in to see Corinne. He'd been fuming too, hating his job, his life, and every one of his students in that moment. But he remembered it as being far more comfortable a situation than the one he was in now.

'Luc, I'm afraid something's happened. Something tragic. Is Aisha in today?' The head teacher's voice sounded strained. Instead of her usual pose, which was to sit on the edge of a desk with her legs crossed, surveying the room and everyone in it, she was standing.

'She's absent.' He was careful to keep his voice neutral, to conceal his agitation. He had no choice but to lie, and pretend he didn't already know about Aisha's brother. It was either that or let the detective and Corinne know that he'd seen Aisha before school. Picked her up from the estate and parked in a quiet spot where they could be alone. He swallowed and made himself look at the police officer.

'What is it? What's happened?'

'The girl's brother was found dead during the night. Stabbed to death.'

'How? Where?'

'At the foot of the building where he lived,' the police officer said. He was still looking at Luc like he hadn't made up his mind about something. 'You probably know a Roma boy died from his injuries too, after taking a severe beating. That's two deaths in a very short time.'

90

'It's dreadful.'

'We've talked to his teachers, of course,' Marchal continued. 'But we thought others might know something. You have the boy's sister in your class. Maybe you can tell us something about the family.'

'I don't know much about them, beyond my interaction at school with Aisha and the parent teacher meetings. There is no father, I believe he died some time ago. I've met with the mother a few times.'

'Any problems in the home?'

'What sort of problems?'

'Drugs. Abuse. Maybe the Mum's found herself a man and the boy clashed with him. Maybe the boy was selling drugs, getting in the way of other sellers on the estate. Any thoughts?'

Luc pretended to mull the question over.

'I really can't say.'

The detective looked at his watch.

'So Aisha is a student of yours?'

'She's one of my best.'

'Smart, then?'

'Very.'

'Close to her brother?'

'I don't know. Sorry.'

'That's fine.' Marchal made a show of looking at his notes, but it was obvious he'd come prepared.

'The family are Algerian,' he said as a statement.

'They're French. Aisha was a couple of years old when she moved here.'

'Is that right?' the detective said. He gazed at Luc with interest.

'You think this is about race?' Luc asked. He hadn't meant to sound angry but it came out that way.

'I have no clue,' Marchal said, smiling. He might have been discussing the weather forecast for the following day. 'What do you think?'

'I'd be reluctant to make those sorts of assumptions. This is the sort of thing that can only cause trouble. Any mention of racism, discrimination, and I can guarantee you'll have your hands full trying to contain things around here, let alone trying to solve a murder.'

'The detective is only asking whether race might be a factor here,' the head teacher intercepted.

'How would I know?' Luc asked.

'You knew the boy Samir?' Marchal asked.

Luc managed to look blank. 'Not really. I've never taught him, but I know who he is.' He added, 'I've been working here for six years, so of course I know the kids a little.'

'Is there anything you might be able to tell us about him? Anything that might help us understand why he was killed?'

Luc shook his head. 'Like I said, I know who he is – but I'm afraid that's about it.'

'No gossip? As a teacher you must get to hear all sorts of stuff.'

'I'm one of those teachers who doesn't pay any attention to that sort of thing. I'm sorry to disappoint.' And Marchal did seem disappointed, like he'd expected a great deal more.

After Marchal left, Corinne asked Luc to stay. In his mind, he was going over the exchange he'd had with the detective. Was it his imagination or had Marchal looked at him as if he didn't believe a word he said? Was it okay to lie, when the truth was complicated?

None of what was happening was his fault. He had to keep reminding himself of that.

Luc took a deep breath and willed himself to relax. The man had no reason to suspect him of anything. When he looked up, he found Corinne looking at him. 'What do we do now?' she said.

'What do you mean?' She looked at him as if he was stupid. 'Luc, you said it yourself. You know this isn't going to end here. This is just the beginning.'

Eleven

Alberto looked out his bedroom window and found the world much as he'd left it an hour earlier, before he'd decided to lie down and rest. It had stopped snowing, but still he felt strange, as if a white mass, something blinding and immovable, prevented him from leaving his flat. There was a tightness around his chest and a numbness in his left arm that made him wonder, briefly, whether he was having a stroke or a heart attack, and whether he should call someone. He had a fear of dying alone.

That morning, when Samir had left after breakfast, Alberto had hoped that he might return. Even after his disastrous exchange with Samir's sister, he'd gone to his flat and waited, thinking that maybe the boy had simply changed his mind about going home and decided he needed more quiet time. Maybe he would return to Alberto's place once he realized there was nowhere else he could comfortably be. Alberto realized now that he had been waiting all this time. Waiting, that is, until he'd heard the dreadful news from the police, snuffing out all hope. They'd knocked on his door just as he was about to head out to the shops. Afterwards, he'd forgotten what it was he wanted to get.

It was nearly two. Out of habit, he turned to the kitchen. There wasn't much in the pantry. Coffee and a tin of stale biscuits. That would do for lunch. He'd lost his appetite, in any case. He couldn't shake the feeling that he'd let the boy down. That morning, when Samir had said he was going home, he should have checked, made sure he was safe. Or made him stay longer instead of insisting he call his mother.

He could hear Emilia chiding him. You can't be responsible for someone else's child. A child, who is nearly a man, at that. No one would think this was your fault. But Samir's sister Aisha did blame him. If only he'd insisted, gently, perhaps the boy would have confided in him. He'd clearly been in some sort of trouble. And he, Alberto, had pretended not to see.

Imbecíl, a voice inside his head said. What difference would it have made, if he'd said something then? When had Samir ever opened up to him, about anything? Alberto bit into a biscuit and pulled a face. It was like eating dirt.

Seven years, he'd known the kid. Since that first time he and Emilia had passed him on the stairs, knowing better than to take the lifts. Already then, the residents had figured out that the construction was shoddy. How quickly the buildings had run into disrepair. '*Qué haces, nino*? What are you doing?' The boy had been sitting halfway down the steps, puffing on a cigarette. Alberto had taken it from him. 'You're too young for this. If you really want to smoke, at least wait till you're a man.'

'What does it matter?'

'It matters.'

The boy had ignored him and Alberto had decided to let it go, continuing down the stairs with his wife. He'd looked back to find the child staring at him through a cloud of smoke, with an expression on his brooding face that could not have been clearer. *Fuck off*.

A week later, when he'd completely forgotten about the kid, Samir had shown up on his doorstep. 'No one's home and I'm stuck outside,' he'd said. 'Can I sit here and watch TV?' Alberto couldn't even remember why he'd agreed to let him in. Emilia had been suspicious, at first. But, gradually she'd grown fond of Samir too.

95

After her death, Samir had come more often. Always alone, and never for long. There had been a spate of robberies in the neighbourhood and businesses were closing. A friend of Alberto's had been mugged outside the building, in the middle of the day. People were locking their doors. With everything he had known falling apart around him, it had felt good to know that trust still existed. For some reason, Samir had trusted him, Alberto. And Alberto had felt he could trust the boy too.

'I think he just felt comfortable here,' Alberto had told the detectives. They'd knocked on his door first thing this morning and asked, in a dozen different ways, why Samir would stay the night at his. He'd tried to explain, though it wasn't easy to describe the relationship, if it could be called that. He could see the police were skeptical. Why would an adolescent like Samir be hanging around with an old geezer like him? He could see them contemplating the worst, because that's what you did when you were a police officer, wasn't it? He imagined their thoughts and felt defiled, revolted.

He plumped the sofa back into shape and picked up the cardigan he had lent the boy. He must have left without it. Stupid kid, he thought. What had he done to keep warm? He reached for the top and checked the pockets, out of habit, before storing it away. In one of them, there was a bloody tissue. When he went to throw it in the bin, something fell that had been contained in its folds, and after a moment's hesitation he picked that up too. He stared at it, his hand shaking slightly.

Mierda, he muttered to himself.

It was a tooth. To Alberto, it looked like it must have belonged to a child.

*

Morel was on his way to the Cité des Fleurs, with Lila. Romain Marchal, the detective overseeing the investigation into the boys' deaths, had called him and asked if he could come by the station in Villeneuve. 'I know you're a busy man, but given what's happened, and given your connection with Samir Ketab's family, I'd like to have a word.'

Morel was tempted to say they could talk on the phone, that he was too busy to drive all the way to Villeneuve. But he might get closer to the investigation by being there. It was none of his business, of course. And Perrin would have a fit if he knew. But there was Virginie, and there was Aisha. He felt, obscurely, that he owed them something.

'Well, it's as lovely as its name suggested. I was right about that,' Lila said as they drove around the housing estate. Before going to see Marchal, Morel wanted to show her where Samir had lived. The four tower blocks that made up the Cité des Fleurs loomed over everything. Morel looked up. Many of the windows were shut. Some were boarded up. On the streets, there was rubbish everywhere. Either the collectors were on strike or they didn't bother coming here anymore.

'Can the city council just do that? Ignore an entire section of their district, and let it go to ruin?' Lila asked, echoing his thoughts.

'It looks that way, doesn't it,' Morel replied.

'You know what the problem is?' she reflected. 'It's that there's no through-traffic. No one needs to come through here. There's no reason to stop, no shops or anything. The only people you see are the ones who live here. There's no link with the outside world.'

She had a point. As far as Morel could tell, there was only one shop in the vicinity, a Leader Price supermarket. And he guessed that the nearest RER station was a twenty-minute walk away. They'd driven past it on their way here.

How long, he wondered, till they tore the tower blocks down? At what point would the authorities decide that a place was no longer fit to be lived in? Other housing estates like this one outside Paris had been replaced with new buildings, though often there was a price to pay: not everyone got a place in the new order. Putting new buildings in place with fewer available units was a way of weeding out the worst elements, by kicking them out on the street.

'Remind me: why are we here, anyway?' Lila asked as they drew outside the Villeneuve police station. Morel didn't bother replying. He'd already told her.

'Tonight I'm going to do the rounds of these clubs Simic and his wife liked so much,' she said. 'Shall I take Vincent with me?'

'Aren't we having drinks? To welcome Akil?' Morel asked, as he pushed the door open.

'Exactly,' she said, striding past him into the building.

Romain Marchal came out to greet them and Morel introduced Lila to him. They followed him to his desk. 'So what do you think of our new premises? How do they compare to the Quai des Orfèvres?'

'I'd say this is a lot more modern than where we are,' Morel replied.

Marchal's laugh was unconvincing. He invited Morel and Lila to sit down. 'Thanks for coming.'

'Not at all,' Morel said. 'How is it all going?'

Marchal scratched his head and pulled a face. 'It's always tough. No one wants to share information. That includes the Roma community. They're afraid of reprisals.'

'From those who attacked the boy?'

'That, of course. And being illegals, for the most part, they're afraid they'll be deported. We've been talking to people in the tower blocks about Samir, too. Either they're telling us nothing, or they're making up stories. It's like wading through pig shit, to be honest.'

Lila snorted. 'I know that feeling.'

'You asked me to come down...' Morel began.

'You came here, the day before Samir was found. How well do you know the family?'

'I don't. I was asked to come by a friend of mine. She's a school counselor and has been seeing Samir's sister Aisha.'

'Her name?' Morel hesitated slightly, then gave Marchal Virginie's details. 'I'm not sure she can help you with any of this. She hardly knew the boy.'

'Why did she ask you to get involved?'

Morel shrugged. 'I guess because we've known each other a long time. She knows what I do for a living.'

'Can you take me through the conversations you had, when you visited the Ketabs?'

'There isn't much to tell.' Morel took him through his meeting with Aisha and her mother.

'Have you visited the family since this happened?' Morel shook his head. 'Good. I'd like to ask that you don't. It might complicate things.'

'If you're worried that I'll interfere in your investigation, don't be. I have no intention of getting involved.'

'Thanks. I appreciate it,' Marchal said. He stood up.

'Is that it?' Morel asked, somewhat surprised. It seemed like a long way to come for such a brief exchange.

'Thanks for coming,' Marchal said again. 'Truly, I appreciate it. Come, I'll walk you out.' Without ceremony, he steered them out of the building, as if he had other urgent matters to attend.

'So have you figured out whether there is a link between the two deaths?' Lila asked him as they were heading out.

Marchal hesitated. 'We've had the Roma boy in here before, for breaking into a couple of flats in the tower blocks. My guess is some of the residents had had enough and decided to take matters in their own hands.'

'What about the link between the two boys?' Lila insisted.

'Like I said,' Marchal replied dismissively. 'We haven't got anywhere yet. There isn't anything I can tell you beyond what I've already said.'

Which is nothing, Morel thought. He was seething.

The silence was ominous as he and Lila got in the car. He knew she was feeling much the same as he was. Outraged, that Marchal should have summoned them here, essentially to tell them to stay away. As they backed out of their parking spot, someone rapped on Morel's window, startling him. He stopped the car and wound down his window. The man standing outside the car was familiar. Morel had seen him in the police station just now, when he'd been talking to Marchal.

'I'm sorry for coming up to you like this. Thierry Villot,' he said, sticking his hand through the open window.

'You work with Marchal?'

'Marchal and I go way back. We started here around the same time. I've had quite a bit to do with the Cité des Fleurs. It's shocking what happened to the Roma kid but I'm not that surprised. He'd been causing trouble, breaking repeatedly into people's homes. The sort of people who don't sit back and wait for the police to solve a problem for them...and there's a great deal of animosity against the Roma people here, and everywhere ... I'm not telling you anything you don't know. But I knew Samir personally. It's terrible what happened to him.'

'How did you know Samir?' Morel asked, taken aback by the other man's chattiness. What was Thierry Romain doing here, talking to them? And why did everyone keep referring to Georghe as the Roma boy? Didn't he at least deserve a name? Morel glanced in his rearview mirror, wondering if Marchal was watching.

'I'm well acquainted with the boys Samir hung out with. That whole gang, I've known them for years. Some of them are down at the station all the time. They don't care. They know we can't keep them inside forever. They just sit tight and wait till we have no choice but to release them. Then a few months later they're back in the cells again.'

'What for?'

Thierry glanced back at the building.

'Drugs?' Morel pressed.

'Yes and no. Boys like Samir, at that age, they're still on the periphery. They get sucked in to the business, but they don't make any of the decisions. From my perspective, they're just pawns. Working for the dealers, running errands for them, acting as lookouts. That kind of thing.'

'It's not what I'd refer to as the periphery.' Lila's comment went unanswered. Thierry was looking at Morel, ignoring her.

'What about Samir?' Morel asked.

Thierry shook his head.

'I don't know, exactly. At least I'm not sure. But I did notice he seemed to have a bit of money all of a sudden. Not a great deal, but enough to make me wonder.'

'So you kept an eye on him?'

'I didn't need to. I'd see him at the station, every few months or so. Marchal hauled him in three, four times. For questioning. Mostly to see if he'd give us anything on the guy Marchal thought he was working for.'

'Marchal never mentioned that,' Morel said, glancing at Lila. 'He never said he knew Samir. In fact, when I first came by the station and mentioned Samir was missing, he acted like he'd never heard the name before. Why is that?'

'I don't know,' Thierry said, looking uncomfortable.

'Why are you telling us all this?' Lila asked.

'I don't really know. Maybe I just wanted to communicate the fact that he wasn't a bad kid,' Thierry said. 'It's frustrating, for me, to see these boys fuck up their lives. Even if there isn't much we can do about it. Some of these kids I've known since before they could walk. I know their families, their siblings … after a while, it wears you down.'

Morel looked at the unhappy man before him. Everything he said seemed heartfelt and genuine, but there was something else too. He thought Thierry was lying. Or maybe not lying so much as holding back. That wasn't what he'd come here to say. He thought back to his earlier comment about Samir, how he'd been hauled in by Marchal and interrogated. Hauled in. Interesting choice of words.

They'd been here for a while now, and Morel felt it was time to stop. Obscurely, he worried he might be getting Thierry into trouble.

'Are you working on the investigation into the two deaths?' he asked.

'No.' Thierry hesitated. 'But I hope they find who did this.' He seemed in a hurry now to end the conversation. 'Nice to meet you,' he said, and turned away before Morel could respond. He and Lila watched the man walk back into the building without turning back.

'What the fuck was *that* about?' Lila said.

'I have no idea.' Morel watched the man disappear into the building. 'But I have a feeling he and Marchal may not be close. Even though they go "way back."'

'In that case, I like him already,' Lila said. 'That Marchal. What a tosser. Making you come all this way so he could tell you, in the nicest possible way, to butt out?'

'I'm not feeling that great about it either,' Morel said, leaving the new police building behind. He thought about the man they'd just met. He felt certain they'd meet again.

*

'What's going on?' Marchal asked Thierry when he returned to the office. 'What did you want with Morel?'

'Just curious. I thought I'd say hi,' Thierry said, doing his best to appear nonchalant despite Marchal's intense gaze. His scalp itched, as it always did in times of stress. He resisted the urge to scratch his head.

'Thinking of working for him? Maybe you're getting tired of Villeneuve?' Marchal looked amused.

'You're joking, right? Can you imagine what it's like, working with that bunch of snobs? Besides, how could one possibly get tired of Villeneuve.' Thierry saw Marchal relax and grin before walking away.

Thierry watched him go. Noted the swagger in Marchal's walk, and the way everyone in the room responded to him.

Careful, Thierry, he told himself. His heart was beating as wildly as it had on that day in the building entrance, talking to Karim.

*

'Can we stop at that supermarket we saw on the way in? I need a drink. I'm parched. Must be all those hours of conversation we had back there with Marchal.'

Morel turned into the Leader Price car park and Lila got out. He watched her stride towards the shop with the air of a woman who had no time to waste. Morel watched her go, wondering what it was that had made it impossible for her and Akil to stay together. Part of the attraction with her, he knew, was the way she seemed to take on the world without hesitation, never caring what people might think. But it was also what made her intractable. Was that what had led to the final break-up - the absence of malleability? In Lila's dictionary, compromise wasn't give and take; it was a word that meant someone caught with their pants down.

While she was gone, he watched people entering and leaving. A man in a coat that looked like he'd borrowed it from someone twice as big as him was leaning against the wall, talking loudly. His face was deeply flushed, and he used his hands eloquently to demonstrate something to an invisible companion. Nearby, a group of teenagers stood in a circle, smoking, obviously skipping school. Morel was debating whether to get a drink too when Lila came back with two bottles of Orangina. She handed one over. 'You know,' she said as she slid into her seat, taking up the conversation where they'd left it, 'I didn't think this was any of our business. I told you as much when your friend Virginie dropped into the office. Marchal is right. It's nothing to do with us.' She took a sip of her drink. 'At the same time, it really pisses me off when someone tells me what's my business and what isn't.'

'I didn't enjoy that either,' Morel commented. They sat in silence for a moment before Morel backed the car out of the parking lot.

'We could drive past the Roma camp on our way back? Just, you know, to take a look?' Lila suggested.

'Lila, you know that's a bad idea.'

'What can I say?' She finished her drink and grinned. 'I'm full of bad ideas.'

The Roma camp was easy to find. Less than 500 metres from the towers, it was a sprawling vista of improvised dwellings. Morel wound his window down to get a better look. The place looked like a giant dumping ground. There were shopping trolleys, stray dogs, burning fires. Lengths of copper cable, and rubbish everywhere. The Roma earned a living with scrap metal and garbage. A kilo of copper could go for five euros, Jean had told Morel. That's if you could find a buyer willing to do business with a seller who didn't have a French ID card.

A garage stood next to the camp. A man in dirty overalls leaned into a car with its bonnet open. As they watched, he stopped whatever he was doing to stare at them.

'Do you think he's worried we might rob him?'

'I think it's more likely he's worried we'll talk to him,' Morel mused. 'It'd be interesting to find out how much he knows about his neighbours. Whether he knew Georghe's family.'

'Shall we have a chat then? Drop in on some of the friendly locals while we're at it?' Lila asked. The man lit a cigarette without taking his eyes off them. His shirtsleeves were rolled up and there were tattoos on both arms. From where Morel and Lila sat, it was hard to know what they depicted.

'I think it's best we leave it,' Morel said. 'If Marchal finds out we stopped here on our way out, he'll be unimpressed. Plus, I can't see us getting a warm welcome.'

'Well, not in that get-up,' Lila said, looking pointedly at Morel.

Self-consciously, Morel adjusted his tie and the cuffs of his jacket. 'Virginie said the same thing. Everyone's very concerned about the way I dress all of a sudden.'

'That's because, when you dress like that in an area like this, it's like waving a big red flag at a grumpy bull,' Lila said.

'Really?' But inwardly Morel was thinking about his visit to the Cité des Fleurs with Virginie. She had said to him, as they were leaving, 'do you want to get killed? Is that it? Because coming in here dressed like that, you're begging for a beating. At the very least.'

Twelve

'Thanks for being here, Aisha,' Virginie said. Aisha was not supposed to call her Virginie, it was too familiar, but sometimes she did, when the woman was getting on her nerves. 'I know you didn't want to come today.'

Aisha knew it was rude, but she couldn't stop looking at Virginie's hair. Why did she dye it, when the colour was so obviously fake – too bright for a woman her age? It made her look cheap and vain. Surely her hair should be starting to turn white by now? Why were people always trying to cover up who they really were? It was the sort of thing Karim would probably do when he was older, colour his hair to look young.

She wished she hadn't come. She had nothing to say.

'You're right,' she said, looking down at her hands. 'I didn't want to come. I don't really feel like talking about anything.'

'That's fine. You don't have to talk.'

Aisha thought that was funny. What was the point of being here if all she was going to do was sit and say nothing?

Virginie put her notebook and pen away and crossed her legs. She had rubbish taste in clothes but you could tell she spent a lot of time choosing what she wore. Not so that men would notice her, that wasn't it at all; but so people would look at her and think she was strong and independent and didn't care what other people thought was cool or trendy. Today, Virginie was wearing purple stockings and a red skirt, and a short, rust-coloured leather jacket. Her earrings were little orange foxes that peeked out of her hair when she moved, then disappeared again, as if they were alive.

To Aisha, there was something sad about Virginie, like she was trying very hard to project a particular image, to make people believe something about her that she knew was bullshit. *Maybe we all do it*, she thought. *Me, Virginie, Monsieur Clément. Maybe Samir did it too.*

She leaned forward and Aisha could see Virginie was waiting for her to say something meaningful. Instead, Aisha was focusing on not staring at the woman's cleavage. It was too much for a woman her age. Too much for any woman. Aisha didn't believe women should cover up but neither did she believe that it was necessarily freeing to reveal so much. When people talked about the hijab they said women had no choice and it was the men who dictated how they should dress. But when a woman showed half her breasts or wore clothes so tight, heels so high she could barely walk normally, who dictated that? Was that really a choice?

'You seem very far away, Aisha,' Virginie murmured. Aisha knew for a fact that Katarina, that hyena, had regular appointments with the school counsellor too. She wasn't *supposed* to know. These meetings were supposed to be confidential. But Virginie had let it slip once when they were talking. Very unprofessional. Aisha would have paid to know what they talked about. She couldn't imagine what problems Katarina might have, though she liked to think that her issues were all related to the fact that even she had trouble liking herself.

'Aisha, you came today and I'm glad you did. If you don't want to say anything, if you just want to sit here for a while, that's fine. The important thing for you to remember is that, in this room, there is no judgement, no expectation. There's no rule about what you have to say or do when you're in here. It's completely up to you.'

'That's not true.'

'What isn't?'

'That it's up to me. Nothing's up to me. Everything that happens is beyond my control.'

Virginie nodded. 'I can see why you'd think that. After what's happened to Samir. But we do have some say in what goes on in our lives. A great deal, in fact.'

'You would say that.'

'Why?'

'Because you're an analyst. You have to believe that people have some control over their thoughts and actions. It's the basis of your work.'

'You're very perceptive. That's true. I do have to believe it. And I do. Maybe it's the reason I chose this profession.' Virginie cocked her heard and looked at her. Aisha knew that look. It meant the psychologist found her *interesting*. She looked away so she didn't have to meet Virginie's gaze, and let hers wander around the room. How much longer before the session was over? She couldn't risk looking at her watch. Virginie never took her eyes off her. And there was very little to look at in here. It was more of a closet than a room, really. Right now, it felt particularly cramped. The walls seemed thin, made of paper. She pictured someone ripping them open, leaning their head in. Next door, the head teacher must be eavesdropping. In her shoes, Aisha would definitely be listening in. Just to escape the boredom of sitting in an office all day, running this school. The walls were bare and the only window looked out onto the fenced area where the school kids spent their free time. There were two basketball hoops, and benches on either side of the quadrangle. Someone had left their jacket on one of them. It would be soaked by the time they got it back. It had warmed up a bit since the morning but the snow was still everywhere. You could see the footprints left by school kids and teachers earlier, and there were areas where the grey surface showed.

All of a sudden, she felt really tired. She looked back at Virginie. 'You talked about choice. What choices did I make that affected Samir? What did I choose that makes him dead?' she asked.

'Do you feel responsible for his death?' Virginie responded.

'You're missing the point. I'm saying I had no influence on what happened to him.'

'And I'm trying to tell you that you can influence the shape of your own existence.'

'Do you think I actually care about that at the moment? The shape of my existence?'

'What *do* you care about?'

For the first time, the psychologist sounded impatient. Aisha felt a bit bad. She must be getting fed up; this exchange was going nowhere. She took a pen from the notebook where it rested, on her lap, and started playing with it.

'How is it going at home?' she asked.

'How do you think? My Mum's not coping.'

'I wouldn't expect her to be coping. She's grieving, and that's only natural.'

'Your policeman friend. The one from Paris. Is he going to do anything, now that my brother's dead?'

'The police here in Villeneuve...'

'Spare me.' Aisha stood up. She was never this rude, but she couldn't help it. Something big was swelling inside her, making her lips move and articulate words that didn't belong to her. *I have to get out of here, before I say something I'll really regret,* she thought. 'Look, I've got to go.'

'Aisha – '

'I'm fine.'

'Have you got anyone you can talk to?'

She couldn't help thinking about Luc Clément but of course she didn't mention him. Virginie would go straight to the head teacher, probably, even though everything that happened in this room was supposed to be confidential. Besides, he wasn't a friend. A friend was someone your own age. Aisha could see Virginie wasn't satisfied with the way things had gone, but she stood up anyway. The foxes were caught up in her hair and Aisha pictured her extricating them later, looking in the mirror with that same impatient look she had earlier. 'You have my number,' Virginie said. She sounded a bit desperate. 'Please call me anytime. I mean it. Day or night. If you want to talk.'

'Sure, I'll do that,' Aisha said. If there was one thing she knew, it was that she would never call.

*

What a relief it was, to be out of there. It was all she could do to walk and not break into a run on her way to the bus stop. Occasionally, she looked over her shoulder to make sure she was lengthening the distance between herself and that poky little room full of secrets. The things people didn't want to share eventually being dragged out of them. As far as she could tell, it was to do with all the things you didn't like about yourself. When you told your secrets, did it actually make you feel any better?

If someone saw her, they'd think she was being chased. She wanted to get as far away from the school as she could, but it was hard to walk fast. Her feet hurt. If it hadn't been so cold, she would have taken her shoes off. All morning they'd been killing her. The new boots looked good but they were a size too small. Half the original price. That was something at least. She'd bought them and a bottle of black nail varnish with the money she'd earned from babysitting. She'd also bought perfume for her mother, who'd told her it was frivolous to waste money on stuff like that, but later when they'd been getting ready for bed, Aisha had smelled it on her. Aisha and Samir had been together that day. They'd taken the train together, to the nearest suburb that had decent shops. Three stops on the RER, heading towards Paris. She remembered it well because it had been Samir's idea to go out together after lunch on a Saturday, but then when they'd got there he'd said he had something to do and would she mind walking around for a bit on her own until he came back? Of course, she'd told him she didn't. He'd disappeared for an hour and returned in a really good mood. Where had he spent that time? Who had he met with? She was beginning to realize there was a lot she didn't know. And now he was dead she had so many questions. Who would answer them for her?

While she waited for the bus to show up, she undid her laces and loosened them so she could wiggle her toes. Her nose was dripping and she searched her pockets for tissues, but she didn't have any so she had to keep sniffing. It was something Antoine, who was kind of her mother's partner and kind of just a friend, and always around, did constantly when he got a cold, and she had to bite her tongue then not to show how irritating she found it. She sniffed again, and used her sleeves to wipe her eyes. She tried to imagine Samir showing up, frowning at her when he saw her at the bus stop with her shoes undone and her face a mess. How she wished he would show up and she wouldn't care if he was in a bad mood or said something to make her feel bad.

Her phone beeped. It was a message from Eloise, saying that there was no need for her to babysit her daughter tonight; that she should be with her mother and look after herself. And that she was sorry. Everyone was sorry. Aisha wondered who had told Eloise, though it could have been anyone. News travelled fast on the estate. She texted back to say she was happy to babysit. No one seemed to realize that she would much rather be busy than sitting around thinking about what happened to Samir. Thinking about how he'd looked when she'd seen his body, her mother reaching out for her too late to prevent her from seeing. The way her mother had collapsed when she'd realized what she was looking at. They'd stood outside in the cold and her mother had started screaming and the lights had gone on in the tower block so fast, almost as if one person had turned them all on at once. When something bad happened, everyone wanted to know.

Another text came from Eloise. *Honestly, there's no need. Stay with your mother.* They went back and forth like this a couple more times and in the end Aisha gave up, because the whole exchange was going nowhere. She couldn't stop shivering and when she finally caught sight of the bus she felt a surge of relief. She scrolled down her contacts to find Karim's number, and sent him a message. *Meet me outside the supermarket in an hour.* He didn't send a reply but she knew he would come.

On the bus, she recognized some of the older boys from the estate. They were around Ali's age, and she guessed they didn't have jobs because they tended to hang around the tower blocks during the day, watching people and making smart-ass comments. She knew their faces, but not their names, though one of them was related to someone in her class. They sat at the back of the bus, and one of them had headphones on, though the music was so loud everyone on the bus would be able to hear it. The seats were all taken, so Aisha stood by the door in the middle section and put her own headphones on, mainly to block out the crap that was playing. She hadn't started playing music yet when one of the boys came up and tapped her on the shoulder.

'Can't you see I'm busy?' she snapped, and immediately regretted it. What was she doing? She normally tried to keep a low profile and stay out of trouble. And here she was, being rude to a guy twice her size, while his friends watched.

'What is it?' she said, softening her tone. The bus stopped and more people got on. The boy looked like he wasn't sure what to do or say next. She stared at his face, waiting for him to get angry or at the very least to start telling her to learn some respect.

'We're all really sorry about what happened to your brother,' he said. It sounded practiced. Empty words. She kept her expression soft but inside she felt like spitting in his face. She glanced over at the others. They were all pretending not to notice. She turned back to him. It wasn't his fault if he had to stand there like an idiot pretending he was sorry. She guessed the others had sent him because he was the one with the least courage.

'Thanks.' She was about to pop her headphones back on but he wasn't finished.

'He didn't deserve it. Let's hope they find the sons-of-bitches who did this to him.' He raised his voice as if he wanted to make sure his friends and everyone on the bus would hear, and she felt her face go red. 'Too many of our brothers are getting killed. This shit needs to stop.' She nodded quickly so he would go away and he did, at last, but now people were looking at her as if somehow, she was to blame for the boy's stupid comments, and she could see in their minds they'd lumped her in with him, just another troublemaker they hoped would get off the bus really soon. Her eyes darted around the bus, hoping to see one friendly face, and that was when she spotted one of Katarina's friends. She was sitting behind the driver, but she'd turned so she was looking straight at her. An anorexic blonde in skinny jeans and a white puffer jacket with fake fur around the collar. She was smirking and Aisha's heart caught in her throat, because she knew the girl would be on the phone to Katarina the second she got off the bus.

Aisha got off at her stop and checked her phone. Nothing. She tied her laces and started walking towards the supermarket, thinking about what had just happened on the bus. She wished she'd caught a different one, or just walked. She could still see Katarina's friend watching her, that air of mild triumph and impatient excitement. She'd looked like a kid with a story she couldn't wait to share with someone. Aisha told herself she shouldn't care, but what the boy had said was so dumb. She was ashamed for him, ashamed for herself. What *brothers* was he talking about? Where had he learned his lines? In some action movie? On one of the news channels the night before, someone had referred to the Roma boy and Samir as victims of the system. What did that mean? Samir's killer wasn't some abstract concept. It wasn't the system that had killed him, it was a real person, someone evil who had hurt him and left him to die. Just like someone had hurt the Roma boy and ended his life.

As she walked, the snow began to fall, and it grew dark. Other people were on the street. An old woman hurried past her, looking at the sky. Aisha's mother would be waiting for her. She should probably call and let her know she would be a bit late. Aisha knew her mother wouldn't take it well, would insist she come straight home; but right now she really needed to stay away. The thought of another night at home was unbearable. It was easier when Antoine was around, looking after her mother like he always did, but he'd been acting weird these past days. One minute he was there and the next he was making excuses not to stay, and it was obvious he was lying. Maybe he too was finding it hard to hang around, given the atmosphere. Last night, Aisha had had to listen to her cry for hours. That was what you got for sharing a room with your mother. There was nowhere to go to escape another person's grief, or to give in to your own. At some point, when Aisha thought her mother must have fallen asleep, she'd started talking. She said the two of them would have to move back to Algeria now. That there was no point staying in France.

'What are you talking about? And what would we do there?' Aisha said, horrified.

'There's nothing for us here now. Nothing,' her mother wailed. Well, Aisha thought, there's me, for a start, and maybe I'm not ready yet to be considered dead, to be buried alongside my brother. I know what returning to Algeria means. I've seen a few families do it. As a girl, everything I do, everyone I see would be scrutinized. I want to choose my own future. And even if it's hard here in Villeneuve, it's what I know and where I belong.

Karim was waiting where she'd asked him to. 'Thanks for coming,' she said. They kissed on both cheeks. 'Where to?' he asked.

She had to think. It was privacy she wanted, and suddenly it was clear to her where they needed to go. The wasteland, behind the tower blocks. 'We'll make it quick,' she said.

'You're crazy. No way.' Karim would never admit it but she knew what he was feeling. Since they'd found the Roma kid there, the place freaked him out.

'Yes. It'll be fine. We won't be there for long.'

The wasteland was where people went who had something to hide. It seemed fitting. Aisha didn't want anyone to know what her intentions were. Not now, in any case. She was scared too but she'd try to hide it. And she couldn't stop shaking, but it was only because she wasn't suitably dressed. Karim was wearing his leather jacket that looked warm. He caught her looking at it and after a moment's hesitation took it off and handed it to her.

'Here.'

'No. Keep it.' He shrugged his shoulders and put it back on.

They reached the wasteland quickly, walking fast. There was no one there except the two of them. She dug her hands into her pockets and bounced up and down to try to warm up and to hide the fact that she was nervous. Karim seemed on edge too, but then again, he had every reason to be. Samir was dead. Karim was the closest person to him, so maybe he was worried about himself. He kept looking around, as if he thought maybe someone might turn up. His clothes looked brand new and like they would have cost a lot of money. How had he paid for them? Aisha thought she knew. She'd always had some idea of what he and Samir were up to, but she'd never known for sure. Samir had never bought fancy clothes - so what had he done with the money?

She'd always wondered what her brother saw in Karim. It was obvious the two of them got on. She didn't really get it. It wasn't that she didn't like Karim, she just didn't think there was much to him.

Maybe in every friendship there was one person who was stronger than the other. That was just the way things went. One strong, one weak. Just like Samir had been stronger than her. When she looked at Karim, in some ways it was like looking at herself. The part that she despised, that would never stand up for itself. Even now, she could see that both she and Karim felt the same. Helpless. Sad. So sad, it hurt, like that time she'd had the flu and all her joints had ached, and there hadn't been any position she could sit or lie in that would make her forget the pain. The difference was that she wasn't going to give in to the helplessness. For her brother's sake, she would be brave.

'Let's keep this short,' Aisha said. This was her first time in the wasteland. She'd never had any reason to come here before. She'd never been late going home either, not without calling her mother. So much had changed in a very short time.

She'd brought a notebook and a pen, and when she pulled them out, Karim looked worried.

'What's that for?'

'Taking notes.'

'What fucking notes?' He saw the look on her face and shut up. The fact was that she wanted to write everything down. She wanted to do this properly. And it helped, to be methodical. The feel of the pen in her hand steadied her.

'Question number one. What was Samir doing on the first day he didn't come home? Karim shook his head. 'What, the two of you weren't together?'

118

'No.'

'Was he even at school?'

'I wasn't there, but I hear he didn't show up.'

'Why wouldn't he go to school?' It wasn't really a question, she was thinking out loud. 'Was he in trouble? Tell me.'

'Honest to God, I don't know. I'd tell you. I would,' Karim said. But Aisha could tell he was lying. Why else would he look away? She'd have to come back to that, but there were other things she wanted to know. Like, was her brother seeing anyone? A girl?

'Maybe,' Karim said reluctantly.

'You mean yes. Who was it?'

'I don't know,' Karim said, and his face turned red. 'But I think he had someone. He kind of hinted at it, but he didn't want to say.'

'Why not? Why would he keep it secret?'

'How would I know?'

Aisha thought about this. Karim went on.

'Maybe the girl was married or something. Maybe she was cheating on her boyfriend, or on her husband.' Aisha knew about Karim's Dad cheating on his Mum, from something her mother had said once, but she'd never told him she knew. She nodded. Karim had a point. 'Maybe you're right. How are we going to find out who it was, then?'

'Why do you want to know?'

'I want to know everything,' Aisha said fiercely. 'How else are we going to figure it out?'

He looked scared again, and she wanted to kick him. 'What about Ali?' she said, and that seemed to freak him out more. Still, he replied. 'It was Ali who told me about Samir. He said they'd gone and killed him. I don't know what he meant by they. That's what he said.'

Aisha knew Ali. Everyone did.

'What have you and Samir been doing for Ali?' she asked. If Samir were still alive, she would never have asked. She would never have interfered in her brother's business. But he wasn't around to get mad at her. Karim, though, looked like he'd seen a ghost. He shook his head.

'You're going too far. You're going to get me into a shitload of trouble.'

'You promised,' she said, but he just kept shaking his head. She wanted to tell him that now Samir was gone, they needed to be strong. But she quickly realized there wasn't any point, not now. This was as far as he would go for the time being. She needed him to be her friend. Who else was there that could help her resolve this? Karim had always liked her, probably because of who her brother was.

'This is what you'll do,' she said, even though he was still shaking his head, and refusing to look at her. 'Listen. One: find out who Samir was dating. Two: find out where he was sleeping the night before...' she swallowed, and stumbled over the next words. 'Before he died.'

'And you? What are you going to do?'

She stared at him till he lowered his eyes. 'Don't worry about what I'm doing.' She felt she had to be honest with him. 'The thing is, Karim. I don't know yet whether I can trust you. Maybe I can. We'll just have to see.'

Thirteen

'I don't know about you guys, but I'm thirsty. I could use that drink now. Are we ready to go?' Jean pulled on his leather jacket and wrapped a scarf around his neck. The scarf looked like it had seen better days but the jacket looked pretty good for something that had been worn almost daily for three or so decades. Every scuff mark, every cigarette burn told a story. Morel had heard them all over the years.

'Ready,' he said. He waited for Akil and Vincent to get their jackets. Vincent hesitated.

'I could come with you,' Vincent told Lila for the umpteenth time.

'What for? It's just a swingers' club. I hear single women are always welcomed with open arms. I'll be more popular if I turn up unaccompanied. '

'It could wait,' Morel said. 'You could do this later. At this hour, there'll be no one there anyway.'

'All the same.'

'Suit yourself. Okay, let's go everyone.' He couldn't keep the annoyance out of his voice.

'I might catch up with you later,' Lila called out. But they all knew she had no intention of joining them.

*

Morel was right about one thing. It didn't look like much was happening at the club. It was too early for that. Lila pushed open the door of the first place on her list – the one closest to the river and to the spot where a passing jogger had seen Simic's body in the water and alerted the police. She found herself in a reception area manned by a kid who couldn't have been more than 20 years old. His eyes were glued to an iPad screen and he barely looked up when she walked in. It was just the two of them.

'Hi,' she began. 'What's your name?'

He looked up from his screen and gaped at her. 'Ludovic.'

'Looks like a quiet night, Ludovic. Is anyone around?'

The boy gave her an uneasy look.

'I haven't seen you here before.'

'No, you haven't. Is the boss in? The manager?'

'She is,' he offered reluctantly.

'In that case I'll go in and find her, if you don't mind.'

Ludovic clearly did mind, but lacked the courage to confront Lila. While he considered his reply, she looked at his screen to see what he was watching. It was an animated film. An astronaut and a cowboy were in a tiny car, chasing a truck.

'Any good?' she asked him, nodding towards his screen.

'I – '

'See you in a little while, Ludovic.'

Before he had a chance to answer, she had turned her back to him and was making for the door that led further in to the club.

'Can I help you?' Before Lila stood a woman squeezed into a black dress two sizes too small for her, with a mass of black hair swept into a chignon and the sort of cleavage that made it hard to look elsewhere. She was no longer young but she clearly devoted a generous amount of time, money and effort to holding back the years.

'This is a private venue,' the woman said. She stood in the doorway, effectively preventing Lila from going any further. Behind her, a woman wearing nothing but a vest was leaning over a pool table, preparing her shot. The sight of her dimpled buttocks was so unexpected that Lila forgot for a moment what she'd meant to say. Over in the far-right corner, a TV screen projected a different sort of movie from the one Ludovic was enjoying out in reception.

'I'm a police officer,' Lila said. 'I want to ask you about one of your members. Gregory Simic. My understanding is he and his wife were regulars here. Gregory may have been here five nights ago. I'd like you to check your records and see if he was. Also, I'll need your name.'

The woman gave Lila a look of intense dislike.

'My name I have no problem giving to you. It's Béatrice de la Motte. But I'm not in the habit of giving out information about our guests. A place like ours wouldn't last very long if I did that, would it?'

'You might find that business slows down a bit once people find out that one of your guests was killed on his way out of here, just last week.' Lila had spoken loud enough for the woman playing pool to hear. There was a crash as she dropped the cue on the ground.

'Killed?' The club's manager seemed genuinely horrified. 'My God.'

'Gregory is dead?' The pool player had come over and she stood before Lila now wearing nothing from the waist down, with an air of utter devastation. 'How?' She started to sob, and the manager drew her close.

'It's okay, Bijou. There now, calm yourself.'

Lila took a closer look at the sobbing woman. She was a softer, plumper version of Valérie Simic. She seemed genuinely distressed. Well, that was easy, Lila thought.

'So you're Bijou. You and Gregory were close, weren't you? I'm sorry.'

'She did this,' Bijou wailed.

123

'Who did this?'

'His *wife*. It must be. She knew he didn't love her anymore. It was only a matter of time before he left her. She couldn't stand the idea.'

The words were delivered so spitefully, Lila felt a wave of sympathy for Simic's wife. Béatrice de la Motte was making a show of comforting the other woman. There were people arriving, Lila could hear them talking to Ludovic. Glancing at the TV screen, she saw that more people had joined in that action too. For a moment, she was distracted. What would Akil say if he were here? How would they talk about it later? They would either laugh or get frisky. Or a bit of both.

It only took three seconds to remember that would never happen, and to realize where she was. Not in some fantasy world with Akil, but in this sad venue on her own, doing her job.

'Bijou. I'll need you to put some clothes on,' she said quietly. 'Then Béatrice here is going to find us a room where we can talk about all this. I've got questions for both of you. For a start, Bijou, I'm going to need your real name.'

*

The bar Morel took his team to was a ten-minute walk away. There was a closer one, but it was where you'd find many of the detectives from the Crim', as the *brigade criminelle* was known, and Morel didn't want to have to spend his evening trapped in idle chatter with other colleagues. Or worse, with the superintendent, who liked to stop for a drink on his way home and was always on the lookout for company. Most people went out of their way to avoid drinking with Olivier Perrin.

The bar was doing a brisk trade, with a crowd that included locals who seemed to be on a first name basis with the bartenders, and tourists taking a rest from their sightseeing activities. Morel watched a man and a woman at a nearby table scroll through their photos on an iPad and reflected there must be thousands of the same ones being taken in Paris at any given moment. The Eiffel tower (captured from a distance, from its base, or going up the elevator), Notre Dame, the bridges over the Seine and the Louvre pyramid. And no picture was complete without a pose. You couldn't walk out without seeing someone taking a photo of themselves, armed with one of those ridiculous selfie sticks people carried with them nowadays. A fitting symbol, it seemed to him, of the narcissistic age they were living in.

'When you're ready,' Jean said, sounding mildly tetchy. 'A few of us are getting seriously parched.' Morel realized he'd been miles away. He ordered and paid for the drinks, and the four of them stood around, waiting for their order. When the drinks came, Morel handed Akil his glass before raising his own.

'*Bienvenu dans l'équipe*. I'm very pleased you've joined us.'

Bienvenu, the others echoed, and raised their glasses. Akil looked like a child on Christmas morning. '*Merci*. I won't disappoint you, I hope.'

'How long ago is it now, dear Akil, since you first came into our lives?' Jean mused. One drink – the first one generally went down fast - and already he was becoming sentimental. His face was flushed and Morel wondered whether it really was just one drink or whether Jean had sneaked a couple in earlier.

'Two years, right?' Akil replied.

'Two years.' Morel remembered his first encounter with the young Moroccan officer well. A sweltering day in August; a dead woman's flat, not far from where Morel lived. It had been a strange and unsettling case. The sort of case where, even after it was solved, a sense of unease remained. It had taken Morel months to get rid of that feeling, though he wasn't normally one to brood on old investigations. You did your best, you covered all the bases, and then you moved on. The victims had been particularly vulnerable. Elderly, frightened, alone. Akil, a Neuilly police officer at the time, had been the first on the scene of the first murder and soon he'd joined the team in its investigation, impressing Morel with his diligence.

'And now you've bloody done it, joined this ship of fools, and your life is about to get a hell of a lot more complicated,' Jean said.

'Let's drink to that, to complication,' Morel said, and raised his glass again.

Jean and Vincent left the bar after an hour, Vincent promising to drop Jean home ('as long as he doesn't tell me that excruciating story again of how he could have been a musician – I swear I'll throw him out of the car then, and he can walk home.') Morel was in no hurry and he stayed with Akil, ordering a cognac for himself and a beer for the young man. The crowd was thinning. The tourists were long gone and the others were heading off for dinner. 'Any dinner plans?' Morel asked. Akil shook his head.

'Let's get something to eat, then. Are you hungry?' Akil started to say something but Morel's phone rang and he stopped, gesturing for Morel to take the call. Morel checked to see who it was. He didn't recognize the number and was about to ignore it, but changed his mind, thinking that maybe it was his younger sister Adèle, who was with their father this evening, calling from the landline at home. Instead, it was Lila's voice he heard.

'You should turn your TV on,' she said. 'They're setting cars alight in Villeneuve.'

'I'm having a drink, with Akil. You should join us. Whose number are you calling from anyway?'

She said something but it was noisy in the bar and he didn't hear what it was. 'You're not still in the office, are you?' he asked, but it seemed she had hung up.

He turned back to the bar and found Akil, who was on his way back from the bathroom. 'Things are heating up in Villeneuve.' He told the younger man what he knew about Samir, and he told him about the incident with Thierry Villot, who had approached him and Lila outside the Villeneuve station following his meeting with Romain Marchal.

'It sounds like you're pretty involved,' Akil said. 'Why?'

'I don't know if they can handle something like this,' Morel said. It was the first time he'd said it out loud and he realized he'd been thinking it ever since he'd first heard about Georghe's death. That, on its own, was serious enough. Samir's murder made things a great deal more complicated.

He ordered another round of drinks for the two of them, then tried Lila's number. The call went straight to voicemail and he left a message asking her to call back. 'It would be good to have you here,' he added.

There was no need for it. It wasn't like there was anything urgent to discuss, either about Simic or about the events in Villeneuve. Nothing that couldn't wait till the next day. But he hoped she would come.

Morel finished his drink and together with Akil they left the bar. They parted ways outside, Morel striding quickly towards the Metro station, thinking about what Lila had told him. He tried to picture it. The burning fires, the wailing of car alarms going off, people from the housing estate out on the cold streets, venting their rage.

Everything he'd feared. It had begun.

BOOK TWO

AISHA

One

No one quite knew when it started or how it went from a handful of bored and unruly teenagers tagging walls to a mob lighting fires across the housing estate and screaming death threats at the police. It was only much later that people started putting the pieces together and making sense of them.

The sequence of events in the early part of the evening, cobbled together with the help of a handful of eye witnesses who were willing to talk, was as follows: sometime after nightfall, around six p.m., six young men aged between 15 and 20 met by the skateboard park at the foot of the tower blocks. It wasn't unusual to see kids there. They messed around in the snow, drank and passed a joint around, but quickly grew bored. It was the wrong night to be out, the coldest in three weeks, but no one felt like going home. One of them suggested walking over to the Roma encampment, and they all agreed, though none of them quite knew what the point of that was.

When they got there, frozen to the bone, they shouted insults and threats, expecting someone would hear them and get mad. But no one came out, or responded, and after a while that became boring too. They headed back the way they'd come, feeling cheated. Setting fire to a brand-new Renault Clio parked outside the tower blocks seemed like a good idea. They smashed a window, doused the interior with lighter fluid, and tossed a match in. Then they lit another joint and passed it around while the Clio burned. The fire set off car alarms along the street and brought residents in the tower blocks to their windows. When, ten minutes later, the owner came bursting out of Tower A, the youths scattered rapidly, laughing as they ran. The leader of the group, easily the swiftest, stood a foot taller than the rest of them. He looked like someone who spent time lifting weights. He was wearing a grey tracksuit and hoodie and he'd covered his face, though no one had any trouble recognizing him. He had the lighter fluid, which seemed to indicate some forethought. The others seemed to look up to him and they followed his instructions. All through the night's events, he remained calm.

The police showed up shortly after 7 p.m. Their numbers grew over the following hours. The evening news at 8.30 showed dozens of protesters facing off against riot officers armed with shields. The youths threw rocks and flares at the officers. They flipped cars and set them alight. They sprayed every wall they could find. The tags were the generic sort. *Fuck the state. Fascist pig.* As the violence spread, faster than anyone could have imagined, the messages became more specific; the language shifted. Sometime around midnight, the words *R.I.P. Samir* appeared along the walls of the first tower block. There was no mention of Georghe, the 12-year-old boy whose body had been found in a shopping trolley in the wasteland behind the tower blocks. Word on the street was that he'd had it coming to him. Samir's name though was on everyone's lips. Shortly after midnight, it became a chant.

The riot police were trained to be disciplined and not to over-react, but many had no experience of the level of anger directed at them here. To withstand the hatred, without charging or retreating, simply to stand their ground, was barely possible. When the first policeman was injured, and fell to his knees, the man standing next to him, a 23-year-old officer who had scored well in all his tests, lost his cool and fired teargas into the mob.

All hell broke loose.

Two

The way she saw it, they were setting the *cité* alight because two people were dead and one of them was Samir. Aisha had no idea why anyone would want to hurt her brother, or that boy Georghe. Some people were saying there was a link between the two. Some were even saying Samir had killed the Roma boy, which was crazy. She wished she could stand up for Samir and tell them all how wrong they were about him. She was useless at this, just as useless as she was at defending herself against Katarina. That crazy girl, at least, had left her alone these past days. Could it be she felt sorry for Aisha? Either that or she was planning something terrible, worse than anything she'd done before. Since her brother's death, Aisha found it hard not to feel paranoid. Over the past few days, Katarina had appeared alongside Samir in her dreams. She and her brother would be talking about something, and often she didn't get what he was saying. It was as if he spoke a foreign language, or he mumbled and she couldn't hear properly. Then Katarina appeared in the background, walking down a street towards them or looking out a window. Spying. Sometimes Aisha didn't see her but she knew Katarina was there. In the dreams, Katarina never spoke, but Aisha sensed she wanted to hurt her. Aisha always woke up before anything happened, but each time it was crystal clear somehow that whatever was going to happen next would be bad. The worst thing about these dreams was that she never knew what was coming.

She took her empty plate to the kitchen – tonight, after meeting with Karim, she'd cooked for herself and for her mother - and finished her glass of water. It was the first time she'd sat down and had a proper meal since Samir's death and she'd made the effort for their mother's sake. But her mother was so far away Aisha didn't think she would notice if her daughter went on a hunger strike. It was lonely at home without Samir or Antoine. She washed the dishes with the radio on, listening to someone telling her about what was happening right where she lived. The way they described it, Aisha thought they were describing a place on a different planet. There was nothing familiar in the words.

Washing. Drying, Putting things away where they belonged. Glasses, cutlery, plates. Given what was happening in the *cité* tonight, it seemed strange to be carrying out such mundane tasks. Though going by her mother's reaction, you would have thought this was an ordinary day and nothing unusual was going on. She'd turned the TV on to her favourite soap opera and now sat still as a statue, her eyes trained onto the screen. Aisha had liked it better when the apartment was filled with wailing women. They'd got in the way and insisted on making tea and bringing food, and watching Aisha and her mother eat and drink. Aisha had prayed they would leave the two of them alone to grieve in peace and it had been a relief when, at the end of the second day, her mother had sent them all away. Now Aisha missed the noise.

A part of her wanted to shake her mother, wipe that blank look from her face. Another part was frightened to be anywhere near her. Her lack of responsiveness was chilling. And the apartment didn't feel like home anymore. It was so stifling and she couldn't breathe easily. She needed to get out. Tonight, she was supposed to be at Eloise's babysitting, so she had a good excuse to go. But she couldn't leave Maman like this. Where was Antoine? He should be here. Only then did she realize Antoine would never make it to the tower blocks and to their apartment, not with what was happening in the street.

Aisha crossed into the living-room. Her mother was still staring at the TV screen, her eyes unseeing. Aisha knelt beside her mother and reached for her hand. Stroked it for comfort.

'What pills did you take, Maman?'

'Samir...'

'No, the pills. Where are they?'

'His pills.'

'Antoine? What did he give you?' Her mother gave her a helpless look, and Aisha sighed. Antoine had said the medicine would help her relax, but this was too much. Aisha needed her mother back. The one who checked on her and nagged her whenever she thought Aisha wasn't paying attention. The one who noticed everything.

'You know, I've just thought of something,' she said. 'Antoine isn't going to come, I think. He might find it impossible. Given what's happening.'

'What's happening?' her mother asked. Aisha turned away. There was no point trying to have a conversation. She dialed Antoine's number but he wasn't answering, so she left a message warning him, in case he didn't already know, that it could be dangerous coming through the estate tonight.

Once she'd finished tidying up, she went to the bedroom and looked out the window at the street below. It was hard to understand what was going on, to make any sense of it. She could hear shouting, and people below were running. She heard the police sirens in the distance, drawing near. They reminded her of the police cars outside the building, after Samir's body had been found in the bushes. So many flashing lights. Someone's hand had been on her shoulder the entire time but she had no idea whose. Two or three people had huddled around the place where Samir lay, unnaturally still, while the man who'd found him stood to the side, blubbering like a baby. Too afraid to look again at Samir's body, too scared to go back to his flat. Some things she remembered so well and others she didn't, like the person who'd kept their hand on her shoulder the entire time.

It was frightening, what was happening below, but in a strange way it made her feel good too, like the anger she was holding on to was being expressed out there. Maybe Samir was right. If you grew up in a place like Villeneuve, where you knew there was a pretty high chance you wouldn't get a job when you left school, where it was hard to stay on a straight path and achieve anything, the only way to be heard was to get really pissed off, and loud, and break things. Otherwise, no one heard. No one was listening. When Samir had said that to her, she hadn't known what he meant, but she understood it now. I don't ever see you do that, she'd told him. Get angry. Lose control. I have my own way of getting back at them, he'd replied. She'd never asked him what he meant. He wouldn't have told her, in any case. She wished her brother were here to see what was happening now. She could tell him that she understood. Torching cars was probably not the best way to start a conversation, but it sure got people's attention. She almost wished she could go down and run in the street too, and release some of the anger inside her, that was making her sick and keeping her awake at night. But she couldn't leave her mother on her own. So instead she sat beside her and put a hand on hers, and tried not to think about how miserable she felt. 'It's alright, Maman,' she said, patting her hand.

Her mother fell asleep. Aisha dozed off like that, holding on to her mother's hand. She was halfway through a strange and complicated dream, when the door opened, jerking her awake. 'Loubna?' It was

Antoine, sounding squeaky and breathless. Aisha hurried to the door and raised a finger to her lips. Antoine looked really stressed. There was a hole in his woolen jumper, right in the middle where you couldn't ignore it. For some reason this made her like him more. 'I got your message but I was on my way. I had to come. I couldn't leave you two alone,' he said. 'My God, Aisha. It's hell out there. I think someone's been badly injured.'

'Who?' she asked, while he struggled with the buttons on his coat, his fingers useless, his eyes wide and unfocused, still caught up in what he'd seen. 'Not a resident. A police officer, I think. I mean, I'm sure. He was in uniform. There was an ambulance and they had him on a stretcher. He wasn't moving. My God.' He pulled a handkerchief from his pocket and wiped his brow.

'Thank you for being here,' Aisha said. It would have taken a lot of courage for Antoine to come. She was so relieved she wanted to hug him. But he would definitely find that strange. Not that they didn't get on, but hugging wasn't the kind of thing they did. 'She's been sitting on the couch. Just sitting there, and now she's asleep,' Aisha said, and she wondered why she was whispering when they were nowhere near the living-room. Her mother's strange behaviour was rubbing off on her. Antoine gave her a weak smile. 'That's fine, I'll just take a minute here and then I'll go to her. You don't have to worry.'

When they went into the living-room, a few minutes later, Aisha was surprised to find her mother wide awake and standing by the window, looking down. 'Loubna, get away from the window, please,' Antoine told her. Aisha had noticed even he'd started talking to her like she was sick, or a kid. Firmly, patiently. He moved nearer to steer her towards the sofa. 'Let's watch a movie instead. What's happening down there is nothing to do with us.'

Aisha couldn't help herself. 'That isn't true,' she said. 'They're down there because of Samir.'

Antoine stared at her in disbelief. 'Is that what you think? This is just an excuse for violence.' Meanwhile, her mother seemed to have suddenly realized that something was different. She was staring out the window, wringing her hands.

'Inch'Allah, it will all return to normal,' she kept saying.

What sort of normal? That's what Aisha wanted to know.

*

Yasmina reached for her hairbrush and ran it slowly through her hair. Every night, one hundred times. It was a ritual – no, more like a superstition – that comforted her. Always one hundred strokes, that exact number, after her shower, sitting cross-legged on her bed in her pajamas. Always alone, once her daughter was asleep. She took pleasure in this, observing her reflection in the mirror, knowing how desirable she was. Samir had been so transparent. Many times, she'd teased him about it, but in truth she'd been flattered. He'd been so passionate, so easy to please. Poor Samir.

There was a loud knock, someone at the door, and she started in surprise. Who else could it be at this time but her brother, coming home? But then why didn't he open the door himself? He had his own key. The knocking grew more insistent and she stopped what she was doing – fifty-seven strokes, she would have to come back and finish what she'd started. She opened the door and took a step back. Swiftly, she adjusted her expression, trying hard not to let her distaste show.

'Réza. What are you doing here?'

He smiled and she raised a hand to her chest. Whenever she saw him, which thankfully wasn't often, he made her feel unclean.

'Your brother home?'

'No. But he will be soon.'

'Then you won't mind if I come in.'

She did mind, but what choice did she have? She opened the door wide and he stepped past her, towards the living-room.

'Can I get you something to drink?' she asked. 'I've prepared some tea, I'll bring you a cup if you like.' It was what she was expected to do, make him comfortable, but mostly she wanted to get away from him. Should she text her brother and tell him Réza was here?

'Is he expecting you?' she asked, when she returned with the tea. Strong, no milk, two sugars. He took the cup from her without replying and looked her up and down.

'I don't need an invitation to visit your brother. What have you been up to, anyway?'

'Working. Looking after my little girl. Nothing much apart from that.'

He sipped his tea. 'That's not what I've been hearing.'

Before she had time to ask what he meant, she heard the key in the front door and the sound of her brother's voice, calling for her.

'Yasmina, I need to talk to you.' Not angry so much as urgent. Quickly, she moved to the hallway. He was taking off his coat. Lately he'd started growing a beard and it gave him a forbidding look. He was strict, but he wasn't a bad person. Whereas Réza, well, that was a different story. 'He's here,' she said in a low voice. 'Who?' 'Réza. Were you expecting him?' Her brother's face changed, became guarded, and then Réza was in the hallway with the brother and sister, stepping into the shadowy space between them.

'Greetings, cousin. Ali sent me. He wants to ask, has your whorish sister told you yet what she's been doing in her spare time, while you're busy earning a living to keep her and her snotty kid fed and clothed?'

*

'Stop. You're hurting me.' Yasmina gripped her brother's hands, tried to get him to release his grip, to prevent him from crushing her skull, which was what it felt like. But it made no difference. He was twice her size. Réza had stepped past them to get into the kitchen, feigning discretion, and come back with a toothpick in his mouth. Her brother's hands moved back and now he was pulling at her hair, so hard she felt like screaming. 'Please, Mehdi.'

'You fucking bitch,' he spat. 'Do you realize what you've done?'

'Let go.'

'You've dishonoured me. You're a whore. Unfit to be a mother.' The pain was unbearable. She started screaming, not caring that Réza was there, not caring if anyone heard. Mehdi clamped his hand against her mouth and shouted at her to shut up.

'Mummy?' Yasmina felt her brother release his hold and she turned quickly to find her daughter staring at her in terror. Before she could reach for the child, Réza appeared in the doorway and pulled her away, before shutting the door in Yasmina's face.

'You're going to let him do that? You're going to leave her in there with him? *Him*?' Yasmina said, looking at her brother. His face was unrecognizable. She wanted to throw up and when she looked at him, she saw that he felt sick too, but his eyes were also full of hate.

'From now on,' he articulated slowly, as if she were deaf, 'you do exactly as I tell you.'

138

Three

Eloise looked like she'd seen a ghost.

'I can't believe you came. I told you there was no need.' She looked shaken, and Aisha wondered if that was just because of her turning up or if there was something else that was bothering her. 'You should be with your Mum, Aisha. Especially with everything that's going on.'

'I'd rather be here.' Eloise's hand was still on the door handle. For a moment, Aisha was worried she would send her home. But instead she put her arm around her and guided her inside.

'So I can babysit for you tonight? You've got plans, right?' she said. No matter what, she didn't want to be at home.

'Jesus, Aisha. Have you seen what things are like out there? I definitely don't need a babysitter tonight. But you could just come in for a coffee and cake. How does that sound?'

Aisha wanted to cry. She didn't want food. She wanted Samir. Eloise's voice was so kind. She took a step towards Aisha and gave her a hug.

They moved into the kitchen and that was when Aisha realized there was someone else there. She stared at the girl sitting at the table. She'd never seen her before but her presence triggered something. A memory or a realization, it was hard to tell.

'Yasmina, this is Aisha, who lives in the building and babysits Lola once in a while. Aisha, this is my friend Yasmina.'

Aisha knew it was rude to stare but really, Yasmina looked terrible. There were bruises around her neck and on her arms, and black streaks down her cheeks where her make-up has run. She looked really shaken. Aisha wondered who had done this to her and why.

'Hello,' she said. 'I'm Aisha.' She felt as though she'd interrupted something. A part of her was embarrassed and wanted to leave, but the other was glad to be here, away from the claustrophobic hell of home.

'Sorry, I don't normally look like this,' Yasmina said, attempting a smile. Eloise touched her arm. 'Take a seat, Aisha. Can I get you something to drink?'

'I'm not thirsty. Is Lola asleep?'

'She's asleep. But seriously, Aisha. I'm worried about you. You're not planning to go outside at any point tonight, right? It's not safe.'

'They're out there because of Samir,' Aisha said. Eloise nodded, but Aisha could see she wasn't convinced. Like Antoine, she probably thought this was just the usual trouble-makers looking for an excuse to break things. Aisha got it. There was plenty of that around here. But this felt different.

'I'm going to make tea. Mint tea,' Eloise said, with a pleased look. 'Yasmina taught me how to make it. You've got to try it, Aisha.'

'I've had mint tea before,' Aisha replied, slightly offended. Has Eloise seriously forgotten where her family came from? She may have been here almost her entire life, but that didn't mean she knew nothing about her roots. Eloise looked uncomfortable.

'Of course you have, Aisha. Take a seat. It won't take a minute.'

Aisha complied. Her heart was so full and she wished the two of them were alone so she could unburden herself. She wished so many things. She wished with all her heart she could go back in time and change the course of Samir's destiny.

She became aware that Yasmina was watching her. 'Don't you think you should call the police?' Aisha asked. Yasmina laughed at that, and Aisha blushed. Even with all the bruises she was really pretty and right now Aisha felt about five years old, clumsy and stupid and unattractive.

'And what good will that do, exactly?' Yasmina said, looking like she felt sorry for her.

'I don't know. But it's better than doing nothing.'

Aisha braced herself for another laugh but Yasmina was silent and when Aisha looked up she saw the other girl's expression was sad.

'I'm sorry about your brother,' she said, surprising Aisha. How did Yasmina know who she was?

'Did you know him?'

She nodded, her eyes beseeching, like she wanted to tell Aisha something but couldn't bring herself to say it. She didn't need to. Aisha got it.

'You're Samir's girlfriend.'

Yasmina laughed again, and Aisha realized it wasn't laughter so much as an expression of pain.

'I guess I am. Was. I probably shouldn't have. Clearly, I shouldn't...' She completely fell apart then and Eloise immediately responded, leaning over to give her a hug. Aisha really didn't know what to say. She felt like crying too but she didn't want to do it here. Eloise was telling Yasmina to try and control herself, that things would be okay. You could tell Eloise was a Mum. She was only 25 but she'd always seemed older than her age to Aisha. Eloise finally let go of Yasmina and looked at the two of them.

'Girls,' she said. 'Forget the fucking tea. I'd say what we all really, really need now is a proper drink.'

'Believe me, there's nothing good about being pretty and having guys notice you,' Yasmina said. The bottle on the table was their second one. Aisha had only had two glasses but that was a lot for her. This was only the second time in her life she'd had alcohol. If Samir or her mother knew, they'd kill her. Well, in the past at least. Now Samir was gone and her mother was a zombie, sleeping and staring into space when she was awake. Aisha was feeling sick and so exhausted she had to prop her head up with both hands or she'd have to rest it on the table, close her eyes and go to sleep.

'That's easy for you to say.'

'I'm serious. You have no idea what I have to put up with. If any guy around here sees me walking around and I'm covered from head to toe, then I'm a slut because it's my fault they like what they see. They tell you to be respectable, have some self-respect. Where's their self-respect? Where's their respect for women?'

'There's no harm in being respectable,' Aisha said, surprising herself. She had no idea where that had come from.

'Well, well. Will you look at that. What a little puritan you are. Are you implying I'm not respectable? And what makes you so superior?'

'You slept with a 16-year-old boy,' Aisha told her. Yasmina narrowed her eyes.

'You have no business judging me,' she said. Aisha held her gaze.

'You're wrong,' she said. 'I have every right. This is my brother we're talking about.'

Eloise leaned towards them. She was looking thinner and paler than usual, and Aisha felt ashamed suddenly, for the things she was saying in the woman's home. But Eloise didn't look angry, just sad. 'You both cared about him. Please don't fight,' she pleaded.

There was a real commotion below, but no one moved from the table to see what was happening. Aisha sneaked a peek at Yasmina. She was crying a little, but trying not to let it show. Aisha realized she was a bit jealous of her. She'd never known Samir like this girl had. With Aisha, Samir had rarely seemed relaxed, and she knew she'd often got on his nerves.

'It's good you could make him happy,' she told Yasmina grudgingly.

Aisha could feel her relax. The girl wasn't so mad at her now. She laughed a little through her tears. 'Oh Aisha. It wasn't like that at all.'

'What do you mean?'

'It wasn't anything serious. Just a bit of fun, you know?'

Aisha didn't know, but she nodded as if she understood.

'When did you see Samir last?' Aisha asked. 'Was he with you when he, you know, went missing from home?'

Yasmina sniffed and looked at Eloise. 'He came on the morning before he died. To my place. My brother wasn't home.'

'You live with your brother?'

She nodded. 'And my baby girl. It's just the three of us,' she added, before Aisha could ask who the dad was.

'What did Samir say?'

'Not much.' A giggle escaped her, and she quickly stifled it. 'We didn't do much talking. Sorry if that sounds bad, but we didn't.'

'Right.' Aisha considered what to say next. She had so many questions, like how long had Samir stayed? Why hadn't Yasmina asked him how he was? Had he seemed upset? Where had he gone? Why hadn't Yasmina kept him close, instead of letting him go and be on his own, when it wasn't safe?

143

'It's getting late, don't you think?' Eloise said pointedly. She pretended to yawn. Aisha ignored her.

'So, who did that to you?' she asked Yasmina, pointing at the bruises. The girl pulled a face and shrank away. Aisha was beginning to realize that, even though she was being friendly now, Yasmina didn't really like her much. That was fine, Aisha didn't like her much either. She was pretty but kind of superficial. Aisha wondered how much she'd cared about Samir, and why he'd never mentioned her. But of course she knew the answer to that. It was a secret, because Yasmina lived with her brother and if he was anything like the other Arab men here on the estate, he wouldn't be happy to hear she was carrying on.

'Was it your brother? Did he beat you?' Aisha asked.

'He didn't mean to.' *Right*, Aisha thought. 'It's true!' Yasmina said, guessing her thoughts. 'He would never do anything like this. But he had to show he was angry.'

'Show who?'

This time Yasmina looked scared, and Aisha felt a bit sorry for her. Her life didn't sound simple either and maybe Aisha was being too hard on her. She felt like a bully, sitting here questioning her when she was looking so rough.

'It's Réza's fault.'

'Réza?' Aisha knew Réza. He was the slimiest person she'd ever met. Aisha wouldn't have asked him for help if she was drowning and he was the last person on earth who could save her. Yasmina nodded.

'Réza came over and told my brother about Samir. Then he waited to see what my brother would do. He had no choice…'

144

'You don't think he would have beaten you anyway if he knew?' Aisha asked. She couldn't help sounding scornful. Yasmina's eyes flashed with anger.

'I'm really sick of sitting here answering your questions. You think you can judge me? Preach to me? You're like a man, Aisha. Just as bad.' She stood up. 'Sorry, Eloise, I have to go.'

'Go where?' Eloise asked, looking horrified. 'Surely you can't go home now, not after what happened.'

'It'll be okay, don't worry ...' Eloise shot Aisha an angry look, like she was to blame. At the door, Yasmina turned around.

'My brother wouldn't have beaten me if he had a choice. You know how I know? Because he knew about Samir before Réza told him. Before he raised his hand to me, I saw it on his face. All that time he knew and never said. Never lifted a finger against me until Réza showed up and forced him to act.'

'You're his sister,' Aisha said with disbelief. 'And he beat you up. Shouldn't he be protecting you instead?'

'He was protecting me. From Réza. If he hadn't done anything, Réza would have taken the matter into his own hands and done much worse. Or Ali.'

'Ali? Surely, he wouldn't do that. Beat a girl up.'

Yasmina looked Aisha up and down like she was born yesterday. 'My God, you're so naïve. Who do you think is in charge in the cité? The gangs, the dealers. And Ali is up there with the best of them. Do you think he got there by being nice?'

Aisha needed a quiet moment to process what she was saying. Ali was courteous. He'd always treated her well, with respect. She knew he could be dangerous. But she couldn't picture his involvement in this.

More importantly, Yasmina's brother had known, and said nothing. He'd been angry with Yasmina and with Samir. As she returned to the table where Eloise was sitting, pale and reproachful, Aisha tried her best not to let her see how agitated she was. She couldn't figure out why someone would want to kill Samir, but now she knew of one person at least who might have had a motive.

The question was, what could she do with that information?

Four

That night in Villeneuve, no one slept. That, at least, was Alberto's impression. He sat in the dark, in his living room, in a faded pair of pajamas and fleece dressing gown, and watched the fires spread below, as car after car was set alight. From this distance, it almost looked like a festive occasion. Normally, at night, it was quiet and dark in the streets, not many lamplights and no pedestrian traffic to make you feel safe if you did have to walk home. No businesses open for customers. Those had left a long time ago. Now the entire neighbourhood was ablaze with light. He saw the vans pull up and riot police pile out of them with all their gear. Helmets, shields. Flash-balls. He'd attended a few demonstrations in his day but these weapons were new. Despite their gear and their numbers, the police looked hesitant and disorganized, but many of the hooded figures seemed unsure too and at the first sign of confrontation, they scurried away. From up here, they looked like insects. *Cucarachas,* Alberto thought, fleeing across the snow.

Cockroaches, the lot of them. There was no other word for the hoodlums running wild down there. No direction, no objective other than causing havoc and polluting the environment. This wasn't about the gipsy boy. No one was spilling any tears over the poor kid. Was this about Samir then? Or was this a bunch of youngsters letting off steam because they felt they weren't being heard? You want to fight the system, fine, Alberto reflected out loud, pulling his dressing gown closer to his chest. But when you started destroying the property of working people - that was vandalism, pure and simple. He sat and watched and muttered to himself, growing angrier all the while, until he could no longer sit and he started pacing, wondering how long it

147

would go on and whether any of the police were going to do their job and allow the decent people of this neighbourhood – there were still many he could think of, despite everything - a chance to get back to sleep.

He got back into bed and picked up the newspaper he'd bought that morning – he still read what Emilia had referred to as that Communist rag. She hadn't minded that much but he knew she found his attitude to politics sentimental. How often she'd told him. *There's no sense remaining loyal to something simply out of nostalgia, because it's part of your history. Your beliefs have to be relevant now, and it's hard to see how they can be, given how much things have changed.* Alberto disagreed. For him, history was everything. It had made him the man he was now. Now that he thought about it, his party card wasn't the only thing he'd held on to. He still believed in equality, freedom and brotherhood. Why wouldn't he remain loyal to the old ideals? Had anyone come up with anything better since? Fine, he could hear Emilia say. But do something, in that case. Don't just sit there.

He didn't want to dwell on this, or to think about Emilia right now. Instead, he turned his attention to a newspaper article about psychology. Something about how the brain worked. Just the sort of thing to help him get to sleep. But the commotion outside was too distracting and he found himself staring at the words without taking them in. Someone shouted, startling him. He folded the newspaper and went to the window again. The cry had sounded like a warning. As Alberto watched, the mood below appeared to change gradually. The hooded figures seemed less hesitant now. Before Alberto's eyes, they scattered and regrouped, again and again, until suddenly their movement seemed more cohesive and purposeful. Before he knew it, there was a mass of people surging towards the police line, which held fast, even when the mob started hurling things at their raised shields. It was too dark to see what they were throwing. In the light of the flames, Alberto saw the police line shift under the assault. Not as steady as it was before.

Things moved quickly after that. It was impossible to know what happened, but one moment the police line was there and the next it wasn't. It was as if the centre had collapsed, and the sides had lost all sense of what they were supposed to do. Then a cloud of smoke went up. There were people on their knees on the ground. Shrieks of rage, or fear, he couldn't tell. And where had the smoke come from? More fires? He couldn't see any flames. He felt a powerful urge to be closer, to understand what was happening. Before he knew it, he had grabbed his keys and left the flat. He walked down, shivering all the way. It was cold and the building was strangely quiet. Get back home now, you foolish old man, he heard Emilia say. She was right, of course. Fear gripped his chest. But his feet propelled him forward.

In the lobby, he paused to catch his breath. How foolish indeed he must look, in his old gown and pajamas, with slippers on his naked feet. He shuffled towards the exit and peered outside. Tentatively, he opened the door.

He had no idea what hit him. His eyes filled up and he staggered back, blindly looking for something to hold on to. Next thing he knew, he was on his back, fingers pressing against his eyelids. Tears streamed down his face. The acrid stench was in his nostrils, he could taste it. He couldn't breathe, at least not without pain and effort. Was this it, then? The end? Would this be what it amounted to? A cold, undignified death, flat on his back in the middle of the building's entrance, in his shabby night clothes. What an idiot he was. He heard the sound of smashing glass and a single, high-pitched scream, and there was nothing he could do except lie there like a cripple. Never in his life had he felt such terror, such humiliation.

'What the fuck ...' He didn't know the voice, not at first, but through weeping eyes he saw a figure tower over him. Big. Then a hand gripped his arm and he was pulled to his feet. As if he weighed nothing.

'What are you doing here, old man?' The voice was familiar but he couldn't place it. He found himself shrinking away, afraid. He was still blind, and with every breath his chest heaved so that he wondered how he would manage the next.

'Who are you?' The sound of his own voice shamed him.

'It's Ali. You know. Your neighbour' *Ali*. The big guy who lived across the hallway from him. Not a kid anymore but he appeared to a magnet for the younger boys on the estate. Often, you'd see a gaggle of them trailing behind him. If you didn't know any better, you might think he was some kind of benevolent uncle. Alberto had seen him once, handing out sweets. He wouldn't have remembered the name if Ali hadn't said it, but his bulk was recognizable. 'So. This is what it's come to. We live next to a drug dealer,' Emilia had said. 'He keeps to himself,' Alberto had replied. 'And that makes it okay?' Emilia had looked at him with something like disappointment in her eyes. 'There was a time you would have said it was important to care, to be involved.' Her words had stung and he'd said something dismissive in return, but she'd been right, of course.

Alone in the empty lobby with Ali, he felt exposed, but relieved too. He remembered that they knew each other, that this man had always been civil to him. For now, this was enough.

150

'You need help getting back to your place?' Ali asked. Alberto heard him curse, and retch. His eyes had cleared a bit and he saw that Ali's were streaming. 'Yeah, I took a direct hit,' Ali said, half-grinning. He was clearly in pain, but he seemed genuinely to be getting some enjoyment out of it all. It helped Alberto pull himself together. Now all he wanted was to get back to his flat, but first he had to know what was going on. 'Is anyone hurt?' he asked. It was a strange question. As if they knew the same people. But Ali seemed to find it completely normal.

'It's tear gas. That's what's making you feel like you're dying right now. I have no fucking clue what's going on, whether anyone's dead or hurt or what. All I know is there are bodies on the ground. I counted four before they fired that shit. But we've shown them who we are,' he added obscurely.

'Good.' The word left Alberto's lips before he knew what he was saying. It astonished him. Back in his flat, looking down at the street, he had despised the lot of them, in their hooded tops, scarves tied around the lower halves of their faces so no one would recognize them, running amok. Now he was – what – showing solidarity? Ali seemed mildly amused.

'I'm going back to my place,' Alberto said, and without another word he shuffled back up the stairs, moving slowly. He was still shaky and didn't want to trip. He'd embarrassed himself enough.

'Wait.' Ali's voice was urgent. Alberto stopped and turned, noting that his sight had cleared, though not completely. 'Word on the street is that Samir was with you. Before he died.'

'Is that right.'

'Yeah. People are saying, "he was with El Chino". It's what I'm hearing.'

Alberto frowned. 'So?' He leaned against the wall.

'What did he say? Anything?' Alberto studied the younger man's face. He thought about what he'd found in the pocket of his cardigan. A child's tooth. Tiny, and insignificant. But the discovery had given him goosebumps. It sat in his bedside drawer now. He had no clue why he was keeping it or what to do with the information.

'Nothing.'

'I just wondered ...'

'I'm sorry but I really need to get home. I'm not well,' Alberto interrupted. Ali nodded and watched him go. He seemed to know better than to offer to help the older man up the stairs.

In the flat, Alberto made straight for the bathroom. For a long time, he stood over the sink, splashing water in his eyes. His legs were still wobbly. He went to the kitchen with his face still wet and poured himself a much-needed drink. A pastis, at three in the morning! Emilia would have had a fit. Or maybe she'd have joined him, given the circumstances. Two boys were dead. Killed. What was the world coming to? You could say they'd been up to no good, maybe they had, but they were just kids, with mothers who'd no doubt done their best to raise and protect them. Alberto thought of his own childhood. It hadn't been easy, exactly, but compared to the sort of environment Samir and Georghe had grown up in, the place he'd known at their age was a treat. The most that had ever happened in his village was two boys drinking the sacramental wine when no one was looking. One of the two had thrown up on the altar steps. The villagers had talked about the incident for months afterwards.

When the riot had erupted, earlier in the evening, he'd wanted the police to react, but not like this. This seemed brutal, and unnecessary. He finished his drink and stood for a while, leaning against the counter, wondering what to do. If only Emilia were here, he could think out loud and she would listen and say something sensible in return. With no one to talk to, his thoughts went around in circles.

'How have we let things get this far? And what can I do, after all. I'm an old man, of no use to anyone,' he said out loud, forgetting that she wasn't in the room. It was nearly five when he finally dozed off in the chair. He awoke two hours later, in pain. He was too old to sleep in a chair and not pay the price. Every limb cried out as he rose to his feet and made it to the kitchen. He made the coffee extra strong, and drank the first cup with one hand gripping the windowsill, looking for signs of life below. Hard to believe so much had happened overnight. There was nothing to see. Except for a couple of burnt-out cars that stood out in all the snow. He'd turn the TV on and watch the news. And then he'd go down there to get a better idea of where things stood. He wondered whether it was over now or whether there would be more. A part of him hoped for the latter. As if he too had things to say, things he'd bottled up these past years. He found that the events of the previous night had given him a sense of purpose.

'It's not so different to what we knew, Emilia, when we first joined the Party,' he said, knowing that wasn't quite the truth, but it would do. This was his community now.

He finished his coffee, realizing that, despite his strangely upbeat mood, physically he wasn't feeling so great. His body was aching in a dozen different ways. In his mind, Emilia was looking at him in despair. When will you ever act your age? He heard her say. Never, he answered her with a ghost of a smile. I intend to die a young man.

Five

The sun rose over the gargoyles of Notre-Dame, over the old insomniac feeding pigeons in the park and the homeless woman cloaked in her own filth, who'd managed, miraculously, to survive the night. Two men stepped out of a houseboat, holding hands as they made their way from the quay up to the road, careful not to slip. Snow everywhere, still. On the radio, they were saying this was the most snowfall Paris had seen in sixteen years. They were saying Villeneuve was a zone of devastation this morning and that there was more to come. The local imam had been seen going in to the mayor's office at dawn, and there was talk of a press conference in Paris later today, with the interior minister. Morel watched a woman walking a pair of Alsatians stop to light a cigarette, take a deep drag and look around her as she slowly exhaled. Like her, he took a minute to commune with his city. Even in its wintry strangeness, it remained *his* – a place so familiar that often he took it for granted.

He was feeling better, clear-headed. Earlier, he'd tried to start his treasured red Volvo, but despite his best efforts – cursing and shivering in the dark - the old thing refused to go anywhere this morning. So he'd caught the train. Before going into work, he stopped to pick up the day's papers from the nearest newsagent. Villeneuve had made the front page, and not in a pretty way.

Good, Morel thought. Things would move quickly now that the story was front-page news. Today, he would pay a discreet call on the Villeneuve prosecutor who was overseeing the two murder investigations and inquire, as diplomatically as possible, about the handling of the case. His guess was that, after the night's events, and with the media attention, there would be pressure from local

154

government for the criminal brigade in Paris to take over. He wanted to make sure that meant his team.

Everyone except Lila had arrived. Jean, Vincent and Akil looked as though they'd been waiting for him. He greeted them and took the coffee that Vincent had set aside for him. It was still warm. A large oil heater gave off a fuggy heat and there were puddles on the floor where the others had stepped earlier in snow-encrusted shoes. Jean, still holding his motorbike helmet in one hand, handed a thick manila envelope over to Morel with the other.

'What is it?'

'Someone dropped it off,' Jean said by way of explanation. 'I didn't see who it was, but must be something important for them to come by so early.' Morel opened the envelope and scanned its contents.

'Now this is unexpected,' he said, sitting down.

'What? A love letter from someone special?' Lila said, entering the room. Her dark hair was sprinkled with snow. She tugged her jacket off and unwrapped her scarf. Her face was flushed. 'Everyone's very punctual today.'

'You been running?' Jean asked.

'Managed a few laps at the pool this morning. Why? Do I look funny?'

'Absolutely not,' Jean said. 'I wouldn't dare suggest that. No. Quite the opposite, in fact. Glowing. Healthy.'

'Right.' She threw her jacket on her desk. It slid across hers and ended up on Akil's. He was staring at his screen like what he saw there was fascinating.

'These are notes relating to both autopsies. Georghe's, and Samir's,' Morel said, looking through the documents. Jean gave a low whistle.

'Who sent them?' Lila asked, surprised.

'We don't know,' Jean said. 'Someone dropped it off downstairs. I picked the envelope up on my way in. It had Serge's name on it.'

'More to the point, why did anyone think of sending it to you?' Vincent asked.

'Thierry Villot?' Lila wondered. When Jean looked at her blankly, she added, 'You know, the Villeneuve detective Morel and I talked to in the car park. Villot seemed keen to let us know what was going on, in his own oblique way.' She took the reports from Morel and started reading through the first one. 'He seemed uneasy. Maybe there's something in here...'

'Are we in charge of this investigation now? When did this happen?' Jean asked. His hair was plastered to his head from wearing his helmet, his beard in serious need of a trim and his eyes bloodshot, as they often were on a Monday morning. Morel thought that perhaps he was drinking more than usual these days. He seemed to have put a bit of weight on too. As he tugged his dark blue roll-neck jumper off, Morel caught a glimpse of his not-so-trim belly before the t-shirt was back in place. Six weeks ago, when Jean had started wearing that jumper, Lila had taken to calling him Haddock, after the character in the Tintin comics, and the name had stuck, much to his annoyance.

'Well?' Jean insisted. Morel smiled. 'I'll tell you what. If we end up being in charge, you'll be the first to know.' Jean raised his eyes to the ceiling and shook his head. 'I can see where this is going.'

Morel took his jacket off and hung it carefully on the clothes stand, which they shared. 'Did you see what happened in Villeneuve last night?' he told Jean. 'You know how this works. The press is all over this story. Which means our Villeneuve friends aren't going to remain in charge of this for too much longer. I want to make sure it's ours.'

'How are you going to wangle that?' Vincent asked.

'I'll ask for it. Nicely.'

Vincent raised an eyebrow. Ever since his wife's death of cancer a couple of years ago, he'd become quieter, more distant, though he remained his good-natured self. Morel knew he was still struggling. He had two young girls to raise, and no one to help him except for his in-laws. In an unguarded moment, he'd told Morel he could no longer stand to be around his wife's parents. They lived under a dark cloud, enraged still by their daughter's death, as if fate had somehow singled them out. Vincent's own parents were long since dead. He refused to meet anyone new, out of a sense of loyalty to his dead wife and to his daughters. It was two years now since her death. Morel had told himself, on many occasions, that he should take Vincent aside and talk to him about how he was doing.

Now Vincent was placing croissants onto a plate — he was always the one to buy croissants, or a bottle of wine, or remember birthdays - and the plate was being passed around. Everyone took one, except for Jean, who helped himself to two.

'It's going to be an interesting one, that's for sure,' Vincent said with his mouth full. Morel raised a hand.

'It's not ours yet. Let's take a look at these reports first.'

'Why do you want this? You know it's going to be messy,' Lila asked, adding, before Morel could respond, 'actually, don't tell me. I know the answer.'

'It's because it's going to be messy that I think we should handle it.'

'Yep, I knew you'd say that.'

'Are you planning to tell the superintendent?' Akil asked.

'Not yet,' Morel replied. 'No point raising his blood pressure before we know where we stand. Look, the fact is that, with the way it's going, it's going to end up here. I want to know we have some control over what happens next.'

*

Taking the autopsy notes he'd been sent anonymously, Morel retreated to his desk. He picked up the ones on Georghe first. The autopsies had been carried out in a hurry, clearly a matter of priority. The reports had yet to be written up though and Morel wondered who had decided it was urgent for him to see what had been written so far.

Whoever had sent these had taken a big risk. If it was someone at the Villeneuve station – Villot seemed the most likely – then that person stood to lose their job. The pages had been photocopied. Morel tried to picture Villot at the station, furtively using the photocopier after hours. Or else getting the reports out of the office and sneaking them back in once he'd copied them. Under Marchal's nose. It seemed so unlikely. How could he have done it without being caught? And more to the point, what would be his motive for doing this?

Morel spread the crime scene photographs of the dead Roma boy on his desk. It chilled him, to look at them. It was a terrible way for anyone, but particularly a child, to die, alone and frightened. The boy's eyes were closed and his knees raised against his chest. He had his arms wrapped around his body, as if he'd tried to keep warm. A pointless gesture, given the conditions and the extent of the boy's injuries. According to the pathologist who'd performed the autopsy, the boy had died of hypothermia, not because of any injuries he'd sustained. But the damage to his body would have accelerated the freezing process. In a weakened state, a person's chances of survival in sub-zero conditions diminished significantly. 'The cause of death was acute hypothermia, as evidenced by the pattern of erosions across the stomach lining. There was discoloration around the elbow and knee joints, which, taken in conjunction with the state of the stomach lining, seemed disassociated from any bruising sustained during the attack, and which I interpreted as further evidence of cause of death.'

Morel made a few notes and wrote down several questions he hoped he might be able to ask if he had the opportunity to speak with the pathologist, then set the notes aside. He then began reading the one on Samir. Multiple stab wounds to the chest and abdomen had resulted in extensive blood loss and organ failure. The weapon, according to the pathologist's description, could be a kitchen knife, the sort you'd find in most households. Ordinary, and difficult to trace, in Morel's experience. No weapon had been found at the crime scene. Unlike Georghe, Samir's body had been cold, but not stiff, when they'd found him, which indicated he had not been outside as long as the Roma boy, though it was difficult to provide an estimate. In both sets of notes, there were question marks and the pathologist's frustration was evident. Freezing conditions did not make her job any easier.

Morel looked at the photos of Samir. He thought of the girl he'd met. Aisha, the boy's sister. How much did she know about her brother? What had the boy been doing out in the middle of the night, in freezing temperatures? Where had he been sleeping, and staying? And why? Maybe he'd been running from something. Maybe he knew something about the Roma boy's death. That would explain the fact that the day he'd failed to come home was the same day Georghe had died.

Morel finished reading and rubbed his eyes. He looked up and found Lila hovering impatiently.

'Shall I update you on Simic?'

'Go ahead.'

She told him about her visit to the club and about Bijou. 'She says Valérie Simic plotted to have her husband killed. That he was going to leave her.'

'You think she's telling the truth?'

'It's hard to say. I find it very difficult to picture Valérie doing something like this. She's nothing like the emotional wreck Bijou described. Plus, I doubt she'd be capable of it.'

'She didn't need to be, if someone did the dirty work for her.'

'Perhaps.' Lila pointed to the papers on Morel's desk.

'What about these autopsy reports? Who do you think sent them?'

'I don't know.' He stood up. 'I'm going to Villeneuve to have a word with the prosecutor who's involved in the boys' deaths.'

'Now? Want me to tag along?'

'No. I think it's best I meet him on my own.'

He buttoned up his coat. 'But if we end up with this case, I'll want everyone involved. You, Jean, Akil. Vincent can follow up on Simic.

Villeneuve is going to be a lot of work. It has to be a team effort,' he stressed, with the emphasis on team, and she nodded, her eyes avoiding his.

*

Villeneuve was desolate. Morel drove past a shattered bus stop, shards of glass glinting in the snow; past several burnt-out cars. The fire trucks had been busy. There were things on the street that had been lost, or left in a hurry. A red woollen scarf. Lighters, and a baseball bat. Tear gas canisters, and cans of spray paint, ditched along the walls. A bicycle lay on the side of the road, mangled beyond repair.

He found the courthouse and parked. Outside, the temperature caught him by surprise. The wind was a fine, cold blade, flicking rubbish off the ground. He strode towards the building, his breath a cloudy trail in the wintry air.

Morel had expected more people. He'd expected police, patrolling the streets. An African woman in bright, traditional clothes and a black coat watched him from the courthouse steps, her expression distant. She seemed to be waiting for someone. As Morel drew nearer, her eyes glazed over and she looked right through him, as if he didn't exist.

The prosecutor's secretary, thin and unsmiling, greeted him and led him into the man's office. Like the rest of the building, it was plain, functional. The prosecutor stood up and the two of them shook hands. He gestured for Morel to sit.

'Come in.' He seemed preoccupied. 'I won't be a minute.' He was writing something on a piece of paper, slowly, in writing so even and tidy it reminded Morel of *maternelle*, those early years of schooling when you learned to draw letters following a trail of dots. There was a photo on his desk. Presumably his wife, and two children, who were clones of their father if the photo was anything to go by.

The prosecutor finally looked up from his desk and gave Morel a bloodless smile.

'You can appreciate that we have a lot on our plate, after last night's events.'

'Of course. Last night's events are why I'm here,' Morel said.

The man lowered his glasses to examine him. His voice was reedy and so quiet you had to pay close attention. Morel found himself leaning forward, all ears.

Watching the man's lips, Morel wondered whether the way he spoke, so quietly, was intentional, some kind of power play. Not for the first time, he thought how glad he was that he'd chosen to become a policeman. Of all the *fonctionnaire* positions he could have aspired to, this was the only one he could see himself taking on. And if you kept your head down, you could leave the politics to others, Morel thought, though even as he formulated this in his head he could hear his father's mocking tone. If this isn't politics – you, in this man's office, smiling falsely, requesting favours behind your superintendent's back – then what the hell is it?

Now the prosecutor was speaking. 'I'm not sure this is very ethical – you turning up here, requesting a case be transferred out of what appears to be personal interest,' the man said. His lips were chapped and he pulled, unconsciously, at his lower one, where the skin was peeling off. His hair was prematurely white and he had a semblance of a moustache, a wispy, uneven hedge that looked like it had grown as much as it ever would.

'It has nothing to do with personal interest,' Morel said. 'Two young boys have died in the space of 48 hours. In an area, where

162

already there is a history of social and racial conflict. The media are having a field day...'

'I'm fully aware of the situation, Commandant Morel. I don't need a lecture from you.'

'My apologies.'

The man continued to tug at his lip. 'You say it isn't personal, but my understanding is that you knew Samir's family even before his body was found.'

Morel froze. *Marchal*, he thought. Marchal, who was in charge of the investigation, must have told the prosecutor about Morel. Well, Morel fumed inwardly, maybe in turn he could tell the prosecutor that Marchal had pretended not to know Samir, when all the while he'd known him well, having 'hauled' him in for questioning on a number of occasions. But it wasn't the right time. *If I get this case, the first thing I'll do is bring Marchal in to the Quai des Orfèvres. See how he likes being summoned.*

He gave the prosecutor a mildly enquiring look, all the while wondering what Marchal's report had said about him exactly. About his involvement with Samir's family. It seemed to him that Marchal had been thinking ahead, covering his bases, making sure the case would remain with him.

The prosecutor was waiting for him to speak. Morel chose his words carefully. 'Sir,' he said, 'I have a very loose connection with the family. To say I know them well would be stretching the truth. The situation is this: I have a friend who has been counseling the victim's sister for some time. I met the family once at her request, when the boy went missing. That's the extent of the connection. My main – my only concern is that the investigation be carefully handled. With your help.'

'I know why you're here Morel, I don't need you to paint me a picture. I'll give it some serious thought, and when I've made my decision, I'll let the relevant people know. I'm sure you're resourceful enough to learn the outcome without my having to inform you. Am I right in assuming you know the way these things work?'

'I think so,' Morel said, resisting the urge to react to the man's sarcasm. 'When do you think -?'

'When I'm ready. This is not something as straightforward as choosing the right tie to wear.'

Morel felt like saying that making the right choice could be tricky when it came to ties, but knew better than to be flippant. 'Of course.'

It seemed the meeting was over. Morel stood up, while the prosecutor remained seated.

'Goodbye, Commandant.'

'Monsieur le Procureur, thank you for your time.'

*

Back in his car, Morel called the Villeneuve police station and asked to speak with Thierry Villot. But the receptionist who answered the call told Morel that Villot had called in sick. Morel considered whether to pay him a home visit, but decided it could wait until he knew whether the case was his.

It was time to get back to Paris. He had a date with Mathilde.

Mathilde was early. There was no one else at the school gates apart from her and a couple of mothers whose faces she knew, but whose names escaped her. It was a bad habit, to repeatedly forget people's names. They always seemed to remember hers.

She looked at her watch. She and Serge had agreed to meet not far from here, in a café they both knew, though it wasn't one they had ever been to together, in the years they'd dated.

She took a book out of her bag and tried to read. Karim Miské's Arab Jazz. Crime novels were all she read. She had no time for the sort of pretentious books her friend Odile tried to get her to read, books full of wordplay and pseudo-intellectual musings on life. This book was great, but she was only reading now to avoid having to engage with the other mothers. They were arriving in twos and threes, and the conversations started, in polished tones, the women impeccably dressed – matching Agnès B. cardigans and perfectly highlighted hair. Mathilde stared at a page and tried not to roll her eyes. When they weren't exchanging notes on ski resorts – Mégève, Courchevel – the women were comparing their children's accomplishments, in ways that suggested it was their own that had got their children there.

Mathilde, you are a complete snob and you judge people too quickly, she chided herself. Not too convincingly. She was fine with being a snob, in her own way, just as these women were too. But she could only blame herself for not having friends here at the lycée. The only people who seemed to tolerate her were her colleagues and Javier. And Emilio too, but you couldn't count your own son. Children loved you no matter what.

And yet, she felt she had tried to be involved with the other mothers. Until it had become intolerable. She didn't belong, she got easily bored and it showed.

At first, there had been invitations to dinner. She and Javier had gone, and done their best to be pleasant. As the evenings wore on, and it became increasingly obvious to them just how little they had in common with their hosts, and with the other guests, they had found themselves drinking a little too much and saying the wrong things. Occasionally, they were invited again, but never more than twice. Never mind. Mathilde couldn't stand it. The ostentatious display of wealth, the insular attitudes she encountered in this wealthy *arrondissement*. Most of the children were prats. Not her Emilio, though.

The sky was clear, the trees brooding and spectacular in their winter coats. Mathilde wore a russet-coloured turtleneck, and sunglasses against the glare. She hadn't wanted to dress up for Serge, though she had taken care with her hair. It was hard to remember Serge and not remember the way he had buried his head in it, gripped it with his hands, nearly – but not quite - hurting her. Sometimes, pain and pleasure were two sides of the same coin. He had known her limits, always. Her hair was still as long as ever, though nowadays she tended to tie it back. In the mirror, she could not yet detect any white strands. A small act of vanity, this examination of herself. Generally, she wasn't the self-indulgent type. Serge had asked her once, long ago, whether her running was a punishment. For what? She'd asked. What on earth do I have to punish myself for? But there was something in it. She didn't really care to figure it out.

The bell rang, and moments later the doors opened and the kids came tumbling out, all talking at once in high, urgent voices. When she saw Emilio's gangly form, the way he slipped on his duffle coat as his eyes sought her out, she felt a wave of love so fierce she had to contain it, mask it with an attempt at humour which made him roll his eyes and scratch awkwardly at his hair where it curled at the base of his neck, something he'd started doing shortly after his 12th birthday. He had his father's dark curls and complexion, his mother's bony frame and unblinking blue gaze.

'You know I could just as easily take the metro home on Wednesdays. I take it every other day of the week,' he said.

'I know. It's one day a week. Let me do it.' They walked away from the school and headed towards the café. Emilio remained silent. 'Everything ok?' she said lightly. Pretending not to notice his preoccupied look.

She had never cared what others might think of her. The tight, insular group standing by the school gate. But now there was Emilio, and seeing him trying to find his place, looking to these boys who were not deserving of his affections, she realized how fragile she had become. With Emilio, she was exposed, susceptible to every slight. She suffered for him and with him. Every letdown, every disappointment became hers as well.

'Where are we going?' he asked, ignoring her question. 'This isn't the way home.'

'We're just catching up with an old friend of mine. One coffee, and then we'll go home.'

'What's his name?'

'Serge. Serge Morel. He's a policeman.' Emilio glanced at her. He was taller than her now. 'You've never mentioned him before.'

'I didn't see any need to. He's a friend from a very long time ago.'

'Why do I need to be there?' Emilio complained. 'Why can't I just go home and see you there?'

'I want to spend this time with you too,' she answered. She did always treasure their time together. But in this particular instance, she knew her answer wasn't the truth.

*

Within minutes of sitting down, she began peeling layers off. The padded jacket, the russet coloured jumper, and the red scarf, bought from Promod the day before on her lunch break, because the wind had been cutting. Initially, she resisted the urge to tie her hair up, knowing he preferred it loose. But then, her vanity irritated her, and she pulled it back into a knot. No makeup, no tricks. She was a married woman, for Christ's sake. And she hadn't spent these past twenty years pining for him, so why play these games now?

She sat with her back to the door, making Emilio tell her about his day though he was uncommunicative, preferring to play with his phone. She knew Serge had arrived from the way her son suddenly looked up, with a flicker of interest, before she felt a hand on her shoulder. When she stood up, the table moved and some of her coffee spilled into her saucer.

'I'll get you another one,' he said.

'Don't be silly.' She sounded abrupt. 'There's no need for that.'

He looked older. It was just a couple of years since she had seen him last, when she'd driven to his home one night to tell him she wanted to be left alone. He had been following her, watching her come and go, like some creep. Who would have thought he was capable of that sort of behaviour? She'd stormed in to his kitchen

168

from the pouring rain and all she remembered now was the look of dismay on his face.

She stole another look at him. Older, but also the same. So familiar, like someone she might have caught up with every other day for the past twenty years.

'I won't be able to stay long,' he said.

'That's absolutely fine,' she said, rushing her words. 'We have to go in a minute as well.'

'What for? We've got nothing on.' This from Emilio, who only a moment ago had complained he wanted to be home. He had an uncanny gift for knowing exactly what would embarrass her. She shot him a furious look.

'This is Emilio, my son.'

'So you're a policeman?' The boy sounded skeptical.

'A detective. With the criminal brigade.'

Emilio nodded slowly. 'Cool.'

Serge ordered two coffees, one for himself and another for her, despite her protests, and then sat so that he was facing her. She was glad then that she had brought her son. Because she could see, immediately, that she and Serge could not easily manage a conversation.

'Your parents are well?' he asked, and leaned forward as if the answer really mattered to him. She could see now that some things had changed. The expression in his eyes, for one. It was prudent, as though he were assessing the situation.

They stumbled their way over a range of neutral topics – her family and his, their work, the way things were going now that Sarkozy was gone and Hollande was prime minister.

169

'You've been following the events in Villeneuve? Those poor boys. It's dreadfully sad.'

'I'm worried things will spin out of control,' Morel said. He told her about the investigation, that it might end up with him.

'That's a heavy load,' she said. 'Are you sure you want it?'

'I don't want it messed up.'

'You're the best man for the job, is that it?' she said, with a quick laugh.

Emilio had been listening, looking bored. His phone rang and when he saw who it was, he blushed slightly and hurried away from the table.

'A girl, presumably,' Morel said. Mathilde followed his gaze to where her son stood, outside the café, shuffling his feet and grinning.

'It looks that way, doesn't it?' she said.

When she turned back to Serge he was smiling at her, in a way that was – what? Apologetic? Happy? It was a smile she recognized. And in that moment, it was as if the past two decades had never happened. Before she knew it, she had reached for his hand. She felt him grasp hers, his eyes never leaving her face.

'It's good to see you, Serge.'

*

The phone rang while he was on the train. It was the prosecutor in Villeneuve, informing him that the dossier was being transferred.

'You should be hearing from your superintendent this afternoon but I thought I would let you know personally.'

'Thank you, I really appreciate it,' Morel said, surprised.

'I don't need to tell you, do I, just how delicate the situation is here. I expect to be closely involved. As closely as if we were working in the same building. On the same floor. I don't ever want to have to find something out about the case from a third party, something that you've withheld. I hope I've made myself clear.'

'You have my word, Monsieur le Procureur.' Morel hesitated. The other man seemed to want to say something more.

'You know, Commandant, I knew your father well when he worked at the Quai D'Orsay.'

'I didn't realize that. You didn't mention it when we met.'

'I didn't want you to assume it would get you anywhere. I'm not in the habit of handing out favours. But I thought I'd mention it now. He and I shared similar taste in music. How is he these days? I trust he's enjoying his retirement?'

'He is.' There was no point talking about his father's illness.

'I had a great deal of respect for him,' the prosecutor mused. 'He was a man of integrity. And I guess that had some influence on my decision today. I feel I'm a good judge of character and I see some of your father in you.'

'Thank you,' Morel replied, thinking, *he's wrong, I am nothing like my father*. Did his father have integrity? Yes, he probably did. But you could have integrity without empathy. You could still be emotionally inept.

Morel walked quickly from the Metro station to his building, enjoying the sun on his face and the memory of Mathilde, her bright, restless presence. It had felt normal, sitting with her. And that was a better feeling than the one that had, some time back, threatened to consume him. He felt happy, until he ran into Perrin at the top of the stairs. The superintendent was on his way down.

'Were you looking for me?' Morel asked.

'Yes. I need a word.' Perrin looked flushed, a sure sign that he was annoyed. He gestured towards the stairs. Morel followed him one floor down, to his office. 'You've seen what's happening in Villeneuve?' Perrin said, gesturing for Morel to take a seat.

'I have.'

'I had a call, ten minutes ago.' Morel kept a straight face. Perrin eyed him suspiciously. 'Can you guess what it was about?'

'I can't, sorry.'

'It was the prosecutor in Villeneuve. Sounds like the case is being handed over.'

'To whom?'

Perrin pointed at him. 'Us. He specifically requested that you be involved. Said he'd heard good things about your team.'

The boss sat back and crossed his legs. He looked at Morel like he was wishing he could get into his head and sift through its contents. 'Tell me. Did you know about this?'

Morel did his best to look astonished. 'I'm as surprised as you are.'

Perrin sighed. 'Jesus, what a mess they've handed over to us. A big, runny one. They're saying on the radio that they expect more of the same tonight. It seems that people will be coming in from some of the other *banlieues*. As a gesture of *solidarity*.' His voice dripped with sarcasm.

'Solidarity,' he repeated, in case Morel hadn't heard him properly.

When Morel didn't say anything, Perrin waved a hand at him.

'Go on, then. You've got plenty to get on with.'

Seven

Once the imam had taken his leave – the mayor stood by her office window and watched him go, impeccably turned out in his white robe and long grey coat - she unplugged her landline, turned her mobile phone to silent, and locked her door. For a minute or two, she stood on the other side of it, breathing deeply and trying not to give in to panic. A part of her wanted to flee. She'd been up during most of the night. Now it was a quarter to six and she hadn't even had a coffee yet. There was none in the kitchen, and she made a mental note to find out who was responsible. At this very minute, she would have sold one of her children in exchange for a double espresso.

The night before, she'd decided to stay late at work and watched things fall apart on the TV screen in her office, in the company of her press attaché, a former journalist whose left-wing politics she'd decided to tolerate when he'd applied for the position years earlier, because he really was good at his job. They got on surprisingly well, both knowing what they wanted and understanding that they could serve each other well. Roland had stayed with her into the early hours of the morning and she'd been grateful for that. He'd remained level-headed while she wondered how the hell they would deal with the situation. By the time she'd thought about going home it seemed like it was too late. Neither she nor Roland fancied driving through Villeneuve on a night like this. She'd taken a nap on a sofa (Roland presumably had found somewhere else in the building to crash), and been woken up at four by a call from the chief of police, telling her that the rioters had finally dispersed and it was over for now. But there were casualties. A police officer had been critically injured in the night's clashes. He'd been knifed and the doctors were saying that the attack had damaged his spine.

'How bad is it?' she asked.

'We don't know yet. But it's not looking good.'

It was possible he would not be able to walk again.

I'll be in touch again as soon as I have more news, Madame le Maire. She'd struggled to sound composed. Please do call again as soon as you have more information, she'd replied, feeling something close to despair. Why, apart from Roland, was there no one in the office yet, she'd wondered? Surely one of her staff had to come soon who she could send out again to buy some coffee. Useless, the lot of them. In the meantime, she was left with the grueling task of having to call the man's wife and tell her how sorry she was. He was a Villeneuve officer, not turned 30 yet. He and his wife were expecting their first child. She should probably also visit the man in hospital, but thankfully that would have to wait a little. Other things required her attention first.

'Is someone going to be with this woman? The officer's wife? I'm presuming she has relatives.' The police chief had assured the mayor that yes, she did. The wife's parents were with her now.

Such tragedy if the man were really paralysed. By then her assistant had arrived in the office and was beginning to take her jacket off but the mayor gestured for her not to. With the phone against her ear, she scribbled on a piece of paper, *coffee's run out, please could you get some, thanks*, sending her on her way. While she waited for her to get back, she had to take an infuriating call from the Interior Minister, asking her what she was doing to make sure the 'hooligans' – his words – would not 'carry on' again tonight. It isn't in my power to prevent them from protesting, she'd said. There's a lot of anger and emotion out there. He'd been unmoved. He had no clue, no clue at all. And now he wanted an extensive briefing from her on the night's events before his afternoon press conference. 'Right now I want you to sit tight, see what happens over the next twelve hours. I don't want you out there making any grand statements.'

'Grand statements?' she asked, truly puzzled.

'This is a social issue, not a political one. The last thing I need is for someone to start talking about Muslims being at war against the state and some such bollocks.'

'And that someone would be me?' she couldn't resist saying.

She yawned loudly and tasted bile. God, she felt like shit. She turned from the door and went to the sofa. Kicked off her shoes, lay back and closed her eyes. That bloody imam, she thought. Where had he learned to speak French like that? He'd made her feel inept.

*

The prosecutor was carefully unwrapping his lunch, wondering what his wife had prepared this time, when the phone rang. He answered straight away.

'I thought it might be you,' he said in a not-altogether-friendly tone, looking at his watch. It was mid-afternoon but it felt like evening. He'd got home late the night before and managed just a few hours' sleep. And today would be just as bad. He felt a surge of irritation, which he did his best to conceal.

'I'm not catching you at a bad time, am I?' the mayor asked. 'I know you must have your hands full too.'

'It's fine, I'm happy to talk,' he lied. 'I should have called you earlier.'

'It's been so hectic. But we do need to touch base.'

'Of course.'

'Did you know we've got one police officer in hospital? Spinal injury.'

'I heard.'

'So you know how bad it is. That he might not walk again.'

'I know.' The prosecutor sat down. He stared at his sandwich. His appetite was gone. Given the circumstances, he guessed it would be near impossible to find witnesses, let alone suspects in the attack against the policeman. Wonderful. As if there wasn't enough pressure on him already, with the deaths of the two boys.

'What with all the commotion last night, I imagine that finding the guy who stabbed him is going to be like trying to find the Holy Grail,' the mayor was saying.

'It's not going to be easy,' the prosecutor said, thinking that had to be the understatement of the year. 'I know we took a dozen guys in last night. Held on to a few. Released them too in the end. Unless we've got evidence, witnesses...'

'What a nightmare.' She sighed loudly. 'Just a minute.' He heard someone in the background, talking to her. Her reply was an impatient murmur. After a while, she came back on the line. 'Are you still there? Fuck, sometimes I hate this job.'

He didn't respond to that, knowing that most of the time she thrived on her job and the power that went along with it. So maybe at the moment she wasn't feeling so confident. But that would pass.

'I had the imam in here at the crack of dawn. Half past six and he breezes in, fresh as a daisy. Luckily, I was at my desk. Don't want him to think we're not taking this seriously. He was looking rather smug, I have to say. Didn't go so far as to say "I told you so" but it was written all over his face.'

'If he can have a positive influence on Villeneuve's Muslim community, help calm things down, then I say it's well worth your while to build a rapport,' the prosecutor said, knowing he sounded pompous. 'So, what's next?' he asked, wanting this conversation to end so he could get on with his day.

'What do you mean? We've got CRS reinforcements. We've probably got more cops in Villeneuve today than in the entire Ile-de-Seine department. Our officers aren't going to take any crap, not after what happened to their colleague. Not that we want them to misbehave.'

'I'm not talking about the police. I'm talking about containment.'

'What is it you're worried about, exactly?' she asked testily.

'My priority is to make sure the cases are solved as quickly as possible. The sooner they are, the sooner we can deal with the riots. And deal with the media.' He paused. 'I had a visit from Commandant Serge Morel earlier today.'

'Did you say Morel? Someone called Morel left a message at my office,' she said. 'Who is he and what does he want?'

'Senior cop at the criminal brigade. I knew his father. But I'd heard about him. Did some digging as well. Impressive record, from what I gather. He asked to take over the investigation.'

'He actually asked for it?'

'Not in so many words. Well … more or less. Yes. He was being coy about it but it was pretty obvious.'

'And?'

'And I think it's probably a good idea to let Paris handle this. I'm not entirely comfortable with the people in charge now.'

'Why? Something I should know about?'

He chose his words carefully. 'Nothing in particular. But it can't hurt to have some distance,' he said vaguely. 'Someone who isn't compromised.'

'Compromised?'

'That's the wrong word,' he said hurriedly. 'It's not what I meant. I meant, someone who has no history with the *cité*. Someone who isn't going to get people's backs up the minute they start asking questions.'

'I doubt a Parisian cop is going to be popular. And surely the local police will know who to talk to better than someone who doesn't live around here.'

'That's part of the problem I guess. Look, it's complicated,' he said before she could ask more questions he didn't feel like answering. 'For your sake, I'd say this is a better thing. This way if things go wrong you can blame Paris. It's out of your hands to some extent.'

'Shall I meet with him then? This Morel?' she said, and he realized that she hadn't been paying attention. She was too busy thinking about what she should do next. It dawned on him that this was why she had called, to get his advice. That gave him some satisfaction.

'I think you should. Today if you can. The sooner Paris takes over the investigation, the better in my view.'

'You're right,' she said wearily. 'This is too big for us to handle on our own. We'll have enough on our hands as it is. How is everything else with you?'

'Why are you asking?' The two of them had had an affair and the prosecutor now felt it had been a big mistake. 'Look, I've got to go,' he said. Now she had admitted to being vulnerable, he felt inclined to be dismissive. 'I'll see you soon no doubt. Save the small talk for then.'

178

Once he'd hung up, he dialed another number on his phone. The person he was calling answered straight away.

'Marchal? We need to talk. Can you come by the office, say in an hour's time?'

*

They started knocking on doors at 3.30 p.m. while it was still light. Morel, Lila, Jean and Akil. But they weren't alone. There were police patrols in the *cité* now, making themselves visible, keeping an eye out for projectiles from the tower blocks and trying their best not to look worried. Marchal had also sent four of his men as personal escorts to Morel's team, on his own initiative. Morel had found the gesture presumptuous, and thought about sending them away, but given the events of the previous night, he felt perhaps it wasn't a bad idea to have some back-up. They were big, burly men, who joked among themselves and seemed disinclined to get to know their Parisian colleagues.

"I don't know that these four meatheads are going to make much of a difference if we run into trouble on the estate,' Jean said.

Earlier, they'd sat down together in the office to figure out how they would proceed.

'We'll start with Tower A, where Samir lived,' Morel told them. 'Lila, you're with me. Jean, Akil, you stay together. I want to stick to the specifics, keep things moving so we don't waste time. Remember we want to be out of there before things heat up. If they heat up. So. Let's focus on Samir for now.'

Lila's head shot up. 'Why? What about the other kid?'

'Because I think we can't do everything at once, not effectively, and I also think Samir is the key. My feeling is that the more we find out about Samir, the more we'll know about Georghe.'

'What if there's no link?'

'Then there's no link. Look,' he said, trying to be patient even though he felt their time was short, and he wanted to get going, 'what happened last night, the rioting on the estate, happened because Samir was killed. I have no favourites. I want to solve both murders. But we're not going to get very far if the *cité* is under siege. So, let's take things one step at a time. Let's find Samir's killer. Get things under control. We won't forget Georghe. Okay?'

Lila nodded, and Morel turned to the others. 'So. Questions for the residents. Did they know Samir, did they know his family, when was the last time they saw him, any idea why someone might have wanted to hurt him. Did anyone notice anything unusual over the past days and weeks?'

'Serge. Where do I fit in in all of this,' Vincent asked.

'I'll get to that in a minute,' Morel said. 'Lila and I will work our way up, from the first floor; We'll talk to the man who found Samir's body. We'll drop in on Samir's family too. Jean, Akil, you start at the top and work your way down, and hopefully we manage to make some headway over the next couple of hours.'

'You're sure you want to do this now? You don't want to wait until things are a bit calmer over there?' Jean asked.

'I've thought about it. But I'm concerned that if we wait we might lose crucial information. You know how it is. The sooner, the better. People's memories fade, as we all know. Details are forgotten. I don't want to wait.'

'Marchal would have spoken to most of the residents when he was still in charge?' Akil asked. 'Have you got his notes?'

Morel nodded. 'I have the notes. I know it's tedious but I want to hear it first-hand. Remember too that Marchal lied. The first time I met him, he acted like he didn't know Samir. I intend to find out why.'

'You're going to bring him in for questioning?' Jean asked.

'I've certainly got some questions for him. I want to know what he's hiding. I want to talk to Thierry Villot, away from the station. Find out if he sent us those autopsy notes. And why he was so keen to talk to Lila and I that day in the car park. Jean, I want you to get the full reports on the two bodies. See if you can get Marchal on the phone tonight. We also need to establish whether there is a drug connection and maybe the report on Samir will give us something. I also want to talk to Antoine Carrère, the man who seems to spend a lot of time with Aisha and Loubna Kateb. The teachers at school, Samir's friend Karim, the Spaniard who saw him two nights before he was killed. The one the boy stayed with.'

'Sounds like we need three teams working together, not one.' Lila raised a finger. 'Just coming back to those tower blocks. There are four of them. Are we going to talk to *everyone*? How long is that going to take?'

'My guess is no one will want to say much and we'll be done in a couple of hours,' Jean commented.

'Like I said. Let's focus for now on the building where Samir lived,' Morel responded.

Morel turned to Vincent, who sat very still, looking out the window. 'Vincent. I need you to follow up on Simic. I'd like you to go back to Valérie Simic with what Lila got at the club. See how she reacts. It would be a good idea to find out more about this woman Bijou. Who she is, whether there's a boyfriend or husband, and anything else that might help us. Let's find out if she's telling the truth. Can you do that? I'm keen to close this one quickly if we can.'

Vincent looked put out. 'Okay. But wouldn't it be best for Lila to do that? Given she's already met with Valérie.'

'I'd like you to do it,' Morel said. He stood up and grabbed his coat.

'We need to go.'

Eight

Aisha opened the door quietly in case her mother was asleep. No doubt Antoine would be awake, waiting for her to come home, making sure she was okay. That was the sort of thing he did. She'd promised him she wouldn't leave the building tonight but he'd still looked worried when she'd left.

The door was unlocked, which was unusual, and she could hear voices. Not Antoine's. Someone else.

'Aisha.' In the narrow hallway, he looked big, his shadow huge on the wall, blocking out the light. Her first thought was that she was glad there was someone else there, aside from Antoine and her mother. Her second thought was that something must have happened.

'Commandant Morel, right?' she said, remembering her manners. Antoine was in the hallway, holding a tea towel and smiling tensely. Aisha started to feel sick. Why were they here? Had something happened to her mother? She started to move down the hallway, looking for her. Commandant Morel seemed to read my mind.

'Don't worry, she's fine. She's asleep.'

Aisha stopped. What an idiot she was. Of course, they must be here because of Samir.

'Is there some news? Did they find out who killed him?'

'Not yet, I'm afraid. The main reason I'm here is to let you know I've taken over the investigation.'

From the kitchen, a woman stepped into the hallway. She had long dark hair tied into a ponytail. Her eyes were bright and curious and trained on Aisha.

'This is my colleague, Lila Markov,' the commandant said. The woman nodded once but didn't move.

'Do you mind if we sit down?' Morel asked Antoine.

'Please. Can we get you something? Coffee, tea? Aisha's mother is resting but I'll get her if you like.'

'There's no need to trouble her right now. And yes, a coffee would be nice. Thank you.'

'Why don't I give you a hand?' Lila suggested. She followed Antoine into the kitchen, leaving Morel with Aisha.

'Is that your partner?' Aisha asked.

'She's part of my team, yes.' Morel remained standing, sensing that Aisha felt more at ease that way. 'How have you been? I hope you're staying safe, with everything that's happening out there at the moment.'

'I am. Are you any closer to finding who did this to Samir? And to that other boy?'

'I'm doing my best.' Morel walked over to the wall with the postcards he'd thought might be from Algeria. With his back to Aisha, he said, 'I really will do everything I can. But if you think you can help me, if there is anything *you* know that you think would be good for *me* to know, then please –' He turned back to face her, and smiled. 'Please share it with me.'

'I will,' she said, and she meant it. She sat down, and Morel moved across the room to be nearer. 'I met a girl just now, who Samir was seeing.'

Morel nodded. 'Go on.'

'It's messy. Her brother beat her up. But he only did it because Réza was there. And Ali and my brother, they were hanging out, which means Samir was up to no good. I never thought about it, it wasn't my business before. But now it is. And - '

'Aisha. Stop for a moment, and take a deep breath.' He watched as she did as he asked, and calmed herself down.

'I want you to tell me all of that again, slowly and in detail, but I also have some questions of my own. Would you mind if I asked you those first?'

'Go ahead.'

'Who was the police officer who talked to you after Samir's death?'

'That was a Capitaine Marchal. I remember. He was rude.'

'Did he come alone or with a partner?'

'Alone. Why?'

'Do you know about Samir's arrests?'

'Arrests? No.' Her attempts to look puzzled didn't fool Morel.

'Your brother was detained on several occasions. The police suspected him of drug-dealing, of doing Ali's dirty work for him.'

Aisha threw him an angry look. 'Well, maybe they were right. I had no clue what my brother was up to. If he was up to anything dodgy, he sure wasn't confiding in me. He never came to me with any of his secrets or worries or any of the important stuff that was going on in his life.'

'You're angry with Samir.' It was a statement, but Aisha took it as a question.

'I'm *really* angry. How could he have been so stupid when he was supposed to be the smart one?'

'Is that what people thought? That he was smart?'

'Sure. Maybe. Well, not everyone. The girls liked him. Maman wasn't always happy about the things he did but she worshipped

185

him. And in this house, he ruled. Even Antoine knew that,' she commented, as if the thought had only just come to her.

'And what about you?'

'What do you mean?'

'I mean where do you fit in in all of this?'

She laughed, as if it was a funny question. 'It doesn't matter where I fit in. What has that got to do with anything? What matters is Samir.'

'You've been so honest with me. But now you're not telling the truth,' Morel said, shaking his head.

'I don't understand.'

'You're telling me you don't care where you fit in. But it's a lie. You care very much.'

'You're saying I'm deceiving you?' Aisha said, looking offended.

'You're deceiving yourself, Aisha. Acting like you don't care that your mother worshipped your brother, or that he ruled the roost, or that he was detained several times for drug-related offences. Or that he's no longer there to walk you home from school. To look out for you.'

Aisha stared at him in shock. He waited for her to say something, but she kept quiet.

'Coffee's ready,' Lila said, entering the room.

'Aisha,' Morel said. 'Why don't you start by telling us about Ali.'

*

It was three-quarters of an hour before they left the Kateb home, and headed back down the stairs. Towards the end of their visit, Antoine had fetched Aisha's mother. She'd sat with them, groggy and mostly unresponsive.

'We should have let her stay in bed. Poor woman,' Lila remarked as they made their way down to see the man who'd found Samir's body. He lived on the second floor.

'What do you make of that guy Antoine?' she asked. 'He's a nervous fellow, isn't he?'

'He gave me that impression the first time I met him. I wouldn't say he was nervous. Timid, maybe. Not that comfortable around people.'

'I'll do a bit of digging. What about him and Loubna? Are they sleeping together?'

'It's hard to imagine,' Morel responded, thinking of the small, fidgety man he'd seen at Aisha's, hovering ineffectively and fretting over the two women he clearly felt responsible for. 'He seems genuinely attached to Loubna and her daughter. My impression is that the mother depends on him, and Aisha seems to tolerate his presence. He strikes me as a lonely sort of man. Maybe this is the closest thing he has to family. I don't know. Let's talk to him again tomorrow. Right now, I'd like to get moving.'

He buttoned up his coat and rubbed his hands to warm them up. He'd sent Marchal's musclemen on their way, quickly realizing that they weren't helping in any way. If anything, they drew unwelcome attention to Morel's team, when he really wanted to keep a low profile. 'I'd like to talk to this Yasmina – the woman Aisha says was seeing Samir. And we need to check out Aisha's story about the brother beating her up, and this guy Réza. Let's pay Yasmina and her brother a visit tomorrow, and while we're at it find Réza. There's not enough time tonight.'

Lila paused two steps ahead of him, and turned.

'So where do we need to be? Which of these beautiful flats does our man live in?'

'Joao Figueras. He lives on the second floor,' Morel said, reading from the case notes he'd brought with him. 'And he lives alone.'

*

It became clear within five minutes of conversation with Figueras that he lived in a fantasy world, though he was perfectly pleasant to deal with. Like most people who lived alone, he couldn't stop talking. It took Morel a while to find an opening.

'You know I was an Olympic athlete,' Figueras said *à propos* of nothing as he ushered them into a dark, cold apartment that smelled of cat urine. 'Representing my country, Portugal. Middleweight boxing. That was my thing.'

Figueras might lack human companionship but not the animal sort, Morel mused. There were cats everywhere. Morel counted five before taking the seat he was being offered. Lila pulled a face. He knew she was allergic to them. It was, Morel reflected, like being in a poorly kept zoo. A pair of budgies rattled about in a suspended cage, leaving a scattering of feathers, droppings and seeds on the carpet below. On the sofa, a black terrier with a doleful expression woke up and rolled over to blink at the visitors, but otherwise showed little interest.

'These are my friends,' the man said, and Morel wasn't sure if he was introducing them to the animals or the other way around. While Lila sneezed, Figueras rattled through his list of achievements at breakneck speed, as if he was afraid of being interrupted. He'd apparently climbed Everest, swum the English Channel and written a French-Portuguese dictionary. All while training intensely as an athlete. Morel found himself losing concentration, though he tried his best to look engaged. He felt feverish again. One minute he was listening attentively and the next he found himself thinking about Mathilde, his father, and the dead boys, his thoughts going in circles until everything seemed tied together, painted in the same, melancholy hue. He snapped to attention, chiding himself internally for his lack of professionalism, and looked for an opportunity to interrupt, but Figueras hardly paused for breath. Lila was struggling too. When Figueras got up to look for the dictionary, she leaned towards Morel and gave him an eye-rolling, I-can't-take-this-anymore kind of look. She whispered, 'he's clearly a nutcase, how are we supposed to believe anything he says?' Figueras returned empty-handed and seemed surprised to find them sitting at his table.

'Are you here about the songwriting contest?' he asked. 'Did I win?'

'I'm afraid we're not here about the songwriting contest,' Morel said, while Lila stared fixedly at an ugly stain on the carpet. Seemingly suppressing a silent scream. 'This is about the boy who was found dead at the foot of the building. Two nights ago. You were the one who found him.'

'Ah yes. The boy. The one with the red sweater and corduroy trousers. He lived in this building,' the man said. He spoke the last sentence in a half-whisper, leaning forward in case someone else might hear.

'Samir,' Lila said.

Figueras didn't answer.

'Is that who you mean? Samir?' Morel asked.

'I hadn't seen him for a while. He lived in this building then he went away. Boys will get into trouble, won't they?' Figueras smiled.

'Could you tell us about the night you found Samir?' Morel asked. If he could get Figueras to focus, even for a few minutes, he might get somewhere.

Figueras' smile vanished.

'I was out walking Dakar,' he began. Lila interrupted. 'Sorry for asking what might seem obvious. Dakar is the dog?'

'Yes. Because she's black, see? Like most people around here. Wasn't like that when I first moved into this *cité*.' He shook his head regretfully.

'Right.' Lila gave Morel a look.

'She has a weak bladder, poor thing,' the man went on, oblivious. 'Sometimes she wakes me at night. I have to take her outside. She gets agitated if I don't. So I took her.' Figueras stopped, looking as if he'd forgotten where he'd put his house keys.

'You were going to tell us about Samir,' Morel urged.

'Ah yes. I went around the block. Quickly, you understand. It was too cold to be out for long. And it was dark. I didn't want to linger. So then I came back to the entrance to go inside, and that's when I saw him.' An air of distress crossed Figueras's face and he reached for the dog, patting its head for comfort.

'Where?'

'Just lying in the bushes outside the building.'

'What did you see exactly?'

'I didn't at first. It was Dakar who went sniffing and when I went to pull him back I saw him. He was wearing the corduroy trousers. Red sweater, corduroy trousers, that's him.'

Morel looked at Lila, shook his head. 'Monsieur Figueras, Samir was wearing jeans when his body was found. Who is this person you're referring to?'

190

Figueras looked puzzled. 'Jeans, yes. Dead, and blood everywhere. That's how I knew. That's the boy who lives in this building, I said to myself.'

'And that's when you raised the alarm.'

'Yes, yes.'

Figueras smiled vaguely. He seemed to be drifting. He clasped his hands, and continued in an urgent tone. 'The year I turned 12, I got a sailboat for my birthday. I don't know why I got such a nice present. It didn't matter. I was just happy to have it. One weekend, my mother and brother and I went all the way to Paris. We took the RER and got on the Metro and went to the Luxembourg Gardens. All three of us. My brother, me, and my mother. And I sailed my boat in the fountain, like the other kids.'

Lila opened her mouth to say something. She wanted to get Figueras back on track, but Morel gestured at her to wait.

'What happened?'

'My brother hated me for that boat. That day when he saw the boat sail away, he started screaming. Not loudly. I thought we were friends, but it turns out I was wrong. He felt threatened. So he destroyed it.'

'What was he like, your brother?' Morel asked, and Lila shook her head, as if to say he was wasting precious time.

'I don't know. Does it matter? He lived in this building. Then he went away. No one knew where, or why.'

'Can we get back to what we were talking about? Samir's death?' said Lila, exasperated.

'Of course.' Figueras reached over and patted her knee. 'You're a nice person, you are. I can tell. My guess is you don't know much about what it means to be a boy. Boys can play rough, sometimes. It's what we do. And sometimes, when we do, people get hurt.'

*

'I felt like telling him that sometimes girls like to play rough too, particularly when someone a little, shall we say, delusional, is droning on about stuff that never happened,' Lila commented after they'd taken their leave. Morel stood in the stairwell, wondering whether to try talking to Figueras again, though they'd spent the past half hour trying to get more from him, without making progress.

'Let's come back to him in a little while, and try again,' he told Lila now.

'Why?'

'Because it's important. What he's trying to tell us. We're missing something important.'

'Let's run through it again, then,' Lila said. They hadn't moved and were still just a few steps from Figueras' door. It seemed eerily quiet. When Lila blew her nose, it came as an explosion in the silent stairwell. Morel wondered where Jean and Akil had got to. He had a vague, ominous sense of time slipping away, of not being in control. But he couldn't escape the feeling that he'd failed, just now, to grasp something major.

'He mentioned the boy who went away. Twice.'

'That would be Samir disappearing,' Lila offered.

'But how would he have known that Samir didn't come home for two nights?'

'Aisha and her mother asked around, didn't they? I'm sure news travels fast.'

'Maybe.' Morel started walking up the stairs. Lila blew her nose again. 'He mixes up his tenses, his stories,' Morel said. 'All the while I felt there was another person there, in his memory. Not just Samir. Maybe someone else he saw that night, when he walked the dog. Only he can't access that particular memory, even though it was only a few days ago.'

Lila wiped her noise, sighed. 'He was also talking about his brother and a sailboat...you don't think he got things a bit mixed up?'

'I think it's just possible Figueras saw something that night. He saw Samir get hurt. He saw two people. Samir and this other person.'

'Or he saw something else. Samir was already dead. He remembers seeing him in the bushes,' Lila reminded him.

'He saw something,' Morel repeated, running Figueras's words over in his mind. They continued slowly up the stairs. Occasionally, they could hear people behind closed doors, conversations, a television. A dog barked and a woman shouted at it to shut the fuck up. 'What I can't believe is that he's living on his own,' Lila said in a wheezy voice.

'He's not alone. He's got the cats and the dog and the birds.'

'Those bloody cats,' she said, shaking her head. 'So, what now?'

'We'll have to get the story from someone else. After Figueras found Samir's body, he raised the alarm. There were other witnesses, who should be able to tell us what they saw. What Figueras was doing. And at some point, I really want to try talking to Figueras again. Maybe we'll get lucky. In the meantime, let's go and talk to Alberto Rosales.'

'Let's,' Lila said. 'I hope that was our only mountain-climbing, song-writing Olympic champion for today. Seriously, how *does* he manage on his own?'

'He probably doesn't have much choice,' Morel replied. He thought about his father. It was clear to him that without Augustine's loyal support, his father would be just as neglected as this old man was. The fact was that the only person actively invested in his father's life was an old woman who cleaned and cooked for him. Here, in this cold stairwell, in the stark lighting afforded by a naked bulb, his failings seemed abundantly clear. *Never mind what the old man is like. Has been like his entire life. He isn't going to change, not now. I need to change. It can't go on like this.*

Nine

Alberto Rosales's place was tidy, scrupulously so. Pet-free, too. It was a nice change from Figueras's apartment. Morel explained that he had taken over the investigation into the deaths of Georghe and Samir.

'I'm glad to hear it,' Alberto said. 'The man who spoke to me – the other policeman...I didn't like him.'

'Why is that?' Lila asked.

'It was just a feeling. He struck me as dishonest. He didn't look me in the eye, not once. I like a man who looks you in the eye when you talk to him.'

In the dining-room, the table was set for one, neatly, as though for a guest rather than the occupant. There was music playing. Morel thought he recognized the Spanish guitarist Carlos Segovia, whom he admired. Alberto went to the stereo and turned the volume down, then invited them to sit at the table. He seemed preoccupied.

'It's a horrible business, isn't it? I can't fathom it.' He pulled a handkerchief from his pocket and, with a shaky hand, wiped his brow. 'I hope they fix those lifts soon. I had to go to the shops and walking back up those stairs with shopping bags feels like quite an effort these days.'

'Would you like me to fetch you a glass of water?' Morel asked.

'I'm quite capable still of fetching myself a glass of water,' Alberto replied, then seemed to realize he'd been abrupt. 'Besides, I try not to touch the stuff,' he said with a smile. He pointed to a cabinet. 'There's a bottle of Xeres in there. Much more invigorating. I expect there's no point offering you two any since you're on the job.'

'I'm afraid so.'

'In that case, carry on.'

'I understand Samir was with you the night before he was killed. What can you tell us about the last time you saw him?' Morel asked.

'Not much,' Alberto said. He had a smoker's gravelly tone; an accent so thick one might think he'd just stepped off the plane from Barcelona. He stood up, took the bottle from the cabinet and poured himself a drink.

'Sure you won't join me?'

'No thanks,' Morel said, and Lila shook her head. She'd stopped sneezing but continued to blow her nose intermittently, her eyes red and itchy, her face a picture of misery.

'That was quite a night,' Alberto said. 'Didn't sleep much. I expect there'll be more trouble tonight. Even though things settled down during the day. I thought maybe the cold weather would be too much for people but it didn't stop them last night.'

'You would have seen it all I guess. From up here,' Morel said.

Alberto nodded. 'It was frightening. You know, back in the days when I still believed in Communism, I was involved in a few demonstrations that turned ugly. But nothing like what I saw last night. I have to admit I was scared. Since Emilia – my late wife – and I came to the cité, so much has changed. I don't share much with these people. I'm not saying there's no sense of community here. But there are challenges. Sometimes I can clearly see myself standing on the outside, looking in. Sometimes I feel threatened. But the truth is that no one here has ever bothered me. And I do understand the anger.'

He finished his drink and set the glass on the table.

'You asked about Samir. He turned up here without warning, but then that isn't unusual. When he showed up, he was cold and wet. He must have been out in the snow for some time. Poor kid, he was

196

chilled to the bone. I lent him some clothes. I had to go to the shops and while I was gone, he got changed. We had dinner together and he slept on the couch. In the morning he had coffee here. I told him he should let his mother know where he was. He told me he was going home straight after that.'

'Why would he lie?'

'I've thought about that. I think maybe he said it so I wouldn't call his mother and let her know where he was. He didn't want that. Don't ask me why.'

'How did he seem? I know you've spoken with my Villeneuve colleagues but I'd be grateful if you could tell me again.'

'He seemed upset.'

'How? Angry? Scared?'

'Scared. Definitely scared.'

'Did he say anything?'

Alberto shook his head. 'I've known Samir for some time. He would come over here every once in a while, spend an hour or two. I think he felt comfortable in this flat. He could watch TV or take a nap without being bothered. But we didn't really talk much. I know that sounds strange,' Alberto added.

'Not strange at all,' Morel replied. 'He felt safe with you.'

Alberto nodded. He'd been expecting the usual reaction. The other detective had looked at him sideways. There'd been a bit of a smirk. But Morel's expression was open, accepting. He seemed to understand.

'Any idea if Samir was dealing drugs?' Lila asked.

'No.' Alberto seemed surprised. 'But there is one thing...when the riots broke out, I went downstairs. I wanted to see what was going on. Not very sensible, I expect. But curiosity got the better of me.

Anyway, I ran into my neighbour. He must have been outside and he came in while I was downstairs. His name's Ali. He asked me about Samir.'

'Who's Ali?' Lila asked.

'He's a young guy who lives next door. Big. Muscly. If you run into him you'll know straight away.'

'What does Ali do? Is he a friend of Samir's?' Lila pressed.

'I don't exactly know what Ali does. I see him hanging around the estate, there's always a gang of kids trailing after him. I've seen Samir with him. I think Ali's dealing drugs, but I couldn't say for sure. I've never seen him do anything like that and my exchanges with him have always been civil. He has manners, which is something I appreciate.'

'What did he ask about Samir, exactly?' Morel asked.

'He asked me if Samir had said anything while he was at my flat.'

'Is that how he phrased it?'

'Yes. "Did he say anything?" was what Ali asked. I don't know what he meant. Either way, I had nothing to tell him. Like I told you, Samir wasn't talkative. If he had any secrets, he didn't share them with me.'

Morel stood up to leave. Lila was still sitting, deep in thought.

'There's something else. The thing I wanted to show you.' The old man disappeared in his bedroom and returned with something in his hand. He opened it and Morel saw what he was holding. A tooth.

'This was in the pocket of a cardigan I'd lent Samir. The boy was wearing it before he left my place. He had it wrapped in a tissue.'

'It looks small.'

'That's what I thought,' Alberto told Morel. 'Samir was 16. It's unlikely he'd still have baby teeth. Either way, this is small.' Morel reached for it.

'We'll take this with us, Monsieur Rosales, if you don't mind.'

'Why would I mind?' Alberto said. 'I'm glad to be rid of it. I can't think why Samir would have had this.'

'Why didn't you give it to the other police officer when he came to see you?' Lila asked.

Alberto shrugged.

'Like I said, I didn't like him. Didn't like the way he spoke about Samir either.'

'How, exactly?'

'Like Samir was nothing. The kid had a mother and a sister. He was going to finish school if they let him. He was more than capable of finishing school and maybe even going to university. Why not? It seems to me the teachers around here give up on these kids too easily.' Alberto's voice was strained.

'Aisha tells me Samir was going to leave school and take up a technical course. Learn a trade.'

'He never said anything about that. That might have been good for him too. That's what I did, after all, and it served me well enough.'

Morel and Lila turned their attention to the tooth.

'What can you tell us about Georghe?' Morel asked.

'You mean the other boy who died? I didn't know him personally. From what I hear he'd been breaking into people's flats. Stealing from them. Those gypsy kids have a bit of a reputation. It was just a matter of time before one of them paid the price.'

'A high price to pay, don't you think?'

'I'm not condoning the violence, if that's what you're implying. I'm just saying it doesn't surprise or shock me as it once did. But I see how things have changed. The kids become hardened at an early age. They lose their way. You can see why. There's nothing for them to do around here. Nowhere to go, no money. Mostly they're bored out of their fucking minds.' He said it with a smile on his face but Morel detected something else, a steely quality to the old man.

Lila wrapped the tooth in the tissue and slid it into her pocket. 'You were obviously very fond of Samir, Monsieur Rosales. It's nice that he had someone like you, looking out for him.' The old man gripped the armrest with both hands, his eyes sliding away from the two detectives.

'I didn't look out for him enough. I should have been more vigilant.'

*

Morel was about to respond, but a cry shattered the silence, followed by the sound of breaking glass. He went to the window and looked down. All he could make out was a couple of figures running across the street. Far away he heard the sound of sirens. Perrin had called earlier to say the neighbourhood would be patrolled all evening. The CRS, the riot police, were on standby.

His phone rang and he picked it up. It was Akil.

'*Chef*, I just heard from Vincent. He says Thierry Villot called the office. He's worried things are going to get messy in a while. Looks like gangs from the estate and also troublemakers coming in from the other suburbs. Maybe we need to wrap up for tonight.'

'Thierry Villot called? Why him? Why not Marchal?'

'Maybe Villot was doing the decent thing, warning us, so we don't run into any trouble. Maybe Marchal couldn't care less what happens to us,' Akil suggested.

'When? Did he say when?'

'No. Just said later tonight.'

'Where are you?' Morel asked, thinking that he hadn't been paying attention to what was happening outside. He looked at the time and realized it was later than he thought.

'Jean and I are on the fifteenth floor.'

'Okay. Let's continue a little longer, then wrap it up,' Morel said.

There was a pause. 'Okay.'

'Stay close to your phones.'

*

They'd been in Villeneuve for over two hours. It was getting darker and the snow, which had stopped for a while, had resumed in earnest. He should have been rounding up his team, leaving this place before the streets became unsafe. Thierry Villot was a seasoned local cop, and even he seemed worried. But instead Morel pressed on. He wasn't himself, caught in a strange state, a combination of daydream and nervy alertness that was clouding his judgment. He touched his forehead but couldn't tell whether he was warm or cold. 'Are you okay?' Lila asked at one point. He told her he was, but in reality, he had lost track of time and it felt to him as though he'd been here forever, knocking on doors and making little headway.

At some point, he left Lila on her own, talking to a family from Mali – five people crammed in a two-bedroom unit, getting ready to sit down to dinner when the detectives turned up - to get a breath of fresh air. He stood in the entrance to Tower A, watching commuters arriving home by car, bus or on foot from the train station. After a while, he became aware that people were hurrying past. Hurrying home before whatever was going to happen tonight happened, he realized. No one looked at him, even when they had to step past him to get inside. The cold air snapped him out of his earlier state. It was time to get going.

Just as he was about to turn and re-enter the building, he noticed a car coming his way, slowly, as if the driver was unsure about where to go. Morel found himself caught in the headlights. The car stopped, then backed into an empty park. A man got out, hesitated for a moment before approaching him. With a start, Morel recognized Vincent.

'What are you doing here? Has there been a new development in the Simic case? You could have called instead of driving.' Morel's voice was unsteady and he was shivering, with cold and tiredness and perhaps a recurrence of the fever he'd done his best to ignore these past days.

'I've come to say something. Look, you can send me back to the office to sift through porn sites and talk to a bunch of middle-aged swingers about whether they shoved Simic in the water because he wasn't a good screw, or because he was too good in bed. Or I can help catch a child murderer. Up to you,' Vincent said. This was a prepared speech. He must have been thinking about what he wanted to say on his way here.

'Simic is dead,' Morel said quietly. 'Solving that case is as important as what we're doing here. You know that.'

'Fine. Then get someone else to focus on Simic. The truth is you've been putting me on the backburner for a while. And I'm tired of it.'

'Lila's been working the Simic case too.'

'But she's here with you now.'

Vincent was the easiest member of his team. Good-natured, but no pushover. Morel could see that he would leave and never come back if he was turned away now. And what would the team be like without Vincent? They needed him.

There was only one thing to do. Morel grabbed Vincent's shoulder, as much to steady himself in his febrile state as to let him know he'd been heard.

'Okay. Forget about Simic for now. Stay with us. But it's late and we need to get going soon. Villot called to warn us things might get ugly.'

'So we're done?' Vincent asked.

'This is not our patch. And in this situation, there's no sense going out there and acting like cowboys. We'll return in the morning.'

Ignoring Vincent's silent opposition, he called Akil and Lila and told them to wrap up and meet him downstairs.

'Are we leaving?' Jean said, when he and Akil reached the lobby. Morel heard the relief in his voice. At the same time, he became aware of someone shouting. Several voices joined in, drawing nearer to the building. Morel recognized the word, a two-syllable chant. *Sa-mir, Sa-mir, Sa-mir*. The tone was angry, each syllable a roar. He opened the door and looked out. A hundred metres from where he stood, the battle lines were being drawn. The police were piling out of the dark blue vans they'd arrived in. The locals were threatening, but they weren't the only ones to worry about. To Morel, there was nothing reassuring about the uniforms.

The rioters stopped fifty metres from the police line. For a moment, no one did anything. There was something about the mood that made Morel step back into the building and urge his team to do the same. Just as the door swung shut, one of the masked youths stepped forward and lobbed a petrol bomb at the police line. Casually, as if he was just passing a ball.

'Fuck,' said Lila who was standing nearest the exit.

She stepped back into the hallway as the flare went up. The next petrol bomb hit a car, not far from the building.

'Your car's nearby, right?' Morel asked Vincent.

'Right outside. You saw where I parked it. Let's go.' Vincent took a step towards the exit but Morel stopped him. 'Wait.'

'Wait for what?' Akil said uncharacteristically. It wasn't like him to disagree with Morel. 'Let's get into Vincent's car while it's still intact and drive to where we parked the other one. The longer we wait, the more difficult it'll be.'

'Wait.' No one moved. They were waiting for Morel to take the lead. He knew he should say or do something, but he had no idea what they were dealing with out there. He wanted to get his team safely out of here, and he wanted to stay and do his job, but even he knew the five of them were in no position to deal with what was happening. He was shaking, he realized. Shaking and sweating. He was still sick. Maybe that explained why he was being so indecisive and why he'd let things get to this point. Lila looked worried. She stepped towards him and touched his arm.

'Chef?'

Before Morel could respond, Vincent was on the move. 'I'm going to get the car,' he said, and stepped past them into the fray.

Ten

Virginie saw the flames before she reached the estate. She pressed on. As she looked for a place to park, somewhere quiet, she counted at least three burning cars. She was driving slowly but still she didn't see the running boys when they suddenly appeared before her on the road, frightening her out of her wits. How old were they? Fifteen, sixteen? The same age as Samir. They came out of nowhere and ran across the road without bothering to check for cars, and she braked hard to avoid hitting them. One of the boys gave her the finger while she clutched her steering wheel and waited for her heartbeat to return to normal.

Kids. Giving her the finger. In the distance she heard the sound of gunshot. Or maybe it was something else. She shouldn't get dramatic. Still, maybe she should turn back now. It was obvious things were getting out of hand. But she wanted to see Aisha. To make sure she was okay. The girl wasn't answering her phone and she'd missed her last session. Virginie had nightmare visions of her hiding away in a room, contemplating suicide. Just like the other girl at the school whom she'd treated for six months. Virginie had thought she was making progress. And then the girl had slit her wrists.

Virginie blamed herself. Then, and now. She'd failed to make a connection and she'd watched Aisha withdraw, little by little, till there was nothing between them. The last couple of times, they'd sat together like two strangers in a waiting-room. And now it was probably too late to rebuild that trust, but Virginie would try anyway.

She parked in a narrow street, a couple of hundred metres from the tower blocks, thinking she would circle the area where the clashes were happening to get to the buildings. With everything that was going on, she reasoned, no one would single her out. Many of the streetlamps were smashed and it was dark. It would have been nearly pitch-black without the fires. There were fires burning too, she saw, down where the Roma encampment was.

She walked quickly, keeping her head down. Despite what she told people, that their fears were exaggerated, she'd always felt unsafe on the estate. The police were here, only a short distance away, she told herself. Nothing would happen. As she moved towards the *cité*, she saw a mob in the distance. Fire trucks, police vans. People running. It wasn't clear what was happening, only that tensions were running high. She'd heard on the morning news that a policeman was critically injured. Were the riot police capable of restraint? As a student, she'd held them in contempt; she'd sided with the underdog. Protest was necessary. You had to contest authority. That was the norm. Now she told herself the officers were the good guys, knowing at the same time how grossly simplistic that was. At some point, she had morphed into the sort of person she despised. How could she be of any help to Aisha, she thought, when secretly, without quite admitting it to herself, she feared everything in the girl's background? When she attached such ridiculous and offensive labels to people? Good guys, bad guys. Insider, outsider.

She heard a sound behind her and turned quickly, certain that she was being followed. But there was no one there. The wind was relentless, blowing over the deserted street. She decided she would go around the back of the tower blocks to avoid the rioters. It meant entering the wasteland, an area that gave her the shivers because it was isolated and because it had something of a reputation as a place you went to for the sort of things you didn't do in public. That poor

Roma boy had died there. The people who'd done that to him were no better than animals.

She picked up her pace. As she neared the buildings from the side, she heard someone whistle and turned to find a couple of boys trailing her. The same ones, maybe, who had run across the road earlier. She'd been right about their age. Close up they really were just kids.

'You lost, lady?' One of them said. She couldn't tell which one it was, whether he was the boy who'd been rude to her earlier.

'I'm fine, thank you. Just visiting a friend.'

'A friend! You mean, like, a boyfriend?'

'No.' A wave of irritation swept over her, but she managed to conceal it. 'You should probably go home. It's not safe out here.'

'We *are* home. It's you who shouldn't be here'.

She noticed then how nervy the boy was. He seemed unable to stand still. What had he taken? She felt the first flutter of fear. Keep calm, she told herself. Don't let them know you're afraid.

'What's your name?' she asked the boy who'd kept silent so far. The other boy snorted, and leered at her.

'Hey. Mourad. I think the slag likes you. What do you say?' Virginie looked at the other boy, hoping to see shame, discomfort, but instead she encountered a face so blank it chilled her. He spoke slowly, staring at her without blinking.

'Nah. Too ugly man.'

'Better than nothing.'

'Nice tits, I guess,' the quiet boy said, eliciting a roar of delight from his friend. 'How about we take her around the back. Into the wasteland. Show her something she's never seen.'

They moved towards her, slowly at first, and she backed away from them, towards the estate. Without thinking, she turned and ran. They seemed to hesitate at first, which gave her an advantage, but then the two of them started running too, calling her names as they got closer. Names she'd never been called before and that terrified her because they came from the lips of two young boys who spoke them as though they were everyday words. One of her shoes came undone and she nearly tripped, but she caught herself just in time and kept on, knowing that it was only a matter of time before they caught up with her. They were younger, faster, spurred on and excited by whatever it was they'd taken.

She had just about given up, her lungs screaming for air, when she realized she was at the tower blocks. All of a sudden there were people everywhere and the noise was deafening. Someone screeched in her ear, but it wasn't for her benefit, he was hurling insults at a policeman who was handcuffing him. The two boys, Mourad and the other, seemed to be gone, but she couldn't be sure. In this crowd, she would stand out. They would find her.

She quickly realized she couldn't expect any help from the police; they had their hands full and would probably just tell her to go home. There was nothing for her to do but get into the block in which Aisha lived. Once she found her, it would be alright.

She started running again. and slammed into a man coming out of the building fast, who caught her as she lost her balance. She was still terrified and thought the boys had finally caught up with her.

'Let me go!'

'It's okay. Calm down. Stop hitting me. Calm down.'

When she looked up, she saw a man she didn't recognize. She broke free and looked around wildly for someone who might be able to help her. The man she'd collided with stepped aside and now she noticed his companion. She stared at him in disbelief.

'Serge?' She wanted to throw herself in his arms. A part of her also felt ashamed and wanted to hide.

'Virginie. Why are you here? What happened?' Morel gripped her arm. 'Come with us now. Quickly. We need to leave.'

She did as she was told. She was vaguely aware of getting into a car, of Morel taking the wheel. Everything else receded, there was only the tension in the car and a resounding silence that sat heavier than words. There were more people in the car than the number of available seats. No one spoke. The car started and stopped minutes later to let two people out. They climbed into another car. She stayed put. They were on the move again. No one spoke. In the rearview mirror, the towers blocked out the horizon. It seemed to take forever to reach a point in the road where she finally lost sight of them.

BOOK THREE

HOMELAND

One

'What were you thinking, Virginie?'

'I wanted to see Aisha.'

She turned her face to his, without making eye contact. They were in Morel's home, or rather the main house - his father's home, as he thought of it now. For years, his mother's shadow had lingered, and everywhere he'd looked, he'd seen only her.

'Your timing was lamentable. You could have been hurt,' he told Virginie. After she had collided with Vincent in the *cité*, Morel had initially intended to drop her home, but she'd been so shaken he'd brought her here instead. His younger sister Adèle, who had come over earlier in the evening to check on Morel senior, had let them in.

Now Morel and Virginie reclined on opposite ends of the same sofa, exhausted and mildly drunk. The cognac he'd poured – the third in a series of single shots - was gone.

'Why? I mean, why then? At night, in the middle of a riot, for God's sake? What was so urgent that it couldn't wait'?

'I don't know why. Same reason maybe that compels you to walk around one of France's most dangerous housing estates dressed in an Armani suit and wearing a Jaeger-Lecoultre watch.' He began to smile but stopped when he saw she was serious. When he didn't say anything, she continued, in a quiet voice. 'I've been thinking about things. I don't think I've been much help to these girls.'

'What girls are you talking about?'

'The schoolgirls I counsel, in Villeneuve. I've had a few referred to me, or who come to me of their own accord. Aisha is the sixth girl I've worked with at the school.' Virginie sat up a little, adjusted the cushion behind her back. 'Each time, it's the same scenario. At first they really want to be there. They have things to say. I listen. I try to empathize, to form a bond. After a while, they lose heart. Eventually, they stop coming. And I think I know why. To do this job well you have to be able to connect with your patients. You need empathy.

'I'm sure that's something you're good at.'

She smiled, acknowledging his comment. 'When I was working in Paris, I managed to connect with the kids. And it wasn't that I could identify with their problems. A lot of these girls were harming themselves. Or dealing with eating disorders. But somehow it was easier to form relationships and to help them work through issues.'

'Are you saying these were lesser problems? Easier to work with?'

'Not at all, that's not what I'm saying. They live in different worlds. And the truth is that, if you've grown up in a lavish apartment in the Rue des Franc-Bourgeois, you might have all sorts of anxieties but you might also have a grounded sense of self-entitlement, something you don't worry about or question.'

'I'm not sure that always works in people's favour.'

'Sure. It doesn't. But what I'm trying to say is that in Villeneuve, I've failed. Again and again. And you know why? Deep down I think I have the same prejudices as anyone else. In my head, I'd written these girls' stories before they'd even told me about themselves. I thought I was listening to Aisha, when in fact I'd already made up my mind that she was a victim of the system and deserved better. No wonder she turned from me. What did I have to offer?' She touched his arm. 'You're a police officer. Maybe you get this. I feel like someone who's committed a crime. What I imagine that must feel like. Uneasy conscience. A sense of being tainted, you know? It's getting worse.'

Morel rubbed his eyes. He felt faint with hunger and tiredness but didn't have the energy to get up. 'I don't know what to say to that, Virginie. To some extent, we're all tainted, aren't we? We all have our notions, some of them ugly. We do the best we can. That's all there is to it. You can't beat yourself up for just being human.'

'Maybe.' She seemed unconvinced.

'You must be exhausted, apart from anything else. So much has happened.' He'd offered her Maly's old room. The nicest in the house, according to Adèle who had spent a major part of her childhood and adolescence taunting her older sister and accusing their parents of favouritism.

Tonight, Adèle was sleeping in her old room – the lesser room, as she'd always seen it. She had got to the door before Morel had a chance to use his key. Which meant she'd sat up waiting for him. She must have seen the headlights. She was pissed off, he could tell. He'd expected a lecture for not calling and letting her know how late he would be. But Virginie's presence had stopped her from speaking her mind. Now the house was quiet, his younger sister resentfully asleep in her childhood bed and Philippe Morel lost in his dreams, just as he tended to be lost these days in his waking hours.

'You should go to bed and at least try to rest,' Morel said gently.

Virginie nodded but stayed put. The lights were turned off and the curtains pulled back, and the snow lit up the room so that Morel could see her quite clearly.

'I can't quite face bed. The adrenalin maybe … do you think I could just stay here, for a little while?'

'Sure. Whatever is most comfortable.' He fetched several blankets from the laundry cupboard and handed them to her.

'Thank you. Tell me: are you any closer to finding who killed Samir?'

'Not really,' he admitted. 'But it takes time. The riots make our job difficult, obviously. And you mustn't forget that we're investigating Georghe's death too. Two deaths, that may or may not be related.'

'Oh God. What happened to that boy was dreadful too.' In the grey light, Morel saw fear in her eyes. 'There's always been an enormous amount of tension between that Roma community and the *cité* residents.'

'The dealers look down on the thieves. Both sides play by their own rules and neither one has any respect for authority.'

'Exactly. And it seems to me that it must be impossible to police.'

'Not an easy place to police, certainly.'

'Are you sure you're not taking too much on? Two murder cases?'

'How can I not take both on? When there's a likelihood – a chance, anyway – that the two are linked?'

'Have you had a chance to talk to the detective who was investigating the homicides before you took over?'

'I have.'

'And?'

Morel thought about the first time he'd met Marchal. The man had been on his guard from the start. In the morning he would find Villot and get him to explain why he'd approached Morel in the car park. Ask him too whether he was responsible for the autopsy notes that had landed on Morel's desk. Then Morel would summon Marchal to Paris. The detective had some explaining to do.

*

It was still dark, and unbearably cold when Ali and Karim walked through empty streets to the Roma encampment. Karim would have preferred to be in bed, but Ali had insisted. He liked to have company.

After what had happened earlier, it was strange to encounter no one. Everyone had left, including residents, police and those who had taken the trains in from some of the neighbouring *banlieues*, as a gesture of solidarity or simply to cause trouble. Sometime during the night, Ali had found Karim and suggested they stick together till things calmed down. Karim felt no need to tell Ali that he'd kept at a safe distance from the violence all evening, watching as others got knocked around, shoved or abused. He didn't like the outsiders, they didn't play by the same rules and were unpredictable. At some stage, and despite his best efforts to remain unharmed, he'd got caught up in a scuffle, and the sleeve on his leather jacket had got ripped. It was stupid to get upset over something like that, yet it had made him cry. Silent tears, which he'd swiftly concealed. His prize possession, irretrievably damaged. He'd spent a month's earnings on it.

When they got to the encampment, Karim stared at what he saw, shocked into silence. He couldn't believe it. Just a few hours earlier there'd been about five hundred people living here, managing somehow to survive in conditions that made the tower blocks seem lavish in comparison. Living with no power or running water. They walked some distance to fill buckets at the sinks near the sports ground. Lugged them back to the camp. Kept to themselves, and put up with constant abuse. Karim had seen Réza once, spitting at a young girl emerging from behind a tree where she'd clearly been doing her business. No toilets either at the camp. How could you live like that?

And now there was nothing left. No sign of life, not even the dogs you often saw wandering around the camp, searching for scraps. The

215

fires had consumed everything. Karim wondered how the gypsies had packed up and vanished so fast. It almost felt as if they'd never been here. Had any of them had time to gather any of their belongings before they were reduced to ashes?

'They'll have to find somewhere else to live now,' he said after a while.

Ali spat on the ground. 'Good riddance,' he said. 'They didn't belong. Thieves, the lot of them. They don't follow our rules, they don't want to be part of the community.'

Karim dug his hands in his pockets. He didn't want Ali to see how upset he was, but it was hard not to. Not that he liked the gypsies. He didn't. He'd despised them too. Had hated the way they pissed and shat everywhere, like animals. There were places you couldn't go anymore because of them. But that kid Georghe, the way things had turned out for him, well, that was different. Karim didn't have the stomach for that sort of violence, the kind you administered yourself and that got your hands dirty. When he thought of that kid, wide-eyed and skinny and scared, it was all he could manage not to throw up.

'Hey! Kevin. Cheer up! You look like someone rammed a hot poker up your arse.' Ali stuck his tongue out, a gesture which seemed strange to Karim until he realized Ali was catching snowflakes in his mouth, happy as a little kid.

As he watched Ali, and waited till he was done goofing around, a single thought went around and around in his head. Aisha. He had made a promise to help find Samir's murderer, knowing full well he could never keep it. He thought that maybe she already knew he wouldn't be much use and that she planned to do some digging on her own. The sort of digging that could get her into serious trouble.

He had to prevent that from happening.

Two

'The lab results are back. The tooth that Alberto found in Samir's pocket. That was Georghe's,' Lila declared happily.

'When did you find out? It's only half past seven. Too early for Richard Martin to be in touch.' The pathologist was not an early riser.

'Come on. You know that sleazebag has a soft spot for me. He called. From memory he said something cute like, "There's no such thing as off the clock when it comes to you, *ma belle Lila*." One of these days someone will get tired of the banter and cut his dick off. But in the meantime, it's good news, no? It proves the two boys were together at some point before they died. There's the connection you were looking for.'

'It does establish a connection,' Morel admitted. He'd woken up after two hours' sleep to find Adèle and Virginie murmuring together in the kitchen while his father hid in his bedroom, as reluctant to join in the female chatter, Morel guessed, as he was. Now he was on his way to Villot's place, and he had Lila on speakerphone.

'How are you feeling?' she'd asked at the start of the call.

'Sleep-deprived and with a long day ahead.' That was when she'd sprung the news about the tooth, expecting it would cheer him up.

'At least now we definitely know he was with Georghe at some point,' she said. 'And the question is, why? That's what we need to be thinking about. And why take the tooth?'

'Maybe he saw what happened. Maybe he was there when the kid was beaten up. Or he found the boy after it happened.'

'And didn't call the police? Or an ambulance?'

'A kid like that isn't going to look to the authorities for help. His experiences have taught him to avoid anything official. No. It's more likely he would have freaked out and run from the scene.'

'But why keep the tooth?'

'As proof, maybe? So he could tell someone what had happened? What he'd seen? I don't know.'

'Hmmm.'

'What?'

'Funny how you won't contemplate the possibility that maybe he did it to Georghe. Beat the shit out of him. Kept the tooth as some sort of trophy.'

'If so, how did he do it? He didn't use his fists then, because we'd know. Nothing came from the autopsy to suggest he did.'

'Maybe he was wearing gloves?' she suggested, half-serious. 'Either way, he could still be guilty. If he watched it happen and did nothing.' When Morel didn't reply, she asked, 'Why are you so uncomfortable with the idea that Samir might be implicated?'

'I'm not uncomfortable with it. But I don't want us jumping to conclusions when we've got no evidence.'

'He had one of Georghe's teeth. In his pocket.' She said it slowly, as if he might have misheard the first time. 'He was there. He's guilty of something.'

*

'How are things with you, anyway? I hardly hear from you these days. I guess you're busy. Still, an occasional phone call to your mother isn't too much to expect, I would have thought.'

'It isn't and I'm sorry,' Luc Clément said, looking in despair at the assignment one of his students had handed in. Half a page of nonsense, riddled with spelling mistakes that even a five-year-old shouldn't make. And the other essays that had been handed in weren't much better. Hobbes must be turning in his grave. Meanwhile his mother carried on in that passive-aggressive way she had, though the passive part seemed to be fading fast as the years went by.

'I've been preoccupied,' he said. 'A boy was killed. Someone from the school. You probably saw it on the news.'

'The gipsy? He was from the school?'

'No, not the Roma boy,' he said, flinching at her use of the word gipsy. At least he'd veered the subject away from himself. 'A boy named Samir.'

'Ah yes. I did see that on the news. Well it isn't all that surprising, is it? Given the neighbourhood and the way we fail to manage immigration.' His mother, who had dismissed Jean-Marie le Pen as common and uncouth, admired the daughter. In Luc's mind, Marine was more dangerous than her father, but of course there was no point in saying it. Or was there? His mother sniffed and Luc emptied his glass in one gulp. Disgusted with her, and by extension, with himself.

'I was thinking I might visit at Easter if that's convenient,' he offered, praying she would get off the subject of foreigners. No such luck.

'We insist on letting people come here without considering how well they'll assimilate, without considering the fact that they come from such alien backgrounds.'

'And with such foreign habits,' Luc said, but the sarcasm – only mild, admittedly - was lost on her. No wonder his father had left her. Had left them, after Luc's sister had died. He'd doted on his little girl, whereas Luc's mother had always had a soft spot for their son.

The two of them, mother and son; same genes, same blood. You didn't get to choose your parents, nor did you get to decide, really, how much influence they had on you.

'It's all so … depressing.' She was looking for sympathy. Wanting to show she too was a person with feelings. He knew it was an act but a part of him wanted to believe. He found himself softening a little. She had left messages, which he'd ignored. That was tough. No wonder she took it personally. 'These past months have been …' Luc searched for the right word '…trying. A few teachers have resigned and we're having trouble recruiting new staff. I've had to take on more classes.'

His mother was silent on the phone.

'I don't think you're telling me the truth, Luc.'

'What do you mean?'

'I mean I think you're not telling me why you're preoccupied. Is this about that student? Aisha?'

'What are you talking about?' He hadn't meant to sound tetchy but the question had shocked him. When had he mentioned Aisha and what had he said, exactly? His mother had a habit of probing and of finding the tenderest spot, and then pressing gently down on it until she made him squirm. There were times he forgot to be cautious, and talked too much, because she was his mother and seemed genuinely interested in his life. Now he tried frantically to remember how much he'd told her, and whether it mattered.

'The last time we talked, you said you were concerned about one of your students. That Aisha. You've mentioned her a few times.'

'I like all my students,' Luc lied. 'She's my best one. I want her to do well.'

His mother said nothing.

'You don't understand what it's like, teaching in an area like this. It can be so demoralizing,' he continued, knowing he sounded defensive. 'But if I can make a difference to the students who want to work and want to make something of themselves, then it's worth all the hardship, the crap wages, the abuse I get, the thankless hours. I wish you had a sense of it.'

'I do understand, you think I don't but I do.'

'But?'

'Never mind.' It was her turn to sound cautious.

'Tell me.'

'I don't know. You just seem, how shall I put it, a little obsessed with that one girl.'

'You make it sound like something it isn't.'

'Don't be silly; I'm not implying any such thing,' she said. 'I just worry about you. I know why you might feel – I mean, your sister…'

'Don't.' He didn't want to hear it. 'I'm fine. There's nothing to worry about.'

'And now this murder. Two murders. And riots! Surely it isn't safe to return to the school. I'm sure they'd understand if you stayed home while all this is sorted.'

Sorted? 'I have no intention of staying home. I intend to go to work as usual.' He didn't tell her that the boy who'd died was Aisha's brother. It would only make things worse.

'I have to get ready for work,' he said, after listening to her for a while, telling him about what she'd been up to and about his siblings, who he never saw. Not for the first time, he felt disconnected from the things and the people that made up his world. Villeneuve had done that. Aisha too. Split him apart. He wished it were otherwise.

'Will you promise to keep in touch more often?'

'I promise.'

'And please be careful.'

'I will.'

He got dressed and ate his breakfast standing in the kitchen. It was a quiet neighbourhood. Most of the people living in his building were older. At this hour, no one was up.

None of his students, not even Aisha, had any clue who he was or where he came from. A privileged background that had included annual trips to a second residence in Aix-en-Provence. The apartment he owned now was a gift from his father, bestowed on his 18th birthday. If his students knew, they would judge him for it and he'd lose all credibility. But sometimes he wondered if he was pretending to be something he wasn't. Playing a part.

He sent Aisha a text.

Everything okay?

Yes.

Any news about the investigation? Have they found out anything?

Nothing.

The night before, he'd been out for dinner with friends, trying a new place in the Trocadéro, when one of his colleagues who lived near Villeneuve had texted about the riots. *It's happening again,* she'd written. *I can actually see the fires from my window.* Without thinking, he'd excused himself to go to the bathroom, where he'd called Aisha, asking if she was safe and urging her to stay home. She had seemed flustered by the call, hanging up as quickly as she could. Stupid move. He should know better than to contact her when she was at home, and place her in an awkward situation.

On the way back from the restaurant, he'd been so preoccupied that he'd had a near miss with another car, veering away at the last minute. The other driver had been livid. Without thinking, Luc had started driving towards Villeneuve. At night, the *périphérique* looked almost pretty, the road painted white with glittering snow. Not long before, the trucks had come through here and sprayed salt across the slippery ground.

Halfway to Villeneuve, he'd changed his mind and turned back. He was tired, a little drunk, and too caught up in what was happening to drive anywhere safely. The last thing he needed was to do something stupid like crash the car and kill himself. What use would that be to Aisha?

He made coffee and toast and ate in front of the TV. The first item on the news was Villeneuve. He wondered how many of the kids would turn up to class today. It didn't occur to him not to go to work. It was important to carry on as if things were normal.

He'd made little progress with the kids over Hobbes. A familiar frustration rose within him, which he tried to ignore. He finished his breakfast and took his plate to the kitchen. His phone went off, signaling two new text messages. On the way back, he checked. One from his mother, telling him she loved him and to please not be annoyed at her, and another from a Commandant Morel. Luc dialed the mobile number he'd been given. Morel replied and asked if Luc would be at the school this morning.

'Definitely.'

'I'll see you there. Later this morning, I expect.'

'I spoke with the other detective, Marchal, when he came to the school. Do you know him personally?'

'We've met. Look, Monsieur Clément, I have to go. I'll see you in a little while.'

Luc took a quick shower and tidied up a little, conscious all of a sudden of the mess. He rinsed his cup and plate and left both in the sink. For nearly a year, he'd shared the apartment with one of his cousins, a bit of a dope but nice enough. Thinking that it would be good to have company and that in any case the place was too big for one person. It hadn't taken long to figure out he didn't like having someone else around.

Books, satchel. A packed lunch, including an apple which one of his students had given him, with a lewd and inaccurate reference to the Garden of Eden. His reply: I would suggest you go back and read the text. Properly this time. A line he used so often, the students had learned to pre-empt him and turned it into something of a joke.

He turned the heater and the lights off and left the flat. Twice, he had to retrace his steps because he'd forgotten something he'd need for class. He wondered what questions the police would ask. Why did they want to speak to him when he wasn't even one of Samir's teachers? It was possible that Corinne Tellier, the head teacher, had told this Morel that he knew the family. He made a mental list of the sort of questions he might have to answer, then forced himself to stop. *I have nothing to feel guilty about, I haven't done anything*, he reminded himself.

In the car, despite his earlier decision not to bother her anymore, he texted Aisha.

Is there anything I can do?

It took her several minutes to reply. It wasn't the answer he'd hoped for.

Nothing.

He waited a while longer with the engine running. Watched the night fade and make way for a frosty grey morning. What should he do? It took him an eternity to decide. His fingers shook when he sent the text.

Will you meet me before school? There is something I haven't told you. It's important.

A pause.

I don't think I can. What's so important anyway?

He was shaking so much he made several mistakes as he typed.

It's about Samir.

Three

Villot lived in a *pavillon*, a modest, two-bedroom house on the edge of Villeneuve. Newly-built, in a street where every house looked the same. It was the sort of place a Villeneuve *flic* might live in. Affordable and unassuming. But the interior took Morel by surprise. It was practically bare. Two chairs, a TV set on the floor. The bedroom door was ajar and he saw a single mattress on the ground, a half-empty coffee cup, and a lamp beside it, still lit.

'Have you only moved in recently?'

'Looks that way, doesn't it?' Villot looked around the room. 'No. My wife left me. Took everything. After fifteen years of marriage, she figured I owed her.'

'I'm sorry to hear that.'

'Don't be. The only thing I regret is the fact we waited so long. We could have avoided a lot of the unpleasantness. We might even have been able to remain friends. Or maybe not. Who knows.' Villot sat down. 'Anyway, I still have a couple of chairs, one or two forks in the cutlery drawer and a bottle of whisky in the pantry.'

'It could be worse, then.'

'My thoughts exactly.'

'How are you finding it, being alone?' Morel asked. The question seemed perfectly natural. He settled on one of the chairs and Thierry took the other. 'I'm sorry if that seems too personal.'

'Not at all. To be honest it's a relief. It was rough in the end. We were always at each other's throats.'

He glanced at Morel. 'You married?'

'No. Though I was once. A very long time ago. It was a mistake.'

'Do you still see her? The ex-wife?'

227

'No. There's no reason to. We had very little in common, from the start.'

Villot nodded as though he understood. He lit a cigarette and crossed his legs. 'I can smoke inside now. One of the perks of celibacy. Anyway, enough about that. You're running the investigation now. Both investigations. Have you got anywhere?'

'Not far,' Morel admitted. 'But we have evidence that indicates Samir was with Georghe at some point, either during or after the beating. He knew something.'

Villot didn't say anything, just watched Morel through a cloud of smoke.

'I'm here to ask about Samir. That day in the car park, outside the police station. When my colleague Lila Markov and I came to see Marchal. You approached me. I've been wondering why. I think something's troubling you. I think you know a lot more about the boy than you've said. I'd like to hear it.'

Villot drew deeply on his cigarette. Morel pressed on.

'I also think Marchal is lying and I want to know why. He knew who Samir was and yet he pretended not to when the name first came up. Why?'

'Do you know what Marchal said when he heard your team had taken over the investigation?' Villot gazed at the ceiling, as if he saw something there that warranted a closer look. 'He said you'd be lucky to get out of this in one piece.'

'I'm touched by his concern,' Morel said. He watched Villot enjoy the cigarette, and resisted the urge to ask for one. 'What made you come up to me in the car park? I'm also guessing you sent me the autopsy notes for both Georghe and Samir. Am I right?'

Villot nodded.

228

'That was risky. Why did you do it?' Morel asked.

'I don't know for sure whether there's anything going on that should concern any of us,' Villot began slowly. 'But I'd be making a mistake if I sat back and said nothing. Only it isn't easy doing this. I'm not particularly fond of Marchal but then again I'm not a snitch.'

Morel waited for more.

'This is how it is. About seven, or maybe eight months ago, we organized a drug raid at the Cité des Poètes. It started out as these things tend to do. A big operation – we had about twenty officers and we were targeting some of the dealers we knew were operating out of the *cité*. We went in early, thinking we'd get them while they were still in their beds. But someone must have alerted them.' He shook his head. 'These guys, they just get cockier by the day. They waited till we got there and saw them, watched us from a distance, then took off. There wasn't the slightest hint of concern. They didn't even run.'

'What happened?'

'We were left chasing the younger kids around the estate. Slippery as eels, but we managed to catch a few.'

'Younger kids?'

'Like I told you the first time,' Thierry said impatiently. 'The younger ones do the legwork – they act as errand boys, or lookouts. We knew it was a waste of time talking to them – even when they give us names they always end up retracting, and without the proof in any case it's a loser's game - but we took them in anyway. It was better than going back to the station empty-handed. Or so we pretended.'

'One of them was Samir.'

'Yes. Marchal was in charge of the raid. Normally we do our interviews at our desks. Same as what you guys do, I imagine. But Marchal, he took the boys into an unoccupied room we use for storage. He took them one by one and did his best to intimidate them. Wear them down. A couple of them wet their pants. One or two gave us something to work with.'

'And Samir?'

'Nothing.'

Morel guessed what came next. 'So Marchal got pissed off. He had it in for Samir. Because he couldn't squeeze anything out of him.'

Villot sighed. 'Samir was a smart kid but he was also proud. Angry. It was a mistake to taunt Marchal. Something in him snapped that day. Not that there was anything unusual about that particular scenario. It's not like it hasn't unfolded many times before. We go in, someone raises the alarm, we leave empty-handed. But I think that day Marchal reached his limit.'

'He's a police officer,' Morel said. 'Restraint is one of the things we're trained for.'

'I know.' Villot flicked the stub on the ground and squashed it with his foot. 'You don't think I know how a police officer should behave? I know everything you're thinking. I'm just saying we're human too. And whatever you think you've dealt with in your neck of the woods, there are things we face here every day that you cannot comprehend.'

Morel stood up. 'When was the last time you saw Samir? You or Marchal?'

Villot hesitated. 'That's the thing. It's been a while since I saw him at the station. That last time, he was in for less than an hour. We had to release him, there was no reason to keep him any longer, even

Marchal knew it. But a couple of days before Samir was killed, I was in the *cité*. Talking to a kid named Karim.'

'I understand he was Samir's best friend.'

'That's right. The two of them were tight. Karim told me the last time he'd seen Samir was with the police. He was implying that the experience had scared the shit out of Samir. That something had happened that might have made him want to disappear.'

'You trust this Karim? Could he be right? That Samir was at the station more recently? Could it have happened without you knowing?'

'Sure. I'm not always in. And I've been unwell, I've had to take time off work. So maybe. As for Karim, it's hard to say how trustworthy he is. Instinctively, I'd say he's making it up as he goes. But given what Marchal's been like with Samir...' He raised his hands in a gesture of helplessness. 'I don't know what to think.'

Morel got up and made for the door, then stopped as something occurred to him.

'Why did you go see Karim?'

'What do you mean? I wanted to know if he'd seen Samir.'

'Why though? Why would you be worried about Samir?'

'Like I said. Marchal had been giving the kid a hard time. I was concerned.'

Villot opened the door, clearly signaling for Morel to go, and reached for another cigarette.

'But you said the last time you'd seen Samir was a month earlier. So why did you choose that particular moment to check up on him?'

'No particular reason.'

'You were alone?'

'Yes I was alone.' Villot looked put out. 'Why so many questions? I thought you wanted to know about Marchal.'

'I do.' Morel buttoned up his jacket. 'Thank you,' he said, shaking Villot's hand. 'I appreciate how frank you've been.'

'Happy to help.' He leaned against the doorframe, sucking on his cigarette. This time, it seemed to give him no pleasure. Morel thought he looked deeply unhappy, and that everything he'd said about enjoying his new celibate status was a lie.

'You were saying you've been unwell.' It was a statement rather than a question.

'This job can really get to you, don't you find?' Villot said in a hollow voice. 'There's no end to the shit you have to deal with. You deal with one thing and immediately something else comes along. Those kids. I've known some of them since they could barely walk. I've watched them change. So many become immunized to the violence. They pretend not to care until one day they stop pretending because that's what they've become: adolescents with no capacity for empathy. It's something I can never get used to. Strange thing for a cop to say, right?'

Morel studied the other man's face. It was an unhealthy shade of grey, creased with fatigue.

'Not strange at all,' he said. 'The day you get used to it is the day you stop being a police officer.'

'Right,' Villot said, as if he'd heard it all before. He walked Morel out.

'Marchal's been in this job for a long time. I guess he doesn't believe an outsider can come in and do the job. No one will talk to you in the *cité*. Tell you the truth about anything, I mean. They'll say whatever it takes to make you go away.'

'I don't think they've been particularly forthcoming with Marchal either. Talking to some of the residents, I didn't get the impression they liked him much. I imagine you're better at establishing some form of rapport with the locals,' Morel added. It was just a guess, but he saw from Villot's face that he'd been right, or that it was the right thing to say, at least.

Villot flicked his cigarette onto the ground, tucked his hands in his pockets and looked away from Morel, towards the street. 'Here's something no one knows about me at work. I grew up in that *cité*. My parents still live there. Forty years in the same apartment. My father worked for the SNCF his entire life, and my mother was a cleaner. She claimed she liked the work because it was straightforward and she didn't need to think. It never entered their minds that there could be more out there. Makes you want to weep, doesn't it?'

'I don't know about that. If they managed to be content with what they had, to keep at it, I'd say that's something to admire.'

'Admire?' Villot turned to face Morel again. 'By the way, whatever I've told you, I'll deny ever saying if someone asks, understand? In my job, it's impossible to survive alone. I'm fucked if my colleagues turn on me. I have to be able to trust you on this.'

'You have my word.'

*

Morel started the car, backed out of his spot and waved to Villot, who waved back before heading back into the house. Slowly, he drove to the end of the street and turned left into another. There, where there was no chance of Villot seeing him from his place, he parked the car again and left the engine running while he thought about the conversation he'd just had, and what to do next.

One thing seemed obvious to him. Something was not right with Villot.

He found the number for the police station in Villeneuve and dialed it. When the receptionist answered, he asked to be put through to Marchal.

'Commandant Morel.' The tone wasn't unfriendly, but it was obvious Marchal wasn't thrilled to hear from him. 'I was wondering when you'd call.'

'Marchal. I hope you're not too busy this morning. I need you to come to the Quai des Orfèvres.'

'Will this be a formal interview?'

'A discussion. I'd like to talk to you about Samir.'

'What time?' Morel named a time that would allow him to meet with the schoolteacher Luc Clément before heading back to Paris.

'Before you hang up, Marchal: what can you tell me about Thierry Villot? Why has he been off work?'

'Why don't you ask him yourself?'

'I'm asking you.'

'The man has never taken a break. Ever. The job is his life. So maybe he's reached the point where he needs one.'

'Do you think it has something to do with his wife?'

'What?'

'I understand his wife left him recently.'

'Well if nine years counts as recently, then yes, she did.'

Nine years?

'Maybe something else is bothering him. About the job, for example,' Morel said, thinking about what Villot had told him about the way Marchal had treated Samir. Had Villot stood up to Marchal, made it clear that he wasn't happy with the way Marchal operated? Maybe Villot was being ostracized, or bullied, for not playing along.

But there was Villot's lie to consider as well. Or was it a lie? All he'd said was that his wife had left him, and taken everything. He hadn't said when.

Still. Nine years. That was a long time to live in an empty house, sleeping on a mattress on the floor.

Marchal was saying something, but Morel cut him off.

'I have to go, but I'll see you at my office,' he said, before hanging up.

He got out of the car and walked back towards Villot's house, thinking it might pay to probe the detective further about Marchal. When he got to the front door, he hesitated. How would he approach this? While he framed the questions in his head, he peered through the blinds and saw Villot. He was sitting on one of his two remaining chairs with his hands in his lap, staring into space. He remained like that for a long time, and Morel continued to watch him, until he became aware of what he must look like, spying through the window.

Thierry Villot, visibly, wasn't going anywhere. There would be time to quiz him again later, after talking to Marchal.

Four

The pool was nearly empty. The only people who showed up this early were the dedicated swimmers; the ones who got up when it was still dark, got dressed, then undressed again in the echoing changing rooms before subjecting themselves to mindless laps in the pale, chlorinated water. Lila sat on the edge of the pool and adjusted her bathing cap. In the next lane, a guy built like a fridge was motoring back and forth as though a shark was chasing him. She watched as his face came up at regular intervals, his mouth, shaped like an o. A humourless sort of guy, she decided. But maybe the same could be said for her. She was here, after all, and in a second she would look just like him, minus the build.

She hesitated for a fraction of a second, then slid into the water. It was surprisingly easy. Not as cold as she'd feared. She swam the first lap at a leisurely pace, enjoying the feel of her body stretching, limbs loosening up, before picking up her pace. She hadn't been here often lately but it wasn't as bad as she'd feared. Her muscles were in good working order, and soon she was matching Aquaman's pace. He knew she was racing him - she could tell by the tension in his back, the direction of his face when he came up for air – and still he couldn't overtake her. She couldn't help feeling a bit smug. He was twice her size and yet no better. She might have neglected herself a little these past weeks, but she was still in good shape. Mentally, she was a rock. Physical strength isn't everything, mister, she thought happily. When they both reached the end of the lane, he stopped and raised his goggles to look at her. He gave her a half-smile. *So he noticed,* was her first thought. Her second was that, without the goggles he was actually kind of cute.

She was about to say something, when she became aware of a pair of familiar shoes, level with her head. Someone was standing over her, at the edge of the pool. 'Hey. The boss wants us.'

'What the fuck, Akil?' she said, pulling her cap off. It was the longest sentence she'd spoken to him in days. 'You couldn't send me a text?'

'This is more fun, surprising you like this,' he said, but he didn't look happy. As Lila pulled herself out of the water, Akil glanced at the man who, just a moment ago had been checking Lila out and was now thrashing the water in the neighbouring lane. Akil cursed him quietly. A sizable part of him hoped the guy would run out of breath, develop a major cramp and drown.

Lila stomped off to the changing rooms. The buoyancy was gone. She found she could barely open her locker, her hand was shaking so much.

A *rock*? You poor, deluded cow.

*

Antoine's view – delivered several times at the dinner table - was that when you looked at what was going on over there - the bombings, the ambushes and kidnappings, and all the talk of terrorism - you could say that Algeria had created its own mess. But you could just as easily look at the way France exploited its territory for decades while treating the locals as second-class citizens, and conclude that maybe the French held a large chunk of responsibility for the way things turned out.

This was Antoine's view, and Aisha's mother subscribed to it. Aisha wasn't sure it had anything to do with her, but she listened with interest all the same.

One minute, Antoine said, the French were practically begging Algerians to come work in their factories. This was after the Second World War, and later around the time of Algeria's independence, when labour was hard to come by. Next minute, when there wasn't so much work around anymore, the French weren't so keen on their Algerian workers. By then, these men wanted to keep their jobs and were in no hurry to leave. Not only that but they wanted their wives and children to join them, even if the rooms they shacked up in were unsuitable for families. Antoine said the French government had tried its best to stop this from happening, and failed. It turned out it was against the law to prevent the workers from reuniting with their families, right here in France.

It was, in Antoine's words, a first-class victory for the underdog.

Antoine talked a lot about the underdog, until one day Samir told him to stop insulting migrants by comparing them to animals.

'Who are you calling an underdog?' he said. Aisha's brother had a way of asking a question quietly, like he was being reasonable, that could make you uncomfortable.

'It's just a term, Samir,' Antoine explained. He was genuinely shocked, and apologetic, that Samir felt insulted. 'It's used to signify a person who is expected to lose.'

'So Algerians were losers.'

'That is not what I'm saying at all, and you know it.' Antoine could be forceful, to a degree, when he needed to be. 'The term says more about the point of view of those who think they are in charge and will win. They are the ones who expect the underdog to lose.'

It didn't sound convincing to Aisha but it seemed to appease Samir. Antoine always talked about how special Algeria was. He said his father had been a teacher in Algiers, before he was married. It made total sense to Aisha that Antoine's dad should have been a teacher. Antoine himself talked like he had a roomful of students listening, and a blackboard behind him covered in neat writing, each line perfectly straight and informative.

'It's sometimes easy to forget that Algeria was once France's most prized possession. Just as India was the jewel in the crown of the British Empire, so Algeria was the jewel of French colonies. A territory so rich, Paris claimed it as an integral part of France. Did you know that Algerians fought alongside the French during the Second World War? That there were around 200,000 Algerians in the French army?'

And then Antoine would go on as if talking to himself, and it wasn't always clear what he meant, not to Aisha at least.

'It's sometimes easy to stop thinking for yourself. It's hard to think about what's happening in the world in a rational, intelligent kind of way, because of how Islam is demonized now and how politics and society and the media work. Look at how information is delivered nowadays. And the world has become increasingly polarized on the issue of Muslims and their faith. It's become difficult to hold any position without stating which side you're on. You have to be for or against a thing. That's the world we live in today. But that doesn't mean we should all walk around with blinkers. It's important to remember what's real.'

And so on. Sometimes Antoine just talked about his father and about Algeria. Observing Samir's face in those moments was like watching a child listen to a lullaby. Aisha wondered why it mattered so much. Going by Samir's reaction, you would think he was being praised personally when Antoine spoke of Algeria that way. Whereas to Aisha, Algeria was just a place on the map. Like Russia, or Spain.

When she tried to picture it, she saw desert. Infinite sand, and heat. An empty horizon.

There was nothing for her there.

*

As she got ready for school, Aisha thought about Antoine's words and their effect on her brother. Samir hadn't minded Antoine, though the two of them couldn't have been more different. And now she understood why they'd managed to get on despite being so different. Antoine had given Samir self-respect. A sense of belonging.

*

In the kitchen, Antoine was making the coffee. Measuring it, leveling each spoonful to make sure he got the exact amount he wanted. She came into the room and watched him. Antoine made the place a bit less lonely, and a bit less frightening now Samir was gone, but how long was he going to be around? And what was he supposed to be to her? She hadn't figured out yet what sort of relationship he and her mother had, but it wasn't like with other couples who ate and slept and talked and fought together. When Antoine came over, he slept on the couch. However many nights he stayed, he never brought too many things with him and he never left anything behind. It was like he didn't want to take up space or leave any trace of his presence.

'What do you think happened?' Her question made Antoine jump. 'Sorry, I thought you knew I was here.'

'I didn't. How did you come in here and make so little noise? Would you like coffee?'

'No thanks.'

'What were you saying?'

'I was asking what you think happened to Samir.'

240

Antoine's hands became still. He looked at the kitchen counter as if he expected to find answers there. 'I don't know,' he said slowly.

'It's okay. Forget I asked.'

'No. It's right to ask. We're all wondering, aren't we? And I don't know, but I wonder if he fell in with the wrong people. If he got hurt because of it.'

'You mean Ali and that?' Seeing Antoine's look of consternation, she added, 'I want to talk about it. I need to find answers.'

'It frightens me to hear you talk about Ali. Your mother wouldn't want you to have anything to do with someone like that. Let the police do their job.'

'How do you know they're doing their job?''

'And why do you assume they're not? You said yourself that Morel seems competent, and trustworthy.'

'Yeah well. I haven't seen any proof yet. Meanwhile I can't sit around waiting for things to happen. I miss my brother.'

'I know you do.'

'I want – I need to know what happened. I can't just sit around and do nothing. And so far I've actually found out things that might lead me somewhere. I know he was seeing that girl Yasmina and Yasmina's brother was angry with her and probably with Samir too. He knew they were together all along. I also think Samir was dealing drugs, or something. Why else would he hang out with Ali so much?'

'You've *found out* things? What have you been up to, Aisha? Do you want to get hurt as well? Is that it? And leave your mother all alone? Hasn't she gone through enough?' Aisha stared at him, stunned by the outburst. She'd never seen Antoine like this. So angry for a moment she thought he might hit her.

It didn't last. He sighed, and went over to Aisha. She was surprised to feel his arm around her shoulder.

'I get it, I really do. It's been dreadful...but I want you to stay away from Ali and those guys. The idea of you wandering around the estate questioning people about Samir's death, well, frankly, it scares me.'

She didn't say anything, and eventually Antoine moved away from her and reached for the coffee cups.

'I'd better get going,' she said.

'Where?'

'School, where else?'

'Aisha, I doubt many people will be at school today. You're better off staying home.'

'I'm going to school. So are all my friends.'

Antoine looked skeptical. 'Which of your friends is staying home?'

She wanted to tell him to mind his own business, that he wasn't her father. He had no authority in this house. Her mother came into the kitchen and sat down. Antoine handed her a cup, which she took from him in silence. Her eyes were like two black holes and her clothes were the same things she'd been wearing for three days now. Aisha wanted to ask when she'd had a shower last but she couldn't talk to her mother, not when she was like this.

'Loubna would probably prefer it if you stayed home.'

'I seriously doubt that.' Aisha pulled up a chair and poured milk into a glass. 'Maman? She asked casually. 'You don't mind me going to school, do you?' Her mother stared blankly and Aisha raised her hands. 'See? She doesn't mind.'

Antoine shook his head. 'Let me drive you at least.'

'You're joking, right?'

'No. Have you been paying attention? Riots. People getting hurt. A policeman's a cripple now because of what's happened. So much violence. It's not safe on the street.'

'And you're going to protect me? Is that it?'

'There's no need to get angry. I care about you and your mother and I want you to be safe. I do what I can.'

Aisha lowered her eyes. 'Sorry.'

Aisha went to get her jacket. Antoine followed her into the hallway and put his hand on her arm. 'Just indulge me. Your mother's lost Samir. She couldn't cope with losing you as well.'

'Okay. But I need to leave in the next five minutes. I have a meeting with my philosophy teacher before class.'

'What for?'

'School project. I just need to talk to him about it.'

'Oh.' While Antoine got ready, Aisha texted Luc Clément.

Being dropped off at the school by family friend. Can't meet elsewhere.

Fine. Will find you when you get here.

She didn't want to meet him before class, it was too near the school and someone was bound to see them talking. But he knew something about Samir. Despite her best intentions, and everything she had told Karim, she had no clue how to proceed. Where did you start, and how did you ask the right questions so that people might give you the truth?

Five

'What is it? What did you want to tell me?'

They were too close to the school, but there was no time to go anywhere else. Luc Clément wished he'd never asked her to meet him. Now she was here he found he couldn't say what he wanted. Aisha stood with her arms wrapped around her shoulders, tense and unhappy. She was close, physically, but so inaccessible she might as well have been in a different country.

'How are you feeling?' he asked. A foolish question, but at least it made her look at him.

'I don't want to stand around here for too long. If someone sees us ...'

'Right, of course. Look, I don't know whether it's relevant, and I don't intend to say anything to the police when I talk to them today ...'

'You're talking to the police? Why?'

'They called. A Commandant Morel. He's coming to the school today. He wants to talk to me. I expect he's talking to Samir's teachers too.'

Aisha relaxed her stance a little. 'I know him.' She frowned. 'What does he want with you?'

Luc Clément stumbled over his words. 'I'm not sure. Maybe – my guess is they're talking to a lot of different people.'

'Why you, though?' Aisha insisted. 'You didn't even know Samir.'

'That's what I want to talk to you about. I've been meaning – I saw something, a couple of days before your brother was killed. Someone was talking to him...'

'Who? Was this at school?' She was listening but she was also distracted, on the look-out for people who might know them.

'Maybe we should talk another time,' he suggested. Her nervousness was beginning to rub off on him.

'Just say what you came to say.'

'Okay. A few days before your brother died, I saw him with the police. It was early, I was on my way in and it was dark. I was looking for a place to park and drove past them.'

'I don't understand. The *keufs* were talking to Samir? I know he'd been in trouble with them...'

'This was different. Samir and this policeman, they were sitting in the car – not a police car. The policeman was sitting in the driver's seat and Samir was in the passenger seat. I remember finding it strange. The two of them sitting there, smoking together. Relaxed, like two friends.'

'There's no way Samir was friends with a *keuf*. I don't understand. Why are you telling me this?'

'Because they're going to ask me if I knew Samir and if I know anything that might help the investigation, and I'll have to say –'

'Why?' The suddenness of Aisha's anger surprised them both. 'Why do you have to tell them anything? Why does that story matter?' She looked at him with something close to despair.

'I'm really sorry, Aisha. I'm not trying to make your life any more trying than it is now. Believe me, I wish I hadn't seen anything. I've spent a lot of time wondering what to do with this information. Until now, I've mostly been worried about you. How you're coping with all this.'

Aisha wasn't listening. Her mind was on what he'd seen. 'Wait. How do you know the other man was police? If it wasn't a police car.'

'Didn't I say? It was that detective. Marchal. The one from Villeneuve who was in charge of the investigation, before Morel took over.'

*

Vincent dropped his girls off at school and drove to the address Lila had passed on for Manon Volkoff, or Bijou, as she preferred to be called. The apartment was on Avenue Mozart, in the 16th *arrondissement*. He parked outside her building and looked up to see if there was any sign of life. According to Lila, Bijou lived on the third floor. Vincent turned the car heater up, delaying the moment when he would have to get out and face the cold. This morning, the girls had woken up earlier than usual and rushed out in their dressing-gowns to play in the snow. He'd been harsh with them, ordering them back inside to get dressed and eat their breakfast.

He wished now that he'd let them have their fun instead of being so uptight.

The building Bijou lived in was a grand affair. Her apartment would be worth millions, Vincent guessed. He didn't like this area. It was dull and exclusive, a *quartier* of little old ladies walking their expensive dogs and nannies shepherding children dressed in Bonpoint and Cacharel. At night, it was dead. Vincent thought about his two-bedroom flat in Rue Lepic, where the bustle and noise were incessant. Many of the *commercants* had lived and worked there for years. The Arab grocer, the Armenian florist; the Breton, who ran the bar downstairs and was emphysemic, but encouraged his customers to smoke, given he no longer could. They all knew Vincent by name. And he knew that this was what had kept him going, in the dark months following his wife's death. To be connected to life, whether you liked it or not. It was all around you, pulling you back from the abyss. He wouldn't swap his messy, chaotic pocket of the city for anything.

It was time to visit Bijou. Before getting out of the car, Vincent texted Morel to let him know where he was and that he would head into work straight after. A man walked past the car, carrying a briefcase. Outside Bijou's building, he punched in a four-digit code and pushed the *porte cochère*. Vincent hurried after him, reaching the door just before it closed again.

He waited in the stairwell, listening to the other man's steps on the stone tiles.

He made his way up, waiting for the sound of a door opening. Eventually, he heard it. The man had entered a flat on the third floor. Could it be Bijou's place? There were only two apartments on each floor. Vincent reached the landing and paused again, outside the flat he knew was hers. Apartment 6. He could hear voices inside. The woman's, shrill, and the man's, low at first, then rising until hers was drowned out. Vincent knocked, and the voices immediately stopped. No one came, so he knocked again. The door opened this time and Bijou appeared, teary and disheveled.

'Good morning, my name is Vincent Laborde, I'm with the *brigade criminelle*. You've met my colleague Lila. I wondered if I could come in?'

'Why? I've already told your colleague all I know.'

'What do you want?' The man had appeared behind her, and he looked like he was ready to slam the door shut. Vincent moved into the doorway to prevent that from happening.

'Your name, Monsieur?' he asked.

'Why should I tell you?'

'He's with the police,' Bijou said, looking anxiously from one to the other.

'If you're a friend, perhaps you'd like to accompany Madame down to the station,' Vincent told the man. 'We'd like to ask her a few questions, as part of a murder investigation.'

'A *friend*? I'm her husband.'

The man took a step forward. Vincent tensed. The two of them were unnaturally close to each other now. Was he going to have to get into a fight? What happened next took him by surprise. The other man shoved him onto the landing and stepped back into the apartment.

'Piss off,' he said, and slammed the door.

Vincent stared at the door in disbelief. He wanted to laugh, and also to pound at the door. 'I guess I'll be back with a locksmith,' he said loudly. 'And you'll be paying. Unless you open up right now. Either way, we're having a talk, you and I.'

Morel's meeting with Luc Clément, shortly after the start of the school day, was brief and illuminating. Now, he was impatient to get back to the *Crim'* and quiz Marchal. He had considered speaking with Marchal here in Villeneuve to save himself the trouble of driving back to Paris, but he felt it was important to talk to the other detective outside his territory. Here, Marchal was far too confident.

What the schoolteacher had told him cast a new light on the investigation. If what he described was true – Marchal and Samir together in an unmarked car, chatting and seemingly at ease with each other – then the relationship was not what Marchal had led Morel to believe it was. Neither was it how Thierry Villot had described it.

It wasn't confrontational. It was an alliance.

*

'Take a seat.'

Marchal smiled. 'That sounds serious. Should I be worried?'

'It depends.' In his mind, Morel was ticking off a long list of people he still needed to talk to. Karim Bensoussan. Ali and Réza. Yasmina, the girl Samir had been seeing. He'd tasked Akil and Jean with searching for the Roma who had left the camp. He had a feeling they would get nowhere and was cursing himself for not approaching Georghe's family earlier.

'Romain, I'm not in the best of moods,' he told Marchal. The detective didn't seem to like being addressed by his first name. Morel decided to keep it up. 'I've got a big day ahead of me, Romain. I'd like this interview to be productive.'

'Fine with me.' Lila stuck her head around the corner of the Chinese screen, which Morel used to separate his desk from the others in the room. Her hair was still wet from the pool and she was flushed. Morel suspected it had something to do with Akil. 'I got your message,' she said. 'Nice of you to send someone, but you could have just texted.' The tone was lost on Marchal, whose attention was focused on Morel.

'I hear the mayor's visiting the *cité* today.' Marchal cocked his head, amused. 'I hope she's not expecting flowers. She's not very popular around there.'

'It's probably good for her show her face. Part of the job description,' Morel replied. It annoyed him that Marchal knew about the mayoral visit and he didn't.

Marchal leaned back in his chair, crossed his legs, and examined his surroundings. 'You weren't kidding when you said this building needed work. Looks much better from the outside. But it's the Quai des Orfèvres, after all. Who cares if it's a bit shabby.' No one bothered to comment. Marchal seemed untroubled. He pointed to the window. 'The view's a bit more uplifting from where you sit, than back in Villeneuve. Mind if I smoke?' He pulled a packet of cigarettes from his jacket.

'Yes, we do mind,' Lila retorted. 'You can't smoke in the building. I'm pretty sure it must be the same in your building. All buildings.'

Marchal slid the cigarettes back in his pocket 'The rules are a bit different in Villeneuve. A lot of things are. Different, I mean.'

'Yeah, I know. People get killed more often.' Marchal and Lila held each other's gaze until Morel spoke.

'Romain. That day I came into the station and reported Samir was missing, why didn't you say you knew him?'

'Should I have? Why?'

'You deliberately pretended not to know who he was.'

'I didn't see how it was relevant, or any of your business at the time.'

'It's my business now.'

'Good for you. And good luck. You'll need it.'

'When did you last see Samir?'

Marchal stretched his legs and sighed. 'I don't remember. Some weeks ago. Yes, it must be three, four weeks ago.'

'Where was it?'

'What do you mean? At the station. I needed information. Samir worked for one of the dealers on the estate, someone we've had our eye on.'

'Who?' Ali?' Morel asked. Marchal raised an eyebrow. 'So you've met Ali.'

'Not yet. What exactly did Samir do for Ali?'

'Let's just say he was one of Ali's minions,' Marchal explained, doing his best to look bored. 'It's a rite of passage. The younger ones have to earn Ali's trust by running his errands, keeping a look-out when transactions are taking place. That sort of thing. I expect Samir was on a couple of hundred a day – my guess is he wasn't smart or ambitious enough to ask for more – but I've seen kids as young as 12 earning twice as much as that, doing the same sort of work. Earning in a week what I'd earn in a month. Easy money, right?'

'So easy he's now dead,' Lila interjected.

Marchal's expression darkened. 'It's a shame. But I'm not going to cry over a boy who was helping to sell drugs to his school mates.' He was trying too hard to sound like he didn't care, Morel thought.

'Tell us about the last time you saw him.'

'I'm happy to do that, but to be frank with you the last time I saw Samir was like so many other times he ended up with us at the station that I'm going to struggle to remember that particular encounter.'

'How about I help jog your memory,' Morel offered. 'I think the last time you saw the boy was when the two of you met up outside the station. This was about a week ago. You sat together in a car, not far from the school. What did you talk about?'

Marchal's expression didn't change. 'You seem to know a lot about it already. Why don't you tell me what we talked about.'

'Okay. I'll tell you what I think, Romain. Samir was there to deliver information. Willingly, of course. You two had an arrangement. What went on at the station – the way you treated him – was just for show. To make sure no one knew he was your informant.'

Marchal gave an impatient sigh. 'You've got it all wrong, Morel. I was doing the boy a favour. There were complaints about some of the boys on the estate slashing tyres, overturning bins. Keeping residents awake. I thought I'd have a quiet word with Samir. Bringing him in didn't seem to do much good. I thought I'd try something different. So I drove around to the estate and picked him up as he was heading to school.'

Morel considered this. It made no sense to him. 'Why would you do Samir any favours?' he asked.

Marchal shrugged. 'This is my job, Morel. I have to try to keep these kids out of trouble.' Seeing the look on Morel's face, he added, 'Look, I'll admit I also hoped to win him over. To get closer to Ali. But there was no arrangement between us.'

'Who filed the complaints?'

'We got a call. Many of the locals just want a peaceful existence. They get fed up with these kids. Some of them would probably like to take justice into their own hands. We try to discourage them.'

'So this particular time...' Morel prompted.

'I got an anonymous call. This guy, saying he would deal with these bastards himself if no one came and got them. His words, not mine. So I went to the estate and found Samir. We went for a drive.'

'Who initiated the acts of vandalism?' Morel asked.

'Who do you think? Samir. It wasn't the first time.'

'So let me get this straight.' Morel thought about what the schoolteacher had said and tried to reconcile it with this. 'The last time you saw Samir, you two had a nice chat. You tried to convince him to mend his ways, and to get him to talk to you about Ali. How did he respond?'

'As expected. I didn't get very far. And I wouldn't call it a nice chat, exactly. He wasn't a *nice* kid.'

'In what way?'

Marchal looked at his watch. 'In what way? Let me see. He was smug. Uncooperative. He seemed to think he was invincible. Above the law. He acted like nothing and no one mattered. Like the world had done him wrong and owed him, somehow.'

'It can't have been easy for him, living without a father. Growing up in that *cité*,' Lila said.

'He had a mother and sister who doted on him. A decent home. That fellow who's there a lot – what's his name? Carrère, right? Antoine Carrère. He took care of Samir too. Tried to be his friend. No, I won't feel sorry for the boy. He was a cocky little bastard.'

'Good riddance, then, I guess.'

253

Marchal remained unmoved. 'I told you. It's a shame. But trust me, that kid had trouble written all over him. You could see it.'

'What did you tell Samir, exactly?' Morel asked. 'That you could help him, if he helped you?'

'All I did was tell him he was making the wrong choices.' He looked from Morel to Lila, shaking his head. 'You're wasting your time talking to me. I've got nothing to do with what happened to the kid.'

Morel ignored Marchal comment, 'Earlier today, I asked you about your colleague Thierry Villot. How would you describe your relationship with Villot?

'How would I describe it? Well, I'd say we trust each other. You have to, in that environment. Have each other's back, I mean.' Marchal clapped his hands on his knees, as if to say the interview was over. 'Look, I need to get going. We're done, right?'

'Sure, you can go,' Morel said. Lila looked surprised. 'Oh, and one more thing: I'd like it if you emailed me any interview notes relating to Samir. Going back to the first time you detained him. When was that?'

'God knows. I'd say about a year, a year and a half ago,' Marchal replied. 'That's a big ask.'

'As soon as you can. I'd appreciate it.'

'Sure. It's your investigation now. And to be frank, I'm glad to be rid of it. Whatever you manage to find, no one's going to thank you for it.'

As soon as they'd seen him off, Lila exploded. 'Why the hell did we let him go? He didn't tell us a thing.'

'I didn't expect him to,' Morel said. 'And I don't think it would help to keep him here any longer. He isn't going to be more forthcoming.

But it did help to give me a better sense of things. I think Marchal was fixated on Samir, like Villot said. Trying to break him, by cajoling him one minute and bullying him the next. What I don't know is whether Samir talked. That's quite important. It gives us motive. If this dealer Ali thought Samir was talking to the police...'

'He'd hurt him.'

Morel sighed. 'Blatant lies, and half-truths,' he said quietly. 'That's all we've been getting.' He glanced at Lila. 'Marchal, Villot. They're lying through their teeth. Aisha and her family don't want to know or don't want to say what Samir was really about. No one in their building wants to reveal anything they might know. My guess is we probably won't have much luck with the Roma either.'

He grabbed his coat. 'Where are you going?' Lila asked.

'There's one person who hasn't deliberately evaded us. I'm going to see if I can get some answers.' Frustrated, she watched him leave.

'Well, are you coming?' he called out. He was already halfway down the stairs. Hurriedly, she threw her jacket on and followed him out the door.

Seven

Akil and Jean walked through the Roma encampment, looking for signs of life even though it was clear everyone had left. Jean peered into one of the homes. 'Jesus, take a look at this, Akil.' The younger detective stepped past Jean into a room – that's all it was, a single room, boarded up against the cold – that looked like it had been used as a rubbish tip. Nothing useful had been left behind. Daily necessities – clothes, kitchen utensils, linen – the Roma had taken it all with them.

'They sure know how to pack quickly.'

'They've had lots of practice. How's things with Lila?'

Akil grinned. 'I was wondering when that would come up. Let's just say things are … uneasy.'

'That's okay then. That's the sort of relationship she has with most people. You still keen on her?'

Akil laughed.

'Sorry, none of my business.'

'No it's not that. Just that it isn't as simple as all that, you know?'

'I do.' Jean took a tobacco pouch from his pocket and began rolling a cigarette. 'Believe me, I do.'

They walked over to the garage that stood next to the encampment. The fire trucks must have got here in time: somehow, the building had been spared.

Inside, a man was tidying up, filling a cardboard box with tools. Jean noticed that the place looked half empty.

'You're closing shop?'

'Without customers, there is no shop,' the man scratched at his stubble, seemingly unfazed by the appearance of two detectives in his garage.

'Everyone left pretty quickly,' Akil stated.

The garage owner looked at him carefully. 'When there is a big fire on your property, it is best to leave fast, no?'

'True. I can't argue against that. Do you know where they all went?'

'I don't know. You are the police, you can find.' When he spoke to Akil, his attitude became hostile. Jean stepped in.

'The people that lived in the camp, they were your customers?'

'Some. I am from Romania, they are also. We speak the same language. This is good for business.'

To Jean, it didn't look like business had ever been particularly good, but he kept quiet about it. 'I'm sure it helps,' he said instead. 'Why didn't you follow them?'

'They're leaving so quickly. One minute here, the next -' he made a sound to indicate they'd vanished into thin air. 'They are my customers. Not my family. Understand?'

'Without your customers, how do you plan to survive? Or is this home?'

The Romanian looked at Jean as if he'd said something strange. 'Home? I am leaving too now. What else can I do here?'

'Did you know the family of the boy who died? Georghe?'

'Yes. Of course. I know everyone in this place. Georghe's family too.'

'Any idea who hurt him?'

The man smiled, bearing a row of tobacco-stained teeth.

'What's funny?' Akil asked.

257

'This question. Is funny. Everyone knows who did this.'

'Why didn't anyone tell the police, if they knew?' Akil asked.

The man snorted, and turned to Jean. 'Your colleague, he is new? Or comedian, maybe. Maybe he is thinking we *gitans* can go to police station and everyone there is welcoming us with open arms and listening to our problems. Maybe giving us big hugs and thanking us for coming.'

'I understand what you're saying,' Jean replied, not giving Akil a chance to respond. 'But we are here to listen and we'll believe what you tell us. So tell us now if you know. Who did this to Georghe?'

'Why? What benefit to me?'

'You're leaving, right? Don't you want to help put Georghe's killer in jail? No one will know you talked to us. And we'll make sure that person doesn't get away with beating a 12-year-old boy to within an inch of his life, then leaving him to die in the freezing cold.'

It was the right choice of words. The man didn't hesitate for long. He made a sign to indicate something big, then flexed the muscle of his left arm.

'Big black man. I seen him before around here. He and his friends like to come and make trouble. He is telling the others what to do and they listen. He drives the car to come here and call Georghe out of his home. The friends watch this. They drag him into car and leave.'

'What kind of car?'

'I don't know. I was not there. My friend, he see everything.'

'Where's your friend?' Jean asked, knowing the answer. The Romanian made a gesture to indicate the man had vanished, along with the other Roma.

'That was the last time someone saw Georghe. Until the next time, when he is dead.'

'Any idea why they took him?'

'They call Georghe a thief. Say he take some stuff from them.'

'What stuff?'

'You think I know? I don't ask. I only know what I tell you.'

'If we bring you a photo, can you identify this man for us? The one who was the leader of the group?'

'Photo?' The man laughed. 'What for? I think you already know this man. No need for photo. Everyone on the estate knows him.'

'His name?'

'Big, black man,' the mechanic repeated, as if that were enough. As if a name was more than this person deserved. 'African. Drug dealer. Big, black bully. In my country, I and my friends, we take this man to an alley and we beat the shit out of him.'

There was a silence, during which the two detectives reflected on the Romanian's choice of words. The man, meanwhile, was looking at Akil as if he embodied all the problems of a multicultural world.

'Where will you go now?' Jean asked, keen to wrap things up.

'Somewhere.' The Romanian shrugged. 'Anywhere. Makes no difference.'

*

It took several minutes for Joao Figueras to open the door. Morel had expected him not to remember them, but he gave a big smile and gestured for them to enter.

'Nice to see you again,' he said. The television was on. Figueras went to turn it off. He sat down, expectant.

'What can I help you with?'

259

'Last time we were here,' Morel began, 'you mentioned someone who was there the night Samir died. It can't have been Samir because he was wearing jeans. You said it was someone wearing corduroy trousers and a red sweater...'

'I did?' Figueras seemed disconcerted. 'Who was it?'

'Well that's what I hoped we might be able to clear up today,' Morel said patiently, while Lila stared into the distance, looking like she was willing herself not to breathe. A single breath, and she was bound to start sneezing again.

'You said,' Morel continued, 'that this person lived in this building and now they were gone. What exactly –' He stopped suddenly, and swore.

'What?' Lila asked. '*What*?'

'Let's go,' Morel told her. He thanked Figueras, who asked whether they were here because of the songwriting contest. 'I'm afraid we're not. But you've been incredibly helpful. More than you know.' Morel shook his hand and steered Lila towards the door.

'Are you going to tell me what's going on?' she asked once they were back on the landing.

He started down the stairs and she followed. 'Well?'

'I think I know who was with Samir the night he died,' he said, keeping his voice low. 'The man Figueras saw when he was out walking his dog. Figueras didn't know him, not well. Not as the adult he is now. But his long-term memory is still sharp and when he saw the man, something jogged his memory and he remembered the child, who *once lived in this building*. Remember, he told us this was someone who lived here and then went away. That distant memory stayed with him somehow. When he was trying to tell us about Samir and the person he saw, he became confused and merged the present

260

with the past, telling us about his brother. What confused him among other things, was that this person did belong in his past.'

'Who are you talking about?' Lila asked, exasperated. By then they were in the hallway, on the ground floor.

'Thierry Villot,' Morel said. 'Thierry, who grew up right here, in the *cité*. That's who Figueras saw with Samir that night.'

*

The mayor stepped gingerly across the slippery surface in shoes that were wholly unsuited to the circumstances and to the weather conditions, followed by her press attaché and a bevy of reporters.

'You're sure this is a good idea?' Roland asked. He was like a faithful old dog, keeping close to her side. Always ready to listen, and offer advice, if she wanted it. He also knew how to keep quiet. It was comforting, in a sense, though she sometimes got the disagreeable impression that he stuck to her like this because he had nowhere else to be.

She hadn't intended to come here initially. When she'd decided, she'd told Roland to call the press. 'Last minute, I know. Do your best.', He knew her well enough not to question it. Besides, she wasn't in the mood for careful considerations. The time for all the usual bullshit – a communications plan, a risk analysis, some key messages and media prepping before going – had long since past. 'I have to be there. I'm the mayor, for fuck's sake.' She would not sit in her office doing nothing. The interior minister, the prosecutor, the reporters with their snarky questions. They all wanted something specific from her. Well they could all go to hell. This was her *cité*.

'Okay so I'm here now,' she told the people gathered around her, who'd left the warmth of their homes to hear her speak. Mostly these were the older residents, though she detected some of the younger people, keeping their distance, a few of them laughing at the sight of her and her entourage. But they were curious, or they wouldn't be here. There was no way of telling how they'd react to her and she felt some trepidation. She hadn't thought this through. For a start, she should have picked a subtler shade of lipstick, and more sensible shoes.

Two nights of rioting. That's all it was so far, but it felt like a lifetime. In total, 87 cars set alight, and the nearest welfare centre, three kilometres from the tower blocks, torched as well. A smashed ATM machine outside a BNP Paribas branch, around the corner from the police station. She hadn't slept much over the past 48 hours and as a result her surroundings took on a vaguely nightmarish quality, like one of those places you ended up in a dream, searching for a way out.

The Roma camp, reduced to ashes. They had left ahead of the flames. That was the one piece of good news. No casualties in that camp, and she couldn't help thinking that now Villeneuve was freed of one problem at least. Let another suburb deal with them.

'They're waiting to hear something from you.' said Roland, leaning towards her so that for a frightful second, she thought he might be about to kiss her. But she realized what he was saying. There was silence. She needed to seize the moment. She cleared her throat. 'I have no agenda. I'm not going to bore you with the same words and speeches you've heard a hundred times. What would be the point of that? When was the last time a politician dropped by to hear what you had to say? No, I'm not interested in making speeches. Instead, I'm going to listen.' The heckling started, but there were expectant faces too, waiting to see what might happen next.

Eight

The bell rang, announcing the end of the lunch break, and Aisha headed for her classroom, not making eye contact. It was easier to be here today, with so many people away. The hallways were unusually quiet. Many of the kids had seized the opportunity – two consecutive nights of rioting - to stay away. Aisha much preferred being here than at home with Antoine and her mother. But she was acutely conscious of being alone. She had only ever had a handful of good friends, but ever since Samir's death, even they seemed to be going out of their way to avoid her. As if death was contagious.

On her way to class, she ran into Karim. The look on his face when he realized it was her spoke volumes: he would rather be anywhere else right now than here with her.

'Karim! Why the hell aren't you responding to my texts? We need to talk. Have you found out anything?'

'Not yet.' He seemed nervous, his eyes darting about the corridor. 'What's going on?'

'Have you been talking to anyone?' he asked.

'I told you I was going to investigate. And guess what? I know who Samir was seeing,' she replied triumphantly. 'I've even met her.'

'Really?' For a moment, he seemed to forget how nervous he was. He looked impressed. 'Who is it?'

'A girl called Yasmina. She lives with her kid, and her brother, who knew she was seeing Samir. He beat her up for it. And he knew the whole time they were seeing each other. Imagine how angry he must have been with Samir.' Aisha hesitated, then dropped her voice to a whisper. 'I told the Paris detective. So he could check it out.'

'You're talking to the police?'

'Why wouldn't I? They're looking for the person who killed Samir. I have to talk to them, don't I? And another thing. Guess who else was there when Yasmina's brother beat her up?'

Karim looked like he didn't want to guess, or know, but Aisha pressed on.

'It was Réza,' she said, her voice dropping to a whisper. 'Réza was there. He wanted her punished for what she'd done.'

Before she knew what was happening, Karim had grabbed her arm and pulled her close, until his lips were right up against her ear.

'Are you out of your fucking mind? Do you want to end up like Samir, is that it?'

She wanted to reply, to tell him not to worry, but there was no time. A teacher opened a classroom door, spotted them, and gestured for them both to step closer. 'Monsieur Bensoussan, I'm sure you and Mademoiselle Kateb are having a delightful exchange but if you could grace us with your presence in the classroom, I'd be infinitely grateful. Now.'

'I'll catch you later,' Karim told Aisha.

She found her own classroom and sat at her desk, aware that heads had turned as soon as she walked in. Towards the back of the classroom where she sat, Katarina muttered something to her friends and they giggled in unison, casting glances her way, just to make sure she knew who they were talking about. There was no sign yet of Luc Clément. She concentrated on her textbook and thought about what he had told her outside the school earlier. She couldn't make any sense of it. What did it mean that her brother had sat in a car with that Marchal, talking like they were friends? If it was true, and she still found it hard to believe, then there could be nothing good about it. Maybe Luc Clément had misread the situation. Wasn't it more likely that the policeman had been trying to put pressure on her brother? Yes. That had to be it. But then what had Samir done, and said under pressure? She thought about Ali. Somehow, he was a part of all this. She needed to talk to him. Without Réza around. The thought of confronting Ali was frightening enough without adding Réza to the mix.

'Sorry I'm late.' Luc Clément dropped his satchel on his desk and grabbed a piece of chalk. He wrote "man is wolf to man" in large letters, then turned to face the classroom. He looked at everyone in turn, and when his gaze fell on Aisha, something passed between them. It was crystal clear, like the loudest of conversations, and Aisha felt the impact of it through her veins. Warmth, friendship. Love. She was thankful that no one seemed to notice.

'We are,' he articulated slowly and with a sweeping gesture across the room, 'primitive beings. We are selfish creatures, driven by emotion. Each and everyone of us is capable of violence.' Aisha thought about her brother and about the person who had planted a knife in his body, over and over again, and felt sick. 'But,' Luc Clément continued, 'we are also rational beings. With the ability to think and to learn. The ability to adapt. We have long understood the need for, and importance of, a social contract. This contract is what makes it possible for us to live together. It protects us, to some extent but not entirely, from misery. This is why laws are so important. When you break the contract, there is no order. Only chaos, fear, and isolation.'

The class listened. No one interrupted or dozed or looked elsewhere. It seemed that today, the teacher had everyone's attention.

Throughout Luc Clément's talk, he didn't once look at Aisha. But she had no doubt he was speaking to her. About Samir. She thought about the look he'd given her moments earlier. There had been nothing in it but kindness.

But all she could focus on right now was the impact of his words.

When you break the contract, there is no order. Only chaos, fear, and isolation.

*

The morning went by quickly. At recess, Aisha hung out in the courtyard with Mélodie, who had been distant lately but now was looking for someone to boast to about a guy she liked, who had invited her to stay with him in Paris for the weekend.

'He lives in the Opéra area, you know what I mean? Like, if you come out of the metro station and go down the boulevard, then take the second left. That's what he said. You should see his place, he showed me photos. From the balcony you can see the Galeries Lafayette. And he drives a Mercedes and runs his own business. Last year he went to the Maldives on holiday. He says he might take me there someday.'

Aisha's mind was on other things but she began listening, suddenly worried about what she was hearing. 'It sounds dodgy, Mélodie. How did you meet this guy? What's this business of his? At this, Mélodie started to look shifty. 'None of *your* business,' she said.

Aisha felt like reminding Mélodie about the girl from school whom they'd both known by name, even if they'd never spoken to her. She'd been sixteen years old and popular with the boys, but never interested in any of them. Then she'd gone with some guy from Paris who had a nice car and next thing everyone knew, she'd disappeared. Months later, someone had spotted her near the périph' at Porte de Clignancourt, standing on the side of the road all tarted up in high heels and a mini-skirt. Aisha had since spoken with her sister, who was a couple of years younger. She'd told Aisha once that her parents no longer talked about their eldest daughter. They acted as though she'd died.

At lunchtime, Aisha sat on her own. She kept hearing her name, spoken in whispers, and catching people looking her way, but maybe they weren't, maybe she was being paranoid. Halfway through the lunch break, Virginie, the counsellor, came looking for her. 'I thought we were catching up today?' she said. Aisha replied that she would rather meet another time and Virginie smiled as if to say it was okay, but her face told a different story. Aisha hated the way she did that, managed to make you feel guilty while pretending to be stoic about it.

She'd done her best to avoid Katarina but when it was time to head home, the hyenas were right there, keeping pace with Aisha on the other side of the road like they normally did.

'Hey, *bougnoule*,' Katarina called out. 'What's with the modern clothes? Shouldn't you be wearing that thing, you know, the potato sack thing your Mum wears? Those are some flattering clothes. I bet you look real nice wearing a potato sack.' The other girls burst out laughing at that.

Seriously? Even knowing Katarina was a bitch, Aisha couldn't believe she was doing this, so soon after Samir's death.

'Knock yourself out, Katarina,' she said. 'Do your worst. I really don't care.'

'You think I care?' Katarina replied feebly.

'I think you care more than I do. I'm not the one following you around. That's you. Tagging after me. You're pretty persistent, for someone who doesn't care.'

Aisha thought she heard the hyenas collectively draw in their breath, shocked at her boldness. She found herself smiling. For the first time, she wasn't afraid. What could Katarina possibly do to hurt her more than she was already? She'd lost her brother. There was nothing that girl could take from her now that mattered.

For a while, there were no more taunts. Katarina and her friends continued walking across the road, keeping pace with Aisha. After a few moments, the abuse started again, and the stupid giggling from the other girls. The gang crossed the road and ended up in front of her, walking backwards so they were facing her. Aisha kept her eyes firmly on the ground. No matter what, she told herself, she wouldn't ever give Katarina the satisfaction again of thinking she had the advantage.

They were close to the estate when Katarina moved closer, forcing her to stop.

'Aisha,' she said. Her voice was soft and quiet, as if she was about to tell Aisha something nice or secret, something just for her. 'I've been meaning to say this. I mean, he was your brother and all that. I wouldn't have picked it.'

Such cold, blue eyes. Aisha found she couldn't look away. 'I mean, he was so persistent it was kind of annoying. He sure didn't get what "no" meant. In the end I had to give in.'

It felt like everything had gone quiet all of a sudden. Where were Katarina's friends? Was anyone laughing? What were they doing? All Aisha knew was Katarina's face, so close she could see every detail. The pimples, the cold sore on her lip, the studs in her ears. Her cold blue stare. She didn't believe what she was hearing for a second, and yet the strange part was that, at the same time, she did. There was no contradiction there. She didn't believe it, but she knew. Had known for a long time, somehow, but refused to make it real by ever saying it.

The anger was like a wave of nausea. It churned inside her, rising fast, and she couldn't do anything to hold it down. The blood was pounding in her head and when she opened her mouth to speak it was as though all the saliva had gone from her mouth. It was an effort to get the words out.

'What did you say?'

'Your brother. Samir. He didn't take no for an answer. So in the end I had to give in. Turns out he was worth it. With those lips, I should have known he'd be the best kisser in the school.'

'You're a fucking liar,' Aisha said, and without a moment's thought she threw herself at Katarina and was tearing at her hair, and Katarina was shouting abuse at her, trying to shove her off and get away. But Aisha knew that nothing on earth would make her let go and she kept tearing, and punching, with every ounce of strength in her body. Katarina flailed and kicked and eventually managed to free one hand. She pinched her arm so hard Aisha cried out. With her hand in Katarina's hair, Aisha pulled the other girl's head close to hers and sank her teeth into her cheek. She tasted blood and heard someone scream, a high-pitched sound that didn't sound quite human, before a pair of strong arms grabbed her from behind and pulled her away.

Nine

Morel and Lila drove to Thierry Villot's house. They knocked and looked through the windows to see if he was home. There was no sign of life. Morel tried Villot's mobile number. The call went straight to voicemail. He called the Villeneuve police station. The receptionist told him Villot had called in sick again.

'What now? Any idea where he might be?' Lila asked.

'Maybe he's just stepped out for a while.'

Morel's mobile rang. It was Jean, calling to let him know about the Roma camp and what the garage owner had said. 'Sounds like Ali is our guy. He killed Georghe.'

'Well done. We've had a bit of a breakthrough as well,' Morel said. He briefed Jean on Thierry Villot. 'I think he was there when Samir died.'

'You think he killed him?'

'If he did, I don't yet know why. All I know is that we need to find him. Quickly.'

Morel tried to think where he might look for Villot. Maybe he'd gone out for groceries and would be back home soon. Or maybe he'd gone away. It was hard to make sense of any of this. If Villot was the killer, what was his motive?

'Shall we bring Ali in?' Jean asked.

'Yes, but we'll have to do this together. It isn't going to be easy.' He suggested that the four of them meet up outside the tower blocks. 'We'll head there now.'

*

Vincent had persuaded Bijou's husband to open the door – it was either that or letting a police officer bang on your door until every one in the building knew your business – and he was sitting in their living-room now, drinking a cup of bitter coffee that the man had offered in a chastened manner, as if he realized now how inappropriate his behaviour had been.

He had calmed right down and was eager to clear things up, he said.

He'd introduced himself as Gérard. Sitting close to his wife, with his arm around her waist, he explained that he was just back from an overseas trip to Singapore.

'These past months have been hell,' he said. 'That bastard Simic. He's been harassing Bijou with calls and texts, begging to see her. He's out of his mind.'

'You and Bijou met Simic and his wife at the club?'

Gérard nodded. 'It was all just a bit of fun. We met three or four times. Valérie is an amazing woman. She was completely wasted on that guy.'

'Right.' Vincent glanced at Bijou. What was she thinking? She was staring at him with pleading eyes, and Vincent realized she was only worried that she'd be found out. Clearly, Gérard had no idea that Bijou and Simic had been secretly involved with each other, that she had fallen in love with the tennis player and that he – if one were to believe Bijou – was planning to leave his wife for her. Vincent gave her a reassuring look. There was nothing to be gained from telling Gérard.

'Gérard, can you tell me where you were on the night of December 28th?' Vincent asked.

'Absolutely. I was in Singapore.' He planted a kiss on Bijou's cheek. 'Missing my wife. Thinking about what I had to look forward to, when I returned.'

271

Vincent left the couple half an hour later, got back into his car and looked up Valérie Simic's address. As he started the engine, he thought to himself that his conversation with the widow would be a lot more difficult than the one he'd just had.

*

It wasn't difficult to find Ali. Alberto Rosales had already pointed Morel in his direction. Rosales and Ali were neighbours. Morel, Jean, Akil and Lila climbed the stairs, Jean and Lila complaining most of the way about the lifts not working. As they got closer to Ali's flat, the sound of pounding rap music grew louder. They knocked and waited for what seemed like a very long time. When he finally opened the door, Lila stepped past him without waiting to be let in.

'Might be a good idea to turn that down a notch or two,' she said.

Ali gave a slow, exaggerated nod, as if he was pondering her comment. 'But then it wouldn't be as enjoyable.' He was wearing grey track pants, a black hoodie with the words New York City written across it, and a pair of red Nike trainers. He opened the door wide. 'Come on in. The rest of you, I mean. I was on my way out, but I can spare a minute.'

Morel led the way, and was relieved to see that there was no one else. Ali fell back on a large leather sofa and lit a cigarette. The music, deafening now, came from two enormous speakers positioned at opposing ends of the room. The windows were shut, making the room stuffy. The air reeked of stale cigarettes, and something else. Marijuana, Morel guessed.

'Your neighbour likes rap music?' Lila asked, moving across to the monster hi-fi system and turning the volume down.

'I guess so. I never asked.'

'I figured you hadn't.'

Ali grinned. 'This is seriously good music. All I'm doing is giving El Chino some musical education.' He cocked his head. 'I heard Villeneuve *keufs* aren't investigating this anymore. What happened? Too crooked, I bet.'

'Why would you say that?' Morel asked.

'No reason. Just messing with you. The truth is they're too incompetent, right? This is too big for them.'

'It's just the way these things work out sometimes,' Morel replied. There was a great deal of hostility in the room, though Ali was trying his best to appear relaxed and amiable. 'They've got a lot on their hands as it is.'

Ali turned to Lila and grinned. 'One thing's for sure, I didn't know they hired chicks like you in the police force. There's no one as pretty as you working in our sector, I can tell you that.'

Morel cut in before things got messy. 'You know why we're here?'

'Yeah. You're here about Samir. Poor kid. He was smart, the girls liked him. He had potential, know what I'm saying? You found who did this to him yet?'

'And Georghe.'

'Who?'

'The Roma kid you beat up.'

'I have no idea what you're talking about.'

'That's funny, because we heard something different. Word is you're the king of the estate. You know everything that happens here.'

'That's right,' Ali replied smugly. 'I know everyone's story. Everyone that's from here. Information is gold. I guess in your line of work you know that.'

273

'I couldn't agree more,' Morel went over to the stereo and turned the power off. 'Ali Kalonga, I am placing you under arrest for the attack on Georghe Laieshi that led to his death. All going well, you'll be charged and tried for manslaughter.'

Ali burst out laughing. 'You're kidding, right? This is bullshit. You're arresting me?'

'Get up.'

'Fuck you.'

Jean and Akil moved to grab him, but Ali pushed them away and stood up, glaring at Morel.

'You're making a mistake.'

Akil moved fast, throwing Ali against the sofa, his foot knocking the table over. He was smaller and lighter than their suspect but quick, ducking in time when Ali tried to punch him, and kneeing him in the groin. Ali roared and lunged at the detective, and they both landed on the table, this time shattering the glass. It took the three men – Jean, Akil and Morel, to finally pin Ali down. He lay on the ground, his head turned sideways to avoid the broken glass spread across the carpet, his face purple with anger.

Akil stood up, panting. Blood poured from his cheek, where the glass had cut it.

'Here,' Lila said, handing him a packet of tissues from her pocket. 'You okay?' He nodded, and she gave him a tense smile.

'You think you're going to walk out of this building with me and people are just going to let you go? You're fucking nuts. You're -' Lila leaned over and cuffed him.

'Shut the fuck up.'

*

274

'So, tell me about Georghe,' Morel asked Ali. They had taken him to the Quai des Orfèvres, after a rapid departure from Villeneuve. Lila had gone to start the car and driven it right up to the tower block, and the three men had shoved Ali in, while he kicked up a fuss. They'd sped away with a dozen youths sprinting in their direction, shouting obscenities and threatening to kill them.

'What did you and your friends have against the Roma kid, Ali?' Morel's tone was calm, focused, but he was distracted. What was it Ali had said? *I know everyone's story. Everyone that's from here. Information is gold.* How well, Morel wondered, did Ali know Thierry Villot? If he could just talk to Villot, it would make things easier. He had sent Akil and Jean out to look for him. Perhaps they'd found him at home and were bringing him in now.

'I've been hearing things,' Morel told Ali. 'I heard Georghe was a thief. He would come into the *cité* regularly, and break into people's homes when he knew they were out. I guess that's how he ended up breaking into your place,' Morel said. He was making a wild guess, hoping he was right. 'Georghe probably waited to make sure you were out, then broke in and helped himself to what he wanted. Poor kid probably didn't realize who you were and bit off more than he could chew. Have I got this right? Yes, I have. I can see it in your eyes.' Morel stood up, apparently deep in thought. The only other person there was Lila, and she was keeping quiet. 'What I'm wondering, Ali, is what he took from you? It must have been something very valuable, for you to get so upset about it.'

Ali didn't respond, just sat back with one hand spread on Morel's desk. The other was handcuffed to the chair. Morel wasn't taking any chances.

'It must have been something very valuable,' Morel repeated. 'For you to get so worked up. For you to lose control, and all of you to gang up like that on someone half your size. Surely a big, important guy like you wouldn't pick on someone so insignificant, so weak. I mean, it would belittle you, wouldn't it? It would be demeaning. I expect that's not normally your style.'

'Exactly. You got that right. It's not my style.'

'Well, that's why I'm wondering what set you off. What made you behave like that? You dragged a kid from his home, in plain sight of his family, his community – and then you took him away with your friends and all took turns beating the shit out of him. And then, to top it all off, you dumped him in a shopping trolley -' Morel paused, imagining the scene '- and left him to die. Think what he went through. A 12-year-old kid. Alone, hurting, terrified. Slowly freezing to death. In that wasteland.'

'You've got no proof.'

'We'll get there, Ali,' Morel said mildly. 'Which takes us to Samir. I've been trying to figure it out. Why Samir was killed. And you know what I think? I think he had proof. He was there all that time you were giving Georghe a thrashing. Maybe he couldn't stomach what he saw. Did you worry he might tell someone about it? Is that why you killed him too?'

'What? You're accusing me of that too? That's funny.'

They watched him laugh, his eyes burning with anger. After a while, he stopped, and leaned forward.

'I'll tell you something.' Spit flew from his mouth when he spoke, and his eyes were full of hate. 'You talk about those gypsies like they're ordinary people. You talk about family, community. None of that means anything to them. They're scum. They have no values.'

'Are you done with your little speech?' Lila asked.

'Oh, I'm done alright. I'm not saying another word. Get me a lawyer. Now.'

It was Antoine who fetched Aisha from the street. Katarina's father arrived around the same time, a big, angry man who shouted abuse at Aisha until Luc Clément told him he needed to pull himself together and drive his daughter to the hospital, so she could get her face seen to.

'She's going to need stitches. Her face will never be the same,' the man wailed.

'It can't get any uglier than it was before,' Aisha murmured, as Katarina's father took her away. Luc Clément told her to stop. 'Enough. It's gone too far already,' he said quietly.

'She said she and Samir got together. That he fancied her. She's lying, he could never like a girl like that.'

'Aisha. He was a 16-year-old boy. At that age, most boys aren't too picky.'

'Samir wasn't most boys.' Aisha dropped her head in her hands. 'You have no idea what she's done to me over these past months.' Luc Clément reached out and placed his arm around her shoulder.

'What? What has that girl done to you? What's going on?' Antoine asked. He looked completely lost.

'You need to get Aisha home,' Luc Clément told him. To her, he said, 'Go, get some rest. We'll talk about this in the morning, at school.'

'Am I in trouble?'

'You shouldn't have attacked her like that. You saw the state her father was in. But I don't want you to worry about it for now. We'll deal with it tomorrow.'

She turned to him, as if something had just occurred to her.

'What were you doing here anyway? Were you following me?'

He looked mildly embarrassed.

'I was worried about you,' he said.

*

'I had no idea what you put up with. I'm sorry.' Antoine perched on the edge of her bed, cradling a cup of coffee.

'Is that for me?' she asked. Only then did Antoine seem to realize he was holding it, and he handed it over, pleased to be doing something for her.

'Two sugars, the way you like it.'

'Thanks, Antoine.'

She sipped her coffee while he waited, neither of them knowing what to say. Her mother had fallen asleep on the couch again, watching one of her shows.

She'd come in here to try to calm down, to think about what Katrina had said. Though he was being kind, she didn't really want Antoine sitting there, looking to connect with her.

'I need to take a nap, I think,' she said, hoping he'd take the hint.

'I want to help.'

'How do you think you're going to help?' She couldn't help herself. 'To be honest, it makes things worse, having you take me to school and hang around. It's hard enough, being Samir's sister, without drawing even more attention to myself by having you shadow me.'

'I'm not trying to make things worse. I only want to help. What you and your mother are going through, I can't imagine. And you know I cared about Samir.'

'I know.'

Antoine stood up. He looked fretful. 'It's not right, the way those girls bully you.'

'It's not *right*? Oh well, I guess we should just tell them that then.'

She could see she'd offended him but she wanted him to leave her alone.

'It's not right,' he repeated. 'Particularly since she was a friend of Samir's.'

'Why would you say that?'

Antoine looked surprised. 'I've seen that girl with your brother, once or twice. No? Maybe I'm mistaken,' he said, clearly regretting saying anything.

'Sorry Aisha, I must be confused.' He'd seen the look on her face and was back-pedalling now, realizing he should have kept his mouth shut. 'I might have just seen her around here. Sorry.'

Stop saying sorry, she thought. Sorry doesn't change a thing.

*

Karim took the RER to Châtelet station and changed trains. He got out at Cité and walked the rest of the way, checking the map on his phone to make sure he was going in the right direction. As he neared the Quai des Orfèvres, it began to rain and he pulled his leather jacket up around his ears. The snow had melted over the past 24 hours. But the rain trickled down his back and got into his shoes – good, expensive shoes, but the soles were worn – and he was frozen to the bone. The street was busy and he felt people's eyes on him. His arm hung at an awkward angle, hiding the spot where the jacket was torn.

Outside the building, he hesitated, awed by its size and by the number of police vans parked outside. His first instinct was to turn around and get away, but the thought of Aisha spurred him on. He crossed the road and went inside. An officious-looking man stood behind a desk. He looked at Karim with a blank expression on his face.

'Can I help you?' He was clean-shaven, courteous, and Karim felt ashamed without quite knowing why.

'I'm here to see someone,' he said. Without thinking, he'd changed the accent, trying to distance himself from his *banlieue* origins. 'Commandant Serge Morel.'

'Is he expecting you?' the officer asked.

'No. But tell him Samir's friend is here,' Karim said, straightening his shoulders. 'He'll want to see me I'm sure.'

*

'Your name's Karim Bensoussan?' Akil checked him out quietly. He was a pretty sort of boy. Dark eyes, long lashes. Designer clothes. That jacket must have cost a lot of money. Vain, by the looks of it. Scared, too. Akil noted the rip in the jacket, the water-logged shoes and felt a wave of pity for the young man. 'You're here to tell us something about Samir?'

'It's Commandant Serge Morel I've come to see.'

'He'll be here shortly. Take a seat.'

Karim examined his surroundings – Akil had invited him to sit in Lila's chair – but remained standing. 'Relax, man. Take a seat.'

'Will he be long?'

'It depends.' Akil crossed his arms. 'He's been talking to one of your friends. Ali.'

'Ali's here?'

'We arrested him a little while ago. He put up quite a fight.'

'I'm not surprised,' Karim said, forgetting himself. He couldn't believe they'd managed to bring Ali in. He also didn't want to run into him. 'Where is Ali? He can't know that I'm here.'

'He won't.'

It was Karim's turn to check Akil out now. He narrowed his eyes. 'You're Arab?'

Akil nodded. 'Moroccan.'

'And you're a *keuf*.'

'I am.'

'How did that happen?'

'You think Arabs can't be cops?'

'Not where I come from. There aren't any Arab police in Villeneuve.'

'Maybe you could train to become one. Be the first Arab police in your neighbourhood.'

Karim burst out laughing, and Akil joined in. 'Good one,' Karim said.

'What is it you want to talk to Morel about? Is it about your friend Ali?'

'He's not my friend.'

'What is he then? Your boss?'

Karim's face became surly, closed.

'I heard Samir was a good friend. You must be pretty upset.' Akil looked towards the door. 'Here's Morel.'

*

It was getting late, and Karim was still talking. Jean and Vincent had left. Morel, Lila and Akil listened. No one moved, except Akil once, to turn on the lights.

'Ali. He made us stay and watch. I didn't touch the kid, I swear. But I was there. Me and Samir and Réza.'

'What did he have against the boy?' Morel asked.

'He sneaked into Ali's place and took a bag of dope. A delivery Ali had been waiting on, for two weeks. Worth thousands.' Karim shivered. 'He said he was going to bash the boy up. He really went for it. And I didn't have the guts to do anything about it, or even to walk away. Mainly because of Réza. He would never have let me go.'

'Réza. Ali's right-hand man. Right?' Morel turned to Karim for confirmation.

Karim nodded, and ran his hand through his hair, looking like he'd just signed his life away.

'Was Samir there?' Akil asked.

'He was there, at first. He couldn't take it. Ali got angry with him but Samir walked away all the same.'

'Did Ali kill him too?' Akil asked.

'I don't know, I swear I don't.' Karim gave Morel a pleading look.

'Do you think he did it?'

'No. I don't know. Maybe.'

Akil drew his chair closer to Karim.

'Why are you telling us all of this? I don't get it. Snitching on your friends. Why now?'

'I'm not a snitch,' Karim said angrily.

'What do you call this, then? Sorry,' Akil said, seeing the look on Morel's face. 'But I don't get it. Why is he here? What's his agenda?'

'Karim?' At the sound of Morel's voice, Karim let out a big sigh that sent a tremor through his body.

'You need to look after Aisha. She's not safe.'

'Why?'

'She told me she would find out herself who'd killed Samir. I think she's going to get herself hurt.'

'Is that why you're here? Because you're worried about her?' Karim nodded. 'So where is she now?'

'I don't know. She could be at home. I think maybe she went to look for Ali.'

'Ali's in custody.'

'It's not just him that can hurt her. Réza...' Karim didn't finish his sentence.

'What do you think?' Lila asked Morel. 'Should we go see Aisha?'

'Let's try calling her.' Morel turned to Karim. 'Thierry Villot, the Villeneuve *flic*. He came to see you not long before Samir was killed. What for?'

'He was looking for Samir. He was worried about him.'

'Why was he worried?'

'He thought the other *keuf* – Marchal, you know the guy I mean? The guy who was running the investigation before you took over – he thought Marchal was giving Samir a hard time.'

'I see.' Morel thought about what Karim was telling him. What was he missing?

'Does Ali know Thierry Villot?' he asked. Karim looked puzzled. Before he could reply, Morel's phone rang and he stepped away to take the call. They all waited in silence for him to finish. When he returned, Lila was the first to notice the change.

'What is it?' she asked.

'Something's happened. I have to go.'

'Are you coming back?'

'I don't know.'

Lila had never seen him so uncertain. 'We can do this without you,' she said.

'Okay.' He considered what should happen next. 'The first thing is to find Réza and bring him in. Find Aisha and get her home if she isn't already there. Make sure you and Akil keep in touch. And be careful. I don't know what it'll be like in Villeneuve tonight. I want you both to stay safe. I'll be there as soon as I can.' To Karim, he said, 'is there anyone you need to call, to let them know you're here? Your mother?'

'What the hell am I supposed to tell her?'

'Tell her the truth.'

'You're joking, right? She'll kill me. Chop me up into little pieces.'

'Karim, look at me.' The boy looked up, reluctantly. 'What that child Georghe went through was terrible. You did something right, by coming to tell us. But you were still there. It's not going away just because you decided to tell us the truth. Do you understand?'

Eleven

The traffic was slow but not as bad as it would have been in the earlier part of the evening, when commuters were heading home. By now, most people would be sitting down to dinner. Morel reached Neuilly in record time and parked behind his sisters' cars. There was hardly any snow left on the ground, and it was raining again, a light, cold drizzle that inched into his collar as he strode across the courtyard towards the well-lit house.

It was the first time in over a year that the three siblings were in the same room together. Adèle and Maly interrupted their conversation the moment Morel entered the living-room. He sensed they'd been arguing and that he was the reason for it.

'About bloody time,' Adèle said.

'Please, Adèle…' Maly turned to her brother. 'Thanks for getting here so quickly.'

'How long has he been gone?'

'Augustine noticed an hour ago. She called all of us -'

'And Maly and I got here straight away but of course you weren't answering the phone,' Adèle cut in. 'More important things to do, I guess.' Morel had noticed the missed calls when he'd answered her call earlier. 'I'm sorry,' he said now.

Augustine came in from the kitchen, crying. Morel went over and put his arm around her. 'It's not your fault.'

'I was getting dinner ready. I thought he was upstairs, resting.' She spoke in a rush. 'Earlier, your father tried to run a bath and left the water running till it overflowed. He flooded the bathroom. I told him it wasn't a big deal but he was a bit upset I think. He told me then that he needed a rest. He must have slipped out quietly. He was in his pajamas when he went to bed. What if he didn't put anything else on before he went out? It's freezing out there.'

'Where's Descartes?'

'That's the thing. He must have taken the dog with him. The leash is gone. It was hanging on the hook, near the front door, where I usually leave it.'

'Well that's probably a good thing. It's hard to miss an old man wandering the streets in his pajamas, with a giant dog. We'll find him in no time,' Morel said, trying his best to sound reassuring.

'What are you going to do?' Maly asked, and he realized they were all relying on him, waiting for him to come up with a plan.

'I'll put a call in to the Neuilly police station. And I'm going to look for him. I don't think he can be very far.'

'Maybe we could make a list of places he's likely to remember,' Maly suggested. 'We can split up the search between the three of us. Augustine, you should stay here, in case he gets home on his own.'

*

It was Morel who found his father half an hour later, sitting in a bar on the Avenue de Neuilly. A couple of hundred metres from home. Morel had spotted Descartes outside, looking stoic. He wasn't tied up and there was no sign of a leash. He just sat with his eyes trained towards the bar where Philippe was. The dog had clearly decided to stay put until the old man decided it was time to go home.

'Good boy,' Morel said, stroking Descartes' head.

He called Maly, letting her know where he was, then went inside. When he drew nearer, his father turned and saw him. There was no hesitation in his greeting, and Morel felt hugely relieved, because he'd wondered whether his father would recognize him. His father had wandered out of the house like this only once before, and that

287

was a few years ago now. It still seemed untypical of him to wander off like this – though there was no sense in looking for typical anymore – and Morel had braced himself for the worst when he'd walked in.

'We've been looking for you,' he told his father with a smile.

'You have? Why? Has something happened?'

'No, nothing at all. But I'm glad I found you.'

'I was taking a stroll,' Morel senior said. 'And then I came here.' His expression as he looked at Morel was uncertain.

Morel stole a glance at his father's outfit. Philippe Morel looked just like any other customer, except for the fact that beneath his coat he was wearing pajamas and slippers. At least he'd thought to put the coat on.

'Can I get you something?' The waiter surveyed the pair of them, but didn't blink, as if he'd seen it all before, even here in Neuilly. Perhaps in a suburb like this one, where so many were elderly, this wasn't such an unusual sight.

Morel ordered a glass of wine to keep his father company. When the waiter was gone, he picked up a napkin lying on the table and started folding it, just so he had something to do with his hands. You couldn't make anything with it, of course. But Morel couldn't think of what to say. He pictured the snowflakes hanging from his window, the last thing he'd made several months ago, and now found himself yearning for a few hours' solitude, his desk and a stack of foldable paper.

'What are you doing with that napkin?' his father asked, and Morel shook his head.

'Nothing.' He dropped it back on the table.

'You're still making those things? With the paper? What's it called, again? There is a name for it,' Philippe Morel said irritably.

'Origami. I am, generally speaking, but it's been a little while. Lately I haven't felt like it. I'm not sure why that is. I haven't felt like it and yet I miss it.' Morel was rambling. His father had never asked or commented before about the origami.

'You've always had a knack for it.' His father's smile was hollow, inward-looking. He was busy remembering a distant time that was sharper in his mind right now than anything that had happened to him in the past hour.

'I bought you an origami book. When you were a kid. You should have seen your face. I've never seen a child so happy. After that we could barely get a word out of you. For weeks.' He sat back, looking pleased with himself.

'I remember it well. It was in Brittany. I loved that book. It was the best present I ever got,' Morel offered.

His father looked away. 'It was your mother's idea. You know how she was. Always thoughtful when it came to gifts.'

Morel waited for more. His father's hand crept across the table, until it found the paper napkin. He scrunched it up and threw it on the ground, then looked around the room, clearly confused.

'Let's go home, Papa.'

'Okay.'

Morel paid for the wine and they headed out together, into the cold night. Outside the bar, his father paused, unsure where to go. Morel slid his arm through his father's.

'Let's walk back together.'

'There's no need, I can find my own way,' Philippe replied testily.

'It's fine. I'm heading home too. We live together, remember?'

289

His father seemed puzzled, then vaguely pleased. 'In that case... so this means you'll be staying a while?'

Morel thought about Akil and Lila, on their way to Villeneuve. He thought about Aisha Ketab. She wasn't answering her phone. Where was she? He hoped she was safe. If she was hurt in any way, he would blame himself. He texted Lila. *Let me know as soon as you have news.*

What should he do? Drop his father at home and leave straight away? He needed to find Thierry Villot. The man owed him some answers. And if he could just have a couple more hours with Karim, Ali, Thierry Villot, and Réza, once they tracked him down, he'd figure it all out. Morel was sure of it. Absently, he reached for his father's arm, and was surprised when the old man gripped his hand. As if he were afraid Morel would take his away.

Philippe's grip was surprisingly strong. Morel thought of the past months and all the time he'd spent avoiding his father. It was painfully clear to him that he'd refused to see what was happening before his eyes, because it meant altering the way things had always been between the two of them.

'Yes. I'll stay a while.'

A look of relief washed over his father's face. 'Good. That's good.'

*

Lila and Akil bickered for several minutes about who should drive and, in the end, Akil won. He drove fast, with both hands on the wheel, hunched forwards. Lila had often joked he sat in the driver's seat like an old man, his nose practically against the windscreen.

'That Aisha,' Lila said. 'She's an interesting girl. Too smart for her own good, I reckon.'

'Let's hope she hasn't got herself into trouble.'

'She's a fool for wandering around the estate running her own murder investigation.'

Akil stared out the windscreen at the périphérique. It was starting to snow. He turned the window-wipers on, and the radio.

'If it's anything like last night in Villeneuve...' he said, without finishing his sentence.

They sat quietly for a while, waiting for the news. Akil turned to observe Lila. She continued to stare straight ahead, acutely aware of his gaze. It was a relief when he turned away.

'Poor kid,' Akil said after a while.

'Aisha? Yeah. Losing her brother like that. Must be tough.'

'I was thinking of Karim.'

'Why? He watched the Roma boy get beaten up. I don't feel so sorry for him. Why are you saying that?'

'Because he's in love with a girl who probably doesn't feel the same way about him.'

'Aisha?'

'Yeah.'

After that, neither one of them said another word.

Twelve

Aisha had to make sure everyone was asleep before she could do what she wanted. Her mother had just gone to bed, and hugged her daughter on the way, making Aisha's eyes water. Antoine, wrapped in Samir's duvet on the living-room couch, was fighting to stay awake. Tonight, he seemed scared. So did Eloise. Aisha had called her earlier, to hear a friendly voice.

'I haven't left the house for two days, because of what's been happening at night,' Eloise said, a note of hysteria in her voice. 'I know it might be okay during the day, but I don't feel safe. Not even then. I'm not sleeping. I can't take this anymore. How long is it going to last?'

Like everyone else, she was worried because of what had happened to the policeman. They were saying on TV that he was lucky to be alive. But it was also clear now that he was going to be in a wheelchair for life. Paralysed from the neck down. It didn't sound that lucky to Aisha.

'If they can't find the guy who did this to him, they'll take it out on all of us,' Eloise said. She'd spent the day on the phone, talking to friends. 'Everyone talked about Samir. How sad it was,' she told Aisha.

While she waited to make sure Antoine was properly asleep, Aisha thought about what Eloise had said. It was true there'd been a lot of support for Samir, from the community. All those people on the street, protesting these past nights. On TV, they were saying the riots were an excuse for violence, or they were a consequence of the way people in the banlieue had been marginalized for so long. Depending on who spoke on TV, it was either a social issue or a race issue.

292

Maybe, Aisha thought. But she saw something else. The rioters had painted Samir's name on the *cité* walls and chanted his name. Surely, that meant something.

And it wasn't just the other Arabs who cared. It had nothing to do with that. Eloise had cried when she first heard. She'd dropped by with a cooked meal and sat with Aisha's mother. El Chino was clearly heartbroken. No matter how angry she was with him, Aisha knew the Spaniard had loved her brother.

Even Ali had dropped by to offer his condolences. Though what that meant, she didn't know.

At the thought of Ali, Aisha tensed. Tonight, she would get some answers.

Outside, there were shouts, isolated flares. Nothing more. The police were outside the tower blocks, waiting. Same scenario as the night before.

Antoine was snoring. Aisha got up quietly and slipped into Samir's room. Everything was in the same place. It was hard to think that he wouldn't just show up any minute now, and ask her what the hell she was doing in his room. For a moment, she thought she wasn't up to it. She couldn't go through his things. But she knew she had to.

She started with the desk. Morel and the female detective he'd come with had looked in here too. There were school textbooks he'd never opened, and pens. A packet of Marlboros, with five cigarettes in it. Nothing else. She'd never seen Samir sitting there, doing homework. Her brother was going to technical college, because his grades were low and he seemed indifferent to the subjects he was being taught in school, his teachers said. At least this way he would get a skill. 'No job, but a skill,' he said once. He didn't think there was much point, but he went along with it. At least he seemed to.

She started searching the cupboard, emptying it so she could get a better look. It was a complete mess. She didn't expect to find anything. Still, she searched, hoping maybe they'd missed something. All she found was shoes and dirty laundry and clean clothes all thrown in there together. A stinky towel, which he'd probably dumped in his closet after a shower. Nothing interesting, but Aisha knew there had to be something. Samir would have been confident that no one would invade his privacy. She guessed he wouldn't have tried too hard to conceal things.

She searched pockets and felt around his clothes. Nothing. There was nothing under his mattress or under his bed either. She stood up, frustrated. Had she been wrong about Samir? Maybe he did have a hiding-place. If he'd been working for Ali, selling drugs, then maybe he had learned to keep secrets.

She looked up at the ceiling, thinking hard. And suddenly it came to her, just as if someone had whispered it in her ear.

She turned around and left, and went to the room she shared with her mother. Softly, slowly, she went through the chest of drawers, running her hands along the back of each one. Her mother turned and pulled the covers up, sighing in her sleep. Aisha opened the cupboard, and searched carefully. Once or twice, she had found Samir coming out of this room and asked what he was doing. He'd said he was looking for her, or for their mother. She hadn't thought anything of it then.

On the bottom shelf, where her mother kept documents and old photographs that she never looked at, Aisha found something. Wedged at the back, behind a stack of albums, was Samir's backpack. Aisha pulled it out and returned to Samir's room to check its contents. She sat on the edge of his bed, her heart beating hard.

294

In the front pocket, in an envelope, she found a stack of notes, held together with a rubber band. She counted it.

There was 6,000 Euros in total.

She sat still for a while, stunned, wondering how Samir had got the money, whether it was his and if so what he'd done to earn it. The more she thought about it, the angrier she felt. He'd been the one to tell her she should sharpen up, use her head, have some courage, or else she would get hurt.

But I wasn't the one who got killed, was I? At least I'm still alive.

She wiped the tears from her face and stood up. What should she do with the money? She decided the best thing was to put it back where she'd found it, at least until she'd figured out what to do with it. She should probably give it to Commandant Morel. It made her nervous just holding that amount of cash in her hand. She wondered whether to tell Karim. But how could she be sure he wouldn't take the money for himself? One thing was obvious: he sure liked to spend it.

She looked in the bag to see what else it contained and found another envelope, unsealed, and a letter in it that looked like it had been folded and unfolded many times before. She opened it and began to read.

Dear son, it said. Absently, she looked at the date. The letter was less than a year old.

Her eyes blurred, as if they'd suddenly stopped working. This can't be what I think it is, she thought. She was wearing her glasses, her eyes were just fine. Still, she had to stare hard to read the words.

Dear son,

I am writing to explain why it is that you and I cannot have the sort of relationship you should expect to have with a father. Your mother will tell you I'm dead. But I'm alive and well.

She read the letter until the end. Her father only mentioned her once. *Look after your mother and* sister, he'd written. Nothing more.

She put the letter back where she'd found it, and the money too. Then she fled the room.

*

Aisha took the stairs two at a time. She wanted to be outside, breathing the cold night air. More than anything, she wanted to be far from the flat and to lose herself in the crowd below. She came bursting out of the building, making the door swing violently, but no one seemed to care or notice. There were lots of people. Too many to count. Familiar faces. Not just the gangs or the troublemakers - their families too. Old men and small kids with sleepy faces, bundled up against the cold. She thought she recognized Mahmoud's Dad, the one who had become obsessed with fixing the playground swing. Most of all she noticed the mothers. Out on the streets, Aisha guessed, because they worried about what the police would do to their sons after what happened to that police officer. Everyone here was expecting the worst. Aisha figured her family wasn't so concerned. For her and her mother, the worst has already happened.

She moved through the crowd, grateful for the numbers and for the familiar faces. A couple of people recognized her and offered words of sympathy. They asked how her mother was doing. The atmosphere was peaceful enough, but the police were out in force and Aisha wondered how little or how much it would take before someone on either side of the divide lost their cool and things descended into chaos.

Here, among her neighbours and the other residents of the *cité*, she managed to calm down a little. The letter and its contents were all she could think about, but as long as she kept moving she could deal with it and with the questions that flooded her mind. How was it possible her father was still alive? Why had he written to Samir, and not to her? Had Samir written back? Why hadn't her brother told her? How much did her mother know, and why had she made her children believe that their father was dead?

Aisha stayed a while, talking to people she knew, then found her way back inside her building. With so many people on the street, it seemed deserted. She climbed to the eleventh floor and knocked on Ali's door. There was no sound coming from inside. She knocked again and waited, feeling nervous but determined.

'What are you doing here?' Réza's voice made her jump and turn quickly. His face, unsmiling, was inches from hers. She'd never seem him this close up. There was no softness in it, nothing malleable. Involuntarily, she took a step back and found herself against Ali's door. The thought of confronting Ali had been frightening, but now she found herself praying that he would turn up.

'I'm looking for Ali,' she said.

'Why?'

'I just am.'

'Anything you tell Ali, you can tell me.'

His breath was sour and his face close up marked by scars that looked like tiny craters. He'd got chicken pox on his 20th birthday and spent the next couple of weeks nearly scratching his face off, Samir had told her once. The only time he'd ever spoken about Réza.

The thought of Samir made her brave. 'Leave me alone,' she said, keeping her voice steady.

Réza gripped her arm. She flinched, and tried to move away, but she was trapped between his body and the door. Réza, meanwhile, seemed to enjoy the closeness.

'Why are you snooping around, huh? I've seen you. Talking to Karim. Watching everyone. Being a little busybody. Why don't you mind your own fucking business?'

Across the hallway, a door opened and someone stuck their head around the frame. With a wave of relief, Aisha recognized El Chino. She had been so focused on what she was doing, she'd forgotten that he and Ali lived on the same floor. He held a mobile phone in his hand.

'How about you leave the girl alone.'

'Fuck off, old man.'

'A man who threatens a woman is hardly a man at all,' Alberto said, looking at Réza with contempt.

'Why don't you go lie down for a while? Take a nap? Before you get hurt?'

'I think you should leave,' Alberto said. 'The Parisian detective is arriving now. He's on his way up. You don't want him to find you here.'

Réza looked like he didn't know whether to believe him, but there was panic in his eyes. He didn't know where Ali was and that made him less certain. He pointed a finger at Alberto. 'I'll be back to teach you a lesson. You have my word. As for you,' he said, turning to Aisha, 'you'll pay for what your brother did.'

Aisha watched him sprint down the stairs. 'What did Samir do?' she called out, but by then Réza was gone and couldn't hear her.

'Aisha.' El Chino's hand was on her shoulder, coaxing her away from Ali's door. 'It's good to see you. Come in for a while.'

He gestured for her to follow him, but she held back, wanting answers. 'What did he mean, I'll pay for what Samir did?'

'I don't know. But they came and arrested Ali earlier. He put up quite a fight.'

'Who came?'

'Commandant Morel and three others.'

'And is it true he's on his way here?'

'I don't know. I just said that.' She saw him for what he was then. An old man, who'd suddenly run out of energy and needed to sit down.

'Thank you,' she said. 'If you hadn't turned up, I don't know what Réza would have done.'

They entered his flat. Alberto shut the door behind Aisha and they stood still for a while, looking at each other. He was reminded of the moment when Samir had stood there, shivering. The memory was painful, reminding him of his incompetence.

'I'm sorry I couldn't protect Samir,' he told her.

'It wasn't your fault. Samir always did what he wanted. You couldn't have stopped him.'

Alberto nodded, unconvinced. 'I should call the police,' he said. 'In case Réza decides to come back.' He found the number that Morel had left and dialed it. 'The commandant isn't answering. I'll leave a message.' He gave Aisha what he hoped was a reassuring look. 'It'll be fine, you'll see.'

She wasn't looking at him and he wasn't sure she'd heard. 'I've been so unhappy,' she said unexpectedly.

What could he tell her? 'It's terrible, losing your brother like that. Simply terrible.'

'It is. But I've been unhappy for much longer than that. So often, I've felt like I can't breathe. There's no space to think. I don't have anywhere to go, anyone to talk to who'll understand.'

He nodded. He wanted her to know he was listening.

'I feel so alone,' she said. At this, he reached out and squeezed her shoulder.

'You're not alone, Aisha.'

Thirteen

Adèle and Augustine had left – Adèle was still angry, even after he'd found their father and brought him home, and promised to stay with him. There was just Maly now. She came upstairs with him and together they kissed their father goodnight. Descartes lay at the foot of the bed and made no move to follow them out.

'He's looking out for Papa. That seems like a recent thing,' Maly remarked.

'It is. He's smarter than I gave him credit for.' Morel smiled but his mind was elsewhere. He was wondering where Thierry Villot was, and how long it would take to get Ali to talk. At least now they had Karim's testimony.

'I can stay,' Maly said.

'What's that?'

'You need to get back to work. I can see that. Go ahead, I'll stay.'

'I can't ask you to do that. You have a family to go home to.'

'And I will. But first, you need to go back to work and wrap up your investigation.'

He hesitated, but she was steering him towards the front door.

'I'm sorry,' he said.

'What for?'

I haven't been thinking of him at all. I haven't wanted to. For so long, we've struggled to talk to each other, he and I. What am I supposed to do now, to help him?

'It isn't easy, Serge. For any of us.'

'When I found him just now, the way he was sitting in that bar – he looked so lonely. And when I said I'd walk him home, he asked if I would stay a while.'

'I know you two haven't been close,' she said. 'But in reality, you're more similar than you think.'

She leaned in and kissed his cheek.

'When this case is closed –' he began, but she stopped him. 'We can talk about all that later. Just go. I'll look after him.'

*

On his way out of the house, Morel checked his phone. There was a message from Alberto Rosales. As soon as he heard it, he called Lila to let her know where Aisha was.

'What do you want us to do?' she asked.

'Maybe check on Aisha, get her home safely. Then find Réza.'

As Morel headed towards Villeneuve, the snow began to fall in earnest. On the passenger seat, he had the notes from Marchal's interviews with Samir, which Marchal had emailed earlier. Morel had skimmed through them before printing them out. At first glance, the exchanges between the two had been so confrontational, it was hard not to think it had all been an act, to mask the fact that Samir was Marchal's informant.

On the way to the *cité*, Morel went past Thierry Villot's house and knocked on the door, but no one came. There was no sign of life, inside or on the street.

He didn't know where to look for the detective, but the *cité* seemed like a good place to start. It was where Villot had started out. A young boy, looking to escape the world he'd been brought up in and the airless sameness of his parents' lives. He'd despised them for not wanting more. Morel wondered whether Villot looked back on his police career as something to be proud of, or whether he felt that he too hadn't wanted enough, had settled for less than he'd hoped for. He had got out of the *cité*, but hadn't made it very far.

It was snowing heavily when Morel arrived at the housing estate. He was exhausted from the drive – the road had been slippery and twice he'd lost control of the car. Luckily the *périphérique* had been deserted.

There were a lot of people out on the street, but this was nothing like the antagonistic crowd of the past two days. Morel parked and stepped out of the car. He was wearing a warm coat but his head was bare and his feet sank into the wet ground. Within seconds, his hair, shoes and socks were soaked. He stopped and looked up at the tower blocks. Most of the residents appeared to be gathered outside tonight. He cursed out loud. What was he doing here? What did he hope to find? He had no idea where to look next. He thought about what Virginie and Lila had told him, about not drawing attention to himself on the estate, but he wasn't worried and besides, no one seemed to be paying him any attention.

He stood under a streetlamp, watching the snow land at his feet and wondering if he had a fever again, because nothing looked remotely familiar. After some hesitation, he stepped out of the light and trudged towards the empty place behind the tower blocks. This was where Ali had beaten Georghe up, while Réza, Karim and Samir watched. What a dreadful place to slowly die, Morel thought. He made his way to the front of the building where Samir had lived and found the spot where Figueras had discovered the boy's body. Samir had been repeatedly stabbed. It was hard to believe Villot could be the killer he was looking for, but Morel knew he was right. The only question was why.

He got back into the car and turned the heater on high. What did he know about Villot? That he had grown up on the estate. That he had always been a *flic*. That he was alone and unwell.

The job was his life.

Morel headed towards Villeneuve police station.

*

There was no one there apart from the duty officer, who told Morel he hadn't seen Thierry Villot come in since he'd started his shift at eight. Two police officers had clocked in but they were out patrolling the neighbourhood, the officer said. They would be back soon.

'You won't mind if I take a look around? Or you could call Capitaine Marchal to check that it's okay.'

The officer didn't seem to find either option appealing, but he didn't try to stop Morel.

There was no sign of Villot anywhere, but Morel kept looking, hoping his instinct was right. He looked at Villot's desk. It was tidy and mostly bare. Morel sat down for a minute. He was so tired he could easily have rested his head on the desktop and gone to sleep. It was an effort to stand up and get going again. Walking down the hallway, his legs felt heavy. He reached the men's toilets and went in, thinking he would splash his face with cold water.

Thierry Villot was in there, leaning over the hand basin. At the sound of Morel's footsteps, he looked up, into the mirror. Their eyes met and Morel was shocked by Villot's appearance. He looked like a dying man.

'I've been looking for you,' Morel said. Villot didn't respond. He turned the tap on and washed his hands carefully, as if a great deal depended on it.

Morel moved towards him and turned the tap off. 'Where have you been?'

'In here.'

304

'For how long?'

Villot stared at his hands. 'For some time. Hours and hours. I don't mean just today. I mean hours and hours over the past months. Just sitting in a cubicle, reflecting on things. And slowly losing my mind.'

'You're not well.'

'I'm not well,' Villot parroted. 'I know.' He looked into the mirror again. 'I can fucking see myself, can't I? And if I ever forget, there's always someone around to remind me of what I've become. Old and grey and used up. Useless.'

Morel didn't speak. Villot went on, talking to his reflection.

'I know. It's a bit pathetic. All this whining. I guess I've been feeling sorry for myself. Not a particularly noble sentiment. But just think about it. Look at me. What have I got? No one to come home to. No friends to speak of. My ex-wife hates me with a passion and blames me for everything that's gone wrong in her life. And the job … ' At this point, the expression on Villot's face went from calm to anguished. 'I invested absolutely everything in my work. I know that *cité* like the back of my hand. I've watched the kids grow up. Watched over them. I know their families and their weaknesses, the things that are likely to trip them up. I've done my best to keep them out of trouble. It isn't always possible, of course, but I've tried. I have given this job my all.'

'No one would deny that,' Morel said, thinking about Marchal's words.

Now Villot had his back to the mirror and was facing Morel, but was doing his best not to look at him. 'The trouble is, all the effort amounts to nothing. Recently I realized I've done nothing but go around in circles. Nothing changes. If anything, it gets worse. The kids are younger, harder than before. To talk about repeat offenders is laughable. When the same person does the same thing 12, 15, 20 times, before they've even reached adulthood, that isn't repeat offending. That's a free fall.'

'What happened, Villot?' Morel asked quietly. 'What happened with Samir?'

'Over the past year, I've thought a lot about getting out,' Villot continued, as if he hadn't heard. 'I thought maybe I'd do something else with my life. But then it dawned on me: who the hell is going to hire a 55-year-old flic? I should have got out ten years ago while I still had the chance.'

'*Thierry*'. This time, Villot reacted by falling silent. 'I want you to take me through what happened with Samir. Help me understand.'

'There's nothing to understand, I'm afraid.' Villot leaned back against the sink and stared in the distance, reliving the scene. 'Ten days ago, I was at the station. Marchal had brought Samir and Karim in, presumably to grill them about Ali. He's obsessed with nailing Ali. We keep trying and he keeps slipping through our fingers. It's driving Marchal crazy. Anyway, I don't know what happened, I wasn't there when Marchal talked to the boys. He must have let them go. I found Karim, he was on his way home, visibly upset. He didn't want to talk to me. And he didn't know where Samir was.'

Villot lit a cigarette. Morel didn't stop him.

'Then Marchal brought Samir in again, the day before he went missing. I was tired of it. The way he treated the boy, it was too much. I decided I'd go looking for him. He was hard to find. Karim couldn't tell me anything. When I finally found Samir, it was very late. I'd been looking for him for hours. He'd come up from the basement. He was upset.'

'This was the day after he watched Ali beat Georghe up,' Morel said.

'It must have been. I knew nothing about it then. I thought he was crying because of Marchal. I told him I would make sure it didn't continue. I expected he would be relieved, or grateful. Instead, he gave me this pitying look. He said:

"You think I need your help?' You think Marchal is trying to cause me grief? You're clueless, man. Marchal is my ticket out of here. So fuck off. I don't need your pity."

'I couldn't believe it. Samir was saying he and Marchal were talking to each other, but Marchal hadn't told me anything. If it was true – and I know now that it is,' Villot said, looking at Morel '- then it means everything Marchal did was for show. He was playing a game, trying to look like he was harassing Samir when all the time he was using him to get to Ali.'

'What did you do?' Morel asked.

'I wasn't thinking straight. I was angry. I decided I would tell Ali that Samir had been disloyal. Effectively, I'd be signing his death warrant. But then I changed my mind. I thought I'd go back to Samir and try to talk.'

'Did you?'

'I did. I found him. He was agitated, full of hate. He said things to me that weren't right. Things I couldn't listen to. He knew all about me. How I'd grown up in the *cité*, who my parents were. My guess is Ali told him. He knew. I felt dirty.'

'He wasn't himself,' Morel said, thinking of Samir. 'After Georghe's beating.'

'I couldn't take it. The hatred, the contempt. I hit him. He came straight back at me, with a knife. I overpowered him easily. He thought he was tough, but really, he was just a kid.'

Morel watched Villot struggle with his emotions. Self-pity and anger, but also horror and a sadness that was eating him alive.

'You sent me the autopsy notes so that I would take an interest in the investigation,' Morel said. 'When the riots started to turn ugly, you called to let my colleagues and I know that it wasn't safe to remain in the *cité*. From the beginning, you wanted me to get involved. You wanted to be found out, didn't you? But you didn't make it easy for us either.'

'I knew it was just a matter of time. I watched, and waited. I wanted it to be over.' Villot hung his head.

'Thierry Villot, I'm arresting you for the murder of Samir Kateb.'

'Do what you need to do. I'm not going anywhere.'

They walked out together, Villot leading the way. As they passed his desk, they ran into Marchal, looking wild-eyed and disheveled.

'So it's true,' he said. 'The duty officer called me to say you were here, Morel, looking for Thierry. I was asleep.' He stared at Villot in disbelief. 'All these years of working together. Did you not think that maybe you could confide in me, tell me you were going off the rails? Instead of which, you screw up this entire department. Do you have any idea what this is going to do to us? How people are going to react, when they realise a *flic* killed the boy?'

'You have a share of responsibility in this,' Morel said. 'I suggest you keep quiet for now.' He cuffed Thierry Villot and called Lila.

'We've got Réza,' she told him.

'Well done. Can you and Akil meet me at the Villeneuve station?'

'We're on our way.'

308

Fourteen

They sat by the river, watching a group of tourists board a Batobus. A family with three kids, a woman in a velour tracksuit and black running shoes. An elderly man and his daughter, or maybe she was his wife, judging by the way she held and stroked his hand. Some were thinking about what seats they might get on board if they were lucky, edging forward, pretending not to be pushy. Others hung back, talking to each other, enjoying the moment. Further along the quay, a boy was chasing his sister. The mother called out to them sharply, worried no doubt that they would fall into the freezing water. Morel wished he had a square sheet of paper in his pocket, to fold and shape. It was so long since he'd made anything that he'd stopped carrying the paper around, as was his habit.

'You did a good job wrapping up the Simic case,' Morel told Vincent. 'I heard from Lila that it took some convincing on your part, before Simic's lover and her husband would speak to you. And that Valérie Simic confessed readily to having plotted her husband's murder.'

'It wasn't that difficult. She *wanted* to tell me. I saw it in her eyes. The relief of admitting what she'd done. It's one thing to seek revenge, but quite another to live with the consequences.'

Vincent hugged himself and leaned forward, watching the woman who'd now caught up with her two children. 'It's absolutely tragic, isn't it? What's happened to these families.'

'Who are you talking about? Georghe? Samir Kateb? Or Simic?'

'All of them. And I don't mean just the victims. Aisha, her mother. Valérie Simic. They're alive. But they've all lost so much. Even Valérie. None of them can ever go back to who they were before.'

Briefly, Morel reflected on the separate cases they'd just solved, replaying recent events in his mind. 'Individuals are destroyed. Families are torn apart. You're right. There's no denying the damage that's done.' He nudged Vincent with his elbow. 'At the same time, 'it *is* possible to move forward. Life goes on.'

'Yes, I suppose it does.' Vincent lowered his gaze.

Morel stood up. 'We should probably head back into the office,' he said. 'I have to go to Villeneuve and tell Loubna and Aisha Kateb what we know.'

'Wait.' Vincent straightened himself. 'First, I need to say something. I was angry with you. For treating me differently to the others. For making me feel like I was underperforming.'

'This is just now,' Morel said. 'Generally, you're very good at your job, Vincent. You don't need me to tell you that.'

Vincent attempted a smile. 'Perhaps I do.'

'I'm just worried about you.'

'I get that. And what I want to say is that I'm trying. I'm trying my best.'

'I know.' Morel waited for Vincent to stand up, but he remained where he was.

'What do you want me to say, Vincent?'

'I want you to promise you won't give up on me just yet.'

Morel shook his head. 'Don't be daft. Of course I won't give up on you. I need you.'

He held out his hand, and Vincent took it. 'Now come on. Let's go.'

*

Outside the tower blocks, a dozen school children were waiting for the bus, wearing their coats and backpacks. Nearby, a group of women were talking, exchanging news. The night's vigil had ended peacefully. There were still piles of rubbish on the streets. But on this grey, cloudy morning, life seemed pretty normal in Villeneuve.

'It's nice of you to drop by.' Aisha led Morel in to the flat. 'Maman's in the kitchen.'

'Is she better?'

Aisha smiled. 'She's up, at least.'

'I heard about what happened with the girl in your class.'

'Her father wants to press charges,' Aisha said. 'But the head teacher is talking to him. She's saying that in the context of Samir's death, and given how Katarina's been bullying me all these months, no one will take the charges seriously. She thinks they'll change their minds.'

'I'm guessing Luc Clément's been busy defending you,' Morel said.

Aisha nodded, embarrassed. 'You'd think he was my brother or father, the way he behaves … still, I shouldn't have done it. Attacked Katarina. That person – that wasn't me.'

'Where's your mother?'

'She's at the shops. It's the first time in days that she's left the house. And Antoine has a job interview this morning. I hope he gets it. He hasn't had a job in two years. I didn't know that till yesterday. All this time he's been too ashamed to tell us.'

'That's quite a secret to keep.'

'Everyone's been keeping secrets.'

'I wanted to tell you in person that we found who killed Samir. And Georghe.' Morel told her about Ali, and about Thierry. He'd wondered whether it was the right thing to do and decided he would hold nothing back from her. 'I'd appreciate it if you and your family kept this to yourself, until we're ready to release the information. It's going to be messy. There's going to be a lot of anger when people find out a police officer was involved.' Morel looked at her. 'Will you be okay?'

'I think so. I don't know.' Aisha reached into her pocket and drew out an envelope. 'Yesterday, I was looking through Samir's things. I found his backpack in the bedroom my mother and I sleep in. Inside it, there was this money and a letter from my father, who's supposed to be dead. You should probably take the money. I think my brother earned it by doing things for Ali.'

'The letter from your father. Was it to Samir?' Morel asked.

'Yes.' She clasped and unclasped her hands. 'I'm going to have to talk to my mother about this. But now's not the right time.' She glanced at Morel. 'What's going to happen to Karim?'

'Nothing much, I expect. He's a minor. He didn't touch Georghe. But he was there. That's something he's going to have to live with.'

'Karim isn't a bad person. He just doesn't have anything that drives him. Nothing meaningful.'

'He has you,' Morel remarked. 'He seems to care about you. Those feelings made him come to us and give Ali up. He did it so you wouldn't get hurt.'

'Really?'

'Really. That took some courage, coming to us.'

'I guess so.'

'I was a little tough on you when we met last. I'm sorry for that. What I was trying to say, is that you seem to undermine yourself. And that you shouldn't. I was trying to be helpful, in a clumsy sort of way.'

'That's cool. I did get it.'

Morel took her hand. 'Good luck, Aisha.'

'Same to you, Monsieur Morel.'

As he was coming out of the building, Morel's phone rang. It was Mathilde.

'I'm meeting friends for dinner this evening. Not far from your office. How about a drink? I don't have to be at dinner till eight.'

'I'd love one.'

*

Morel spent the afternoon buried in paperwork and interviewing both Ali and Réza. Ali wasn't talking, but Morel wasn't troubled. He had Karim's testimony, and it looked like it was only a matter of time before Réza confessed, in the hope of saving himself.

Around 5 p.m., Superintendent Olivier Perrin came in to the office and Morel briefed him. He then called Virginie to let her know what had happened. She told him she was taking a month's leave. 'I need some time to figure out what I want to do with my life,' she said. 'It might be time for a change.'

By a quarter to six, he was on his way out of the building, heading towards the Monoprix on boulevard St Michel where he'd agreed to meet Mathilde. She was waiting outside. She was wearing a short, blue-knit dress and a dark red coat, and her hair was loose, the way he liked it. He kissed her cheek and smelled her perfume.

'Do you mind if we go in for a minute?' she asked. 'I'd like to take a bottle to dinner tonight.'

'Of course.'

He followed her around the aisles, light-headed with exhaustion, and hovered nearby while she chose the wine. After the events of the past week – the murders, the riots, his father's escapade - this moment with Mathilde seemed like a gift. He would worry later about Villeneuve and whether the violence would flare up again; he would worry later about the reporters: the media would have a field

313

day with this case. It was hard not to think about the damage this would do to the police.

'What will you do with the rest of the evening? Should I be concerned about you?' Mathilde asked, half-amused, but he thought he detected a trace of pity in her voice. He bought a bottle of wine and some cheese to take home so he wasn't simply tagging along.

Outside, she looked at her watch. It was dark, and the temperature had dropped further since they'd gone in to the supermarket. He thought she was about to tell him she had to go, that she'd changed her mind about having a drink together, but instead she named a café and suggested they walk there. They wandered towards the river, until they came to the Pont des Arts. Mathilde buttoned up her coat and leaned against the parapet.

'Look. It's beautiful.'

Morel followed her gaze. Against the night sky and the river's dark presence, everything – the classical facades along the quays, the Institut de France, the Louvre, Notre-Dame, and the next bridge across the water – was lit up, and the overall effect was magical.

'I've stood in this exact spot so often. Yet I never tire of the view,' Mathilde said.

Together, they stepped back and examined the thousands of lovelocks attached to the railing. Recently, parts of the Pont des Arts had caved in under their weight, and now entire sections of the bridge were boarded with plywood.

Mathilde shivered. 'It's freezing,' she said. 'Shall we keep going?'

As Morel walked beside her, he pictured the hours ahead. He was looking forward to this drink. He would head back to Neuilly afterwards. If his father was awake, he would sit with him for a while. He thought with pleasure of his flat. Maybe he would sit up and start on an origami project. All he needed was a little time, a little quiet, in the private, orderly world he'd created for himself.

Walking alongside Mathilde, it dawned on him that right now, what he looked forward to most was the place that he'd be returning to alone, after their time together.

Home.

Printed in Great Britain
by Amazon

58209490R00187